THE RETURN

THE WITCH HUNTER SAGA - BOOK TWO

NICOLE R. TAYLOR

The Return (Book Two in The Witch Hunter Saga)

www.nicolertaylorwrites.com

Cover Design: MoorBooks Design

Edited by: Silvia Curry

CHAPTER 1

Lake District, United Kingdom
Autumn, 43AD

Aeriaya was the last daughter of the stars to walk the Earth.

The last of the race known as the Celestines. She was twenty-five of what the humans called years, and she alone held the weight of an impossible responsibility on her shoulders. She was to be the last caretaker of the Earth.

Sunlight filtered through the dense canopy of the forest, casting its dappled fingers through the deep green grass below. It was an abnormally warm day. The earth was still damp from the morning mist, thousands of tiny dewdrops clinging to moss-covered trees.

Aeriaya wandered through the wood, her long pale fingers playing through the light, savouring the small points of warmth. Coming to a clearing, she smiled, her long silver hair blowing across her face in the sudden breeze. The sun had coaxed the little field to come alive with small, white flowers. Pulling her hair back into place, she walked out into the sunlight, gathering as many of the blossoms as she could carry. She knew her mother would love them.

Glimpsing a figure approaching, she shook her head. She wasn't meant to be out walking today, but she needed the peace of the forest...if only for an hour or two.

Smiling, she turned, expecting to see her brother emerge from the forest. He had a habit of following her and playing tricks when she least expected it. But it wasn't him.

She gasped as she caught sight of a menacing figure lingering in the tree line, their form shadowed by the surrounding forest. Dropping the flowers in surprise, she took a hesitant step back. He was covered head to foot in heavy black linen and leather clothing, not an inch of skin showing. A large hood hung low over his eyes, shielding his face from the sunlight.

Aeriaya took a few steps back, fear creeping into her heart, knowing she wouldn't be able to escape even if she ran.

A satisfied smirk pulled at the man's lips as he watched her back away.

How did he get here? He shouldn't have been able to find the clearing, let alone get into the forest. She should've sensed his approach, but even now it was as if she were alone. He was not one of them, nor was he human. He was...dead?

Aeriaya stood frozen in fear, unable to tear her gaze away from him. Something was terribly wrong.

Before she could react, the man lunged forwards, faster than she thought possible, and grasped her around the waist, flinging her over his shoulder. Looking within herself, she sought the coil of power that was the centre of her being. Her parents always taught her to use it for good—that to kill and destroy was wrong—but surely this time was different.

She let her power wash over her, but nothing happened. It sputtered and died, leaving her empty.

"No!" she cried, beating her fists against the man's shoulder. *It couldn't be.* "No!"

Letting out a blood-curdling scream, she beat her fists harder against his back, trying to free herself, but his grip was like iron. He was so strong, her fists and raking fingernails had no effect on him. Even when she tried to bite and kick, he continued to run.

The forest grew dark as he took her farther away from her home, the air colder and more desolate. She pleaded with the man to let her go, but he wouldn't respond, instead he ran faster, never seeming to tire.

She didn't know how much time had passed, but before long, she was dropped like a stone onto a hard floor. Taking heaving gulps, she looked around, her eyes searching for a glimmer of hope, but she found none.

She was in a dark stone room, surrounded by four men and one woman, and she couldn't sense their presence, either. They were dead, just like the man who'd taken her.

Panic overtook her and she scrambled backwards, crashing into something hard. Looking up, she gasped as she realised she'd collided with the man's legs. Jerking away in horror, a satisfied smirk pulled at his lips as he laughed down at her.

There was a scraping sound as a heavy wooden door opened and a woman walked into the room. It closed behind her with a dull thud that echoed off the walls.

Looking around for the first time, Aeriaya realised that the stone room wasn't just any room. Earth was all around her...she could feel it through the walls. She was in a dungeon.

The woman paused just inside the doorway for a moment, a look of triumph plastered on her face. She was tall and slim, with fiery auburn hair that fell in waves over her shoulders. Aeriaya knew she wasn't like the others as her heart beat steady in her chest.

Aeriaya regarded her warily as the woman walked forwards. This woman was very much alive and very much a witch. This was all so very wrong. Just by looking at her, Aeriaya could tell the witch had created the dead creatures who stood around her.

"Well done, Regulus." The woman caressed the man's face with a delicate hand. The man who had taken her from the forest. "*Very well done.*"

"Who are you?" Aeriaya's musical voice sounded misplaced in their dark surroundings. "What do you want?"

"Oh, forgive me," the woman exclaimed. "Let me introduce you to my family. Regulus you have already met on such intimate terms. This is my lovely daughter, Octavia. And my sons, Marcus, Titus, Caius, and Arturius. And I...? I am Katrin."

She knew that name. She was one of the Five. The power she'd been granted had been corrupted.

"What have you done?" Aeriaya whispered, still cowering on the floor.

Katrin laughed. "They're dead. They're vampires. The creatures of myth brought alive by my will. Bound to the night, slaves to blood." She gestured to the six vampires, who moved forwards.

One of the men grabbed her roughly around the waist and hauled her up, holding her lithe form in place. One by one, the vampires came forwards and dragged her head to the side, sinking their fangs into the soft skin of her neck. They took her blood without a care for her.

She tried to fight at first, but each burning tear into her flesh made her limbs heavier.

Why were they doing this to her? She'd never done anything to hurt anyone. Was she to die?

Once they'd all drank, they let her go, and the cell door slammed closed. Alone in the darkness, she sunk to the floor and sobbed, her tears and blood dripping onto the hard, dirt floor.

Aeriaya didn't know how long she was in the cell before someone came. Darkness and fear were her only companions until she heard footsteps approaching.

Scrambling back as far as she could, she curled herself into a ball against the wall. Her neck stung and dried blood flaked off her pale skin and stained her dress.

As the door scraped open, she held her hand over her eyes at the sudden light that filled the cell. One of the vampires stood just inside, holding a flaming torch which he put into the holder on the wall.

She watched him with frightened eyes. There would be no choice for her in what happened next. Her power was gone. Whatever Katrin had done, she had given the means to Regulus to take it away. She was completely at their mercy.

The vampire crouched down, gazing at her, his expression almost sad. She knew he was one of the human people who called themselves Romans. He had that look about him—broad shoulders, dark curly hair cropped close to the scalp, deep-set brown eyes. A long, white, puckered scar began above his right eye and ended below his cheekbone, marring his face. Ugly.

"Are you ill?" His rough voice was a surprise, just as much as his concern was. When she didn't answer he said, "I'm sorry. I don't want to hurt you."

"But you did," she whispered, tears spilling down her face.

"I'm sorry..." He frowned. "But you must understand. I cannot go against the others so openly."

She was confused. Was he really sorry? Would he try to help her? She had to escape this place. Her family had to be warned about the witch and what she'd created. She hadn't been granted this gift to use it in such a way.

"I cannot be here," she said.

The vampire frowned and looked at his hands. Reaching out towards her, he went to grasp her hand that clutched around her knees, but she jerked back, afraid of his touch.

"What is your name?" he asked, letting his hand fall away. She didn't answer, staring at him with unearthly blue eyes. He looked at her a moment, unsure of how to proceed. Finally, he said, "I am Arturius. I must go before I am missed, but I will return."

Standing, he regarded her once more before turning and leaving, the door closing and the heavy bolt driving home with a thud. He left the torch behind, the smoke spiralling upwards towards a grate in the ceiling high above. One small kindness so she didn't have to endure the darkness.

<hr />

Arturius came to see her many times over the coming weeks. He brought food he'd stolen, but he'd eat nothing, content to watch her sate her hunger.

In all that time, she heard nothing of the outside world. Nothing of her family or why she'd been taken. She was at the mercy of the witch and her Roman vampires.

They came to visit her as well, but it was only to take more of her blood. For what reason, she didn't know.

The young Roman, Arturius, told her much about his life before he came to Briton. He told her stories about his family back in Rome, how he became a soldier in the Legion and how he'd come to be here on the other side of the ocean. The ocean, he said, was as beautiful as it was deadly. Blue, sparkling water as far as the eye could see, its surface choppy with waves, the bow of their great ship dipping in and out as they travelled, giant ocean fish racing them and leaping from the water.

He was a commander before he met Katrin. He told men what to do. He was a fearsome leader, respected and admired. He'd fought many battles defending

Rome, the realm of goodness and light, learning and science. The day that Katrin had made them into vampires was the day he realised that the world he knew was a lie. There were no gods. No god would do this to him, he said. Not even all the gods in the underworld would sink that low.

And Aeriaya felt sorry for him. Katrin had betrayed them too, had she not? She'd coerced them into servitude, linking them to her through what Arturius called magic. While all of them had come willingly, they had been tricked into their own prison. Their free will was taken. If Katrin willed it, they had to see it through.

"That," he said, "is why I cannot free you. I want to, so badly. But I cannot." He sat beside her, his back resting against the wall, his arm touching hers. Taking her delicate hand in his, he ran a thumb across her knuckles.

"I would do anything for you," he whispered, letting his lips brush against her cheek.

She shivered and glanced away, suddenly shy where she had become so comfortable with him. Arturius had shared so much of himself with her and she had told him nothing, yet he still gave.

He traced a finger along her jaw, turning her face back towards him. His brown eyes searched hers for a moment before he leaned forward, pressing his lips against hers. She drew a sharp breath as he pulled her close, a powerful hand caressing her waist. Taking the opportunity, Arturius slid his tongue into her mouth. It was a sensation she'd never felt before. She felt herself kissing him back, sliding her tongue against his, feeling him.

Finally, he pulled away, burying his face into the crook of her neck. She jerked back slightly as his lips brushed her torn skin, but he didn't bite down as she thought he would. Instead, he let out a contented sigh.

"She wants to know the secret to your power," he murmured in her ear, kissing the corner of her jaw. "The power of your kind."

No, she could never tell him any of her family's secrets. It didn't work that way; she couldn't tell. Something horrible would happen, something that she didn't understand, but something horrible, nonetheless.

"All you need to do is tell Katrin what she wants to know, then you can go home." Arturius sat on the dirt floor and pulled her against his chest, stroking her silver hair. "I will take you myself so you are safe."

She sobbed into his shirt, shaking her head. Why couldn't they understand? She couldn't. Even if she wanted to, even if it meant her own life.

"Please," he pleaded. "They couldn't learn anything from your blood."

She was confused. Her blood? What did that have to do with anything? The Romans were just tormenting her, drinking her blood to sate themselves. Driving her to give up what she could not.

"Your blood gives us dreams," Arturius whispered as he measured her expression. "They thought to learn what they wanted that way. They hoped... That way, you wouldn't have a choice."

When she didn't speak, he sighed, resting his forehead against hers. "I can't stop her," he said. "She offered your release to your family in exchange for the same information, but they denied her."

Aeriaya froze. Her family had betrayed her? Her parents were strong, they could tell Katrin what she wanted to know. Why hadn't they come to free her, despite the witch's offer? There were too few of them left to leave her to die. Why hadn't they sent someone to rescue her?

"Please, you must, or I don't know what she'll do to you." Arturius grasped her hands in his almost desperately. "Please, my love."

She stiffened in his grasp. *Love?* What did she know of love?

"I cannot," she whispered. "Even if I wanted to betray them, I couldn't. It's impossible."

"What do you mean?" he asked.

"I am bound. I cannot," she stated.

Arturius frowned, trying to mask the anger that'd begun to creep into his features. If they couldn't get the information they needed from her, then what was her fate? Death?

She began to panic, her heart thudding in her chest. Arturius reached out to calm her.

"Come, my love," he beckoned. Falling against him, she gasped as he forced his wrist to her mouth. She gagged at the coppery taste of his blood, but there was so much of it she was forced to swallow several times.

"There, there," he crooned, stroking her silver hair with his other hand. "This will only hurt a moment, my love."

Her eyes widened with panic as he took her head in his large paw-like hands, blood dripping from her chin. Suddenly, he twisted and the last sound she heard was the snap as he broke her neck.

CHAPTER 2

Zac's eyes snapped open, despite how groggy he felt.

He'd been dreaming, which didn't feel right. His nights had been blank since day one. He was a vampire and vampires didn't dream. He tried to remain focused, trying to recall the woman's face—the one whose neck had been broken just as he woke—but it slipped away into darkness.

"Zac," came a familiar voice.

Turning his head, he found himself in his bed, the sun shining outside. Sam sat in a chair beside him, leaning forwards with a concerned look on his tired face. Sam, his little brother, just as undead as he was, always there to patch him up.

"Sam," he groaned, trying to sit up. "What..."

Sam's hand held him down, stopping him from moving. "Easy brother. You've been out for three days."

Zac frowned, trying to remember what'd

happened. They'd been in the forest, guarding the clearing while Gabby and Aya fought Katrin in limbo. Then he was on the ground, dying. This time, he'd had a choice whether he would drink the blood that would save his life.

And he chose her.

"Where's Aya?" he croaked, trying to sit up again.

Sam's expression was pained. "There's no easy way to tell you this, brother."

He rose, pushing away his brother's hands. "What do you mean? Where is she?"

"Zac, she's gone."

"Gone where? She left?"

"No, Zac. She's... She's dead."

The little colour that'd returned to his face drained as his heart twisted.

No. It couldn't be true. Aya couldn't die. She was the strongest vampire he'd ever known. She was over two thousand years old, could walk into anyone's home without being invited, and sunlight didn't bother her in the slightest. Death seemed beyond her.

"I'm sorry." Sam reached out and lay his hand on Zac's arm. "I'm so sorry."

Zac knew his brother better than himself and the look on his face said it all. He was telling the truth.

He tried to speak, but nothing came out.

"While she was weakened from giving you her blood," Sam began, "she had to let her guard down. After everything that happened with Gabby and healing you, I think it took too much from her. It was the moment of weakness that he was waiting for."

"Who? What?" Zac's head was still foggy as he tried to grasp the enormity of what Sam was telling him.

"A vampire named Arturius." He scowled at the memory. "He tore her heart from her chest. He was her maker, Zac. Another founding vampire."

Zac covered his face with his hands, stifling a sob. He ached all over as he dragged in breath after breath to calm himself. His heart was broken; *he was broken.*

He saw her face as she'd hovered over him in the clearing, her tears dripping on his cheek as he died. She'd said she loved him and he realised he hadn't said it back. He loved her so much and he could never tell her.

In that moment, the grief of that realisation made him want to die...but above all else, he wanted Arturius dead.

"We put her in the cave by the lake," Sam said. "If you want..."

Zac turned his face away from his brother and nodded. He couldn't run this time, not from her.

Never from her.

Zac stood at the edge of the gulley that led down to the mouth of the cave. The last time he was here, he'd ripped the head off the woman who'd made him, Victoria.

Was Aya asleep in the cave as he'd killed here? He couldn't remember if the entrance was blocked then or not. Revenge was the only thing on his mind...then and now.

He wondered how different their lives could've been if he'd met Aya that night. He would still be a vampire, but perhaps Sam would've led the human life he was always meant to.

Sam would remember his dead older brother as a hero of the Civil War—a war they'd lost, but a hero, nonetheless. He could've finished his studies, married, had children. He knew Sam would've been successful, continued the plantation in the new United States. He would have righted their parent's wrongs, gone boldly into a new, prosperous future.

Sam should've been the father theirs wasn't. The husband and the businessman. He wouldn't have tolerated the use of slaves like their father had. Sam would've taken the plantation to a whole new level. Employed people, not force them to work.

Sighing sharply, Zac cast his thoughts aside and stared at the rock that blocked the entrance to the cave. Could he go in there, knowing the woman he loved lay cold and dead inside?

He knew he wouldn't rest easy until he did.

Walking forwards, he grasped the heavy rock with

Sam grasping the other side, and together they opened up the cave.

"Go," Sam said. "I'll wait here until you're ready."

Nodding, Zac made his way inside, his steps echoing off the close walls.

As he came into a large room made of pure rock, he saw her lying on a slab of slate, covered with a dark blanket. Her hands were clasped on top of the fabric, her hair cascading over the side of the rock as if she were merely asleep, but her skin was an odd shade of grey.

Zac gazed down at her lifeless form, lingering at her chest, where under the blanket, he knew was a gaping hole. Taking in the features of her delicate face, he realised he'd never seen her look so tranquil. Her gaze had always had an underlying motive about it, like she was aware of more than what her senses revealed.

Reaching down, he ran his finger along her lifeless hand, tracing the length of her index finger.

He wished she would wake up and say something sarcastic; call him out for being an ass. He wished he could go back and change so many things like stop the curse. If he'd done something, maybe she'd still be alive.

So many people had been taken from him—his parents, the plantation workers he'd made friends with, the men he'd commanded in the Confederate

Army. They'd all been casualties of war, outright murdered, or taken by vampires.

Anger swelled in his cold, dead heart and he made a vow to Aya. *The founders would pay for what they'd done to her. They would all pay with their lives.*

He pivoted and left the cave, emerging into the air with a fresh resolve for revenge.

"I'm going to kill him," he told Sam. "I'm going to kill Arturius, and I can't have you standing in my way, brother."

"I figured as much."

"I need to do this for her."

"I know." Sam placed a reassuring hand on his brother's shoulder and together, they sealed the cave for the last time.

The woman standing in the centre of the clearing was strangely familiar. Her skin shimmered an opalescent pearl like the inside of an exotic shell. She stood out like a ray of starlight in the green forest, a beacon.

As she turned, he saw her laughing smile illuminated by the sun through the treetops. Blue eyes as bright as a summer's day and hair so white it was like a fine powder of snow cascading around her shoulders. Her smile faded slightly as she caught his eye and he suddenly felt like an intruder in a place he should never have seen.

Her eyes warmed and she raised her hand in greeting, but before he could raise his own, a black figure emerged from the tree line and seized her about the waist, throwing her over their shoulder.

The horror on her face was gut-wrenching. He went to dash forwards to help, but he was frozen to the spot. He cried out, but she was taken away, her screams growing fainter and fainter until the forest fell silent.

"Zac."

He spun on his heel at the all too familiar sound of her voice. "Aya?"

The forest had become dark, but he could still make out her form in the shadows, her blue eyes sparkling despite the lack of moonlight.

Deep down, he knew this was a dream, but he didn't want it to end.

Reaching out with a trembling hand, he hissed as his fingers connected with the skin of her cheek. The crackle of electricity that shot into him as he pulled her close made his heart skip several beats. Burying his face into her hair, he choked back a sob.

"It's okay," she murmured in his ear.

Zac pulled back, his hands cupping her face and he looked into her eyes, and this time, he really looked. It was as if the entire universe lived inside of her. She was...

He'd hardly noticed he was a hairsbreadth away from her until he felt himself press his lips to hers She kissed him back like her life depended on it, forcing a groan out of him as her hands found their way under his shirt.

Finally, he pulled away. Resting his forehead against hers, he let out a shaky breath. Aya's fingertips traced the edge of his jaw, finally coming to rest over his lips.

"Aya..." He wanted to say so many things. Where would he begin? If this was in any way real, he wanted her to know the one thing he never got to say. "I love you."

She looked up at him, a sad smile on her lips. Why did it feel like she was saying goodbye?

Zac woke with a start.

Sitting up with a gasp, he struggled to catch his breath. Shirtless, his torso glistened with sweat and he collapsed back onto his pillow with a groan. He hadn't dreamed so vividly since... Well, since he was human and even that memory was fading.

Rolling out of bed, he stumbled to the shower and turned on the cold faucet as far as it would go. Stripping, he stepped into the icy water and washed the hot, sticky sleep from his body, the memory of the dream refusing to leave his mind.

He could still feel her lips on his.

He vaguely remembered dreaming of the silver-haired woman before as the water cascaded over his head and down his back. It was Aya, wasn't it? Was that who she really was?

Another vampire had been there with her and

somehow, he thought he'd called himself Arturius, but the memory was still hazy, the details slipping through his mind into nothingness.

He pushed the memory of the dreams away, refusing to think of them. It was a torture he didn't want to dwell on.

Outside, dawn was inching its fingers across the horizon. A new day meant a new problem, and they still had the biggest problem of all to solve—how to kill one of the oldest surviving vampires of all time. Aya was gone and she'd been their only hope, the only way to kill a founding vampire. If they'd been in trouble before, then they were well and truly screwed now.

Drying himself and dressing haphazardly, Zac wandered down the hall to his old bedroom—the one Sam had given to Aya when she first moved in—and opened the door. It was exactly as she'd left it. Bare, except for the furniture and a few items of clothing strewn on the dresser.

Zac sat numbly on her bed, staring into nothingness, his fingers absently clutching the book that was still under her pillow. It was the copy of *Julius Caesar* that Gabby had used to scry with when Caius had abducted her.

He remembered the inscription in the cover and snorted. *For Louis, Many happy returns on the day of your birth, Arthur Risom.*

He understood that Arthur Risom was a

pseudonym and a blatant one at that. Arthur Risom was Arturius. He 'd been here before, manipulating the townspeople, and likely his family along with them. He was here to find Aya and the book was a message.

He wondered if she'd realised and that's why she went to ground. He'd never asked the reason why she slept.

Did it matter now?

Zac didn't know what he should do with the book. It reminded him of her. He had been so angry when he found out that she had it, but now it was a harsh reminder of her killer. He felt burning rage well inside him and he threw the book across the room with all his strength.

He felt so powerless. She'd died while he was comatose. He couldn't protect her. It would've been a suicide attempt, going up against a two-thousand-year-old vampire, but he would have gladly died in her place if it meant she lived.

Standing, he walked over and picked up the book... then tucked it back under her pillow.

Later that night, Sam coaxed Zac into the parlour under the premise of a drink or ten. His older brother had downed almost three bottles so far and was already a little drunk, but he knew that he'd been at it since going to the cave the day before, trying to keep himself under control.

Sam owed his life to his brother. All that time ago, despite what'd happened, Zac had saved his life.

His brother would argue against the point, but Sam had taken to his new life in a vastly different way. He was often told he was all the good things about being a vampire. His turning was horrific, but his first days had shaped him in a way that Zac's hadn't. Without his big brother, who knew what would have become of him?

Sam knew Zac was messed up, but it was beside the point. He would stay with him, regardless. And all of those times he'd let Zac go off on his own... Sam trusted him, of course he did, but it would be foolish to think that he hadn't gone off the deep end and done things he'd later regret.

Zac stood with his back to the room, gazing out of the window into the blackness of the night, swaying slightly as the alcohol blurred his thoughts. "Do you remember the werewolf pack?"

"How could I forget," Sam replied with a touch of sarcasm. How could he forget five mutilated werewolves? Walking into that alleyway and seeing the carnage that his brother had supposedly inflicted on them had been an eye-opener. Zac had been moments from death, and they had suspected that he'd blacked out and tore them apart himself. A frenzy. It wasn't unheard of.

"That was Aya," Zac said without a trace of emotion.

Sam whistled. "Well, that explains a lot. Did she ever tell you why she did it?"

"No," he replied. "I never got the chance to ask her. She compelled me to forget."

"Aya compelled you?"

"Yes."

"And you're only telling me this now because...?"

"I only found out when Gabby cast that knowledge spell. It made me remember what I'd forgotten." He turned, staggering slightly to the side.

"Was it only the once?"

Zac seemed to think about it for a moment and Sam wondered what else he was holding back. Finally, he shrugged and sat down before he fell. Grasping his head, he let out a strangled groan. "I don't know if I ever apologised."

"Apologised for what?" Sam asked, curious what memory the alcohol had procured. Zac had a lot of things to apologise for.

"For what happened when... Victoria," he managed to get out.

"You don't need to apologise for that," Sam said. "It's all water under the bridge."

Sam knew it'd been out of his brother's control, but Zac blamed himself, even though Sam had told him time and again that he didn't blame him. That it wasn't his fault. He had told him the same thing for one hundred and forty-eight years.

It wasn't his fault that she'd chosen him. Victoria... the vampire who'd changed Zac had slaughtered their parents and turned Sam as a message to his brother that he couldn't win against her.

Victoria, the auburn-haired woman who'd pulled Zac from the brink of death into a new life. The monster who had manipulated and brainwashed his brother. The vampire who'd slaughtered their parents. The woman who'd turned Sam.

If anyone was to blame, it was her.

"I'm sorry," Zac slurred as he slumped against him before falling unconscious.

Sighing, Sam laid him out on the sofa and stuffed a pillow under his head. He was worried about what Zac might do once he'd had time to process what'd happened. He would go after Arturius without a second thought and he would be torn to pieces in under a minute.

Sam knew Zac needed to avenge Aya, but they had to be smart about it.

The only thing he could do was be there for his brother and help the best he could.

Sam only hoped he could keep him alive long enough to do so.

CHAPTER 3

P etersburg, Virginia
April 1865

Zachary Degaud was twenty-three years old, born in Ashburton, Louisiana, recently raised to Captain in the Confederate Army. America was at war with itself and he was tasked with the only thing he was good at —fighting.

Much to the disgust of his father, his first-born son had run off and enlisted in the Army of his own free will. He had no mind for business and the society trappings the plantation came with. That was for his younger brother, Samuel, to pursue. He was of a much more logical approach, whereas Zac... Well, he was good with his hands.

They'd stationed his newly appointed infantry unit in Virginia, along with ten others. It was a chance

to see part of America they'd never laid eyes on
before, and to do what they'd been trained to do—
killing Union soldiers in the name of the glorious
South.

Zac had made it through the entire Civil War until
now. If they made it home in one piece, he was
guaranteed to make Major and then, perhaps his
parents would be proud of his accomplishments.
When the Union had attacked Petersburg, it had
landed them nine months in god-forsaken trenches,
until the General had ordered the retreat.

The Confederates had evacuated the entire city
after the Union had overrun their defences. All their
routes were blocked, save for one. Their last remaining
option was to retreat west and that's what they had
been commanded to do by General Lee himself. Zac
thought it was a trap, but they had their orders and
would follow if they valued their lives.

It wasn't going so well. They'd been dogged by the
perusing army and been engaged twice already in
Amelia County. Now, word had it that the Union
cavalry blocked their route to their safe haven in
Danville. Their food was gone and morale was almost
nonexistent. Zac had to move his men as fast as they
could before they were cut off, but that's exactly what
had happened.

It was late afternoon when they realised they'd
been separated from the bulk of their forces. Three
quarters in front and clear, but the last remaining

quarter was behind. Boxed in and cut off, the approach of the enemy in hearing range.

Their only option was to stand and fight for their lives.

The Union cavalry line was advancing through the woods and would be in their line of sight any second. All thirty-five men in Zac's unit scrambled to form a semblance of a line, half their number standing and the other half with one knee to the ground in front. Zac was front and centre, one of the few Confederate captains he knew who would stand and fight with his men. The rest he considered cowards not worthy of their ranks.

As the first of the Unions came into their line of sight, their horses looming over the small infantry unit, he shouted, "*Fire!*"

The crack was deafening as the thirty-six rifles went off, white smoke billowing in front of them, the reek of gunpowder thick in the air. The sharp cries of men and horses in front of them signalled that at least some of their bullets had found their marks, but the line was still advancing. Their rifles were designed for long range shooting, not close range. Most of the shots had gone right over the Union soldiers' heads.

"Reload, reload!" Zac shouted to his men, who hastily dropped the butts of their rifles to the ground, stuffing their next rounds as fast as they could.

"Arms at the ready! Aim low!" he shouted as all thirty-five rifles were cocked and ready to fire. They had to split the cavalry's advance so they could retreat. If they couldn't, then it would have to be hand-to-hand combat until either side was dead or captured.

"*Fire!*"

The crack of their rifles split the air around them as men and horses fell. They were advancing too quickly for another round.

Dropping his rifle, Zac shouted, "Swords!"

Steel rang as all thirty-five men drew without question.

"Legs!" he ordered, trusting his men to understand that they needed to cut down the horses if they had any chance.

They spread out, swords at the ready for when the Unionists would break through their line. The men were thirty-five against an entire regiment of at least fifty—about fifteen had fallen in the wave of gunfire.

As the first wave of cavalry came within range, Zac swung hard and true, hamstringing the mount that came up on his right side. The enormous bay horse fell to the ground behind him, barely missing his head. Its rider was flung headlong into a tree, and a quick glance verified that his neck had been snapped.

The next line was seconds behind and this time, Zac cut his blade to the left, nicking a horse's knee, but not bringing it down. Cursing, he rose to engage a dismounted Unionist who swung his sabre wildly with no aptitude. Zac took advantage and ducked low, bringing his elbow up into the man's gut hard. As the soldier doubled over, he drove his sword through his back, directly into his heart. Not stopping for a moment, he turned to the next man, disposing of him as easily as the first.

Affording himself a quick glance around the clearing, he knew they would be overwhelmed, but they were from the South—all the men in his unit were. They would fight to the end, even if that end meant death. In that moment, he thought about his parents and his brother Samuel. They meant the world to him, but he wasn't good at anything else. He was only good at killing and the Army had swiftly become his life. But... *he had to survive.*

Zac had dispatched of six more men before he felt the biting pain of a bullet imbedding in his chest, but that was only the beginning of his problems.

Falling limply onto the bloodstained ground, he gasped for air—the bullet had passed through a lung. Then Bragg, his second in command, was above him, his palm over the wound, desperately trying to stop the bleeding. As he tried to speak, Zac saw his friend and comrade-in-arms' face shot off in a shower of blood and bone.

At some point Zac had passed out but was brought around when he felt himself being dragged along the ground, none too gently, and heaved up onto something soft and lumpy. He lay on his back, the stars shining through the trees.

Weakly, he turned his head, the blood that'd pooled in his mouth running down his face.

Then he realised two things. One, he was as good as dead and two, he was in a pile of corpses that used to be his men.

He didn't bother trying to figure out how he felt about that. He had maybe twenty minutes left and could probably spend his time pondering more favourable things, like the beautiful lady he'd danced with at ball his parents had held the night before he'd departed for Virginia. She was raven-haired with skin like milk, eyes like the bluest sky. He could ask a lady like that to marry him.

He thought about his brother Samuel. And his parents, even though they'd discouraged him from joining the Confederacy in the first place. What were they doing now?

It was then that he saw a woman look down at him, her chestnut eyes gleaming in the darkness. It had to be a hallucination. He didn't believe in God and angels, only life and death. She straddled him as he lay on top of his dead comrades like some macabre devil.

"Dear Captain," the woman murmured into his ear, "do you want to live?"

He could only cough, blood gurgling in his throat. The woman seemed to take that as an acceptance and to his horror, she sliced open her wrist with his bowie knife and forced the open wound over his mouth, flooding it with their mingled blood. He was forced to swallow several times, groaning as pain shot through his chest.

Then, as far as he could tell, he died. Just as he should have. But the problem was, he didn't stay that way.

Zac's eyes snapped open and he gazed up at the clear night sky. Thousands of stars sparkled through the trees that sheltered him—he'd never seen so many. Rolling over, he coughed loudly, blood splattering the ground. He'd been dragged away from the pile of corpses to a clear patch of grass.

How the hell was he alive? The gunshot wound was enough to kill him. If not, he should've choked on his own blood. Realising he felt no pain, he clutched his chest, ripping his shirt where the bullet had passed through. He was covered in blood, but there was no wound.

Looking around, he found he was alone except for eighty-five corpses.

Everyone was dead.

The Union soldiers who'd survived lay haphazardly around the clearing like they'd been flung there with no regard at all.

The woman he'd hallucinated sat at the base of a tree across the clearing, watching him closely, and he gasped in surprise as his gaze met hers.

He took in her appearance for the first time. She wore a plain green dress that billowed around her waist as she sat, her long, curly auburn hair falling around her shoulders, drawing his eye to her cleavage. He looked away, conscious of her modesty.

Even at this distance he caught the low sound of her laughter. Pulling himself up, he dragged himself backwards, propping his weary frame against a tree. His heart skipped a beat in surprise as the woman was suddenly beside him. He realised she couldn't have possibly closed that distance in a mere second—it was as if she'd appeared out of thin air.

"Who are you?" he rasped, his throat dry.

The woman smiled at him, smoothing his hair back from his brow. "I'm someone who will take care of you." Her voice was soft and musical, her touch reassuring and very real.

His brow furrowed. "Ma'am?"

She laughed again and grasped his arm. "Come, I have a gift for you."

The woman helped him to his feet, but he felt perfectly well, like the entire day hadn't happened at all. The black forest around them seemed clearer, the wind through the leaves louder. He felt better than he had in a long time. It made little sense.

She led him to the opposite side of the clearing where a Union soldier sat against a tree, eyes staring vacantly ahead, the rise and fall of his chest the only sign that he was still alive.

"I saved this one for you," the woman said, coaxing the man to stand. "He's the one who shot you."

The soldier stood rigid and stared straight through

him. Zac waved his hand in front of the soldier's eyes, but there was no response. He didn't even blink.

His eyes flickered warily to the woman who was now standing behind the man, their heights even. As her eyes changed into two black pools of nothingness, she sunk her teeth into the soldier's neck. Zac gasped in horror as she drank the man's blood. Pulling back, she smiled wickedly at him, her mouth and chin red with the soldier's life.

It was then that he caught the smell on the air. Somehow, he knew it was the scent of fresh blood…. and it was intoxicating. His mouth tightened as his teeth ached, and he drew in a deep breath.

Before he could stop himself, Zac lunged for the soldier, sinking his teeth into the open wound over his jugular. Knowing he should be repulsed at the notion of drinking another man's blood, he drank like he could never get enough. When there was no more, he let the man drop limply to the ground.

The woman smiled at him, pleased with the result. As he wiped his face with the back of his hand, he doubled over as pain ripped through him. Grasping his chest, he fell to the ground as his heart raced. The pain was worse than the gunshot by far.

The woman knelt beside him and crooned into his ear, "Don't fear, dear captain. It will pass soon."

He gazed into her eyes as the pain took him into unconsciousness and he knew no more.

When Zac finally woke, he found himself lying in a bed, the curtains of the simple room tightly drawn over the windows.

Rolling onto his side, he dragged himself to his feet. The room seemed to shimmer around him, every little detail sharper and more defined. Rubbing his eyes didn't seem to change anything. The clarity made his head ache something fierce.

Getting up, he walked towards the window and opened one side of the curtain, letting daylight flood into the little room. Suddenly, he jerked back into the corner, away from the direct sunlight with a yelp. It was hot... so hot it felt as if it had burned him.

Reaching out tentatively, the warm sunlight fell over his hand. He wrenched his hand back as his flesh seared, holding his hand against his chest. The bright light seemed to hurt his eyes and tingle his skin.

Looking down, he expected to find a burn there, but he stared in shock as his hand healed in front of his eyes. Seared flesh disappeared into smooth, unblemished skin.

Leaning back against the wall, he caught sight of the woman sitting in the shadows, watching him. Startled, he jumped.

"What have you done to me?" He grimaced, cowering back into the darkness.

"I've given you an incredible gift," she replied. "You will never age, and you will never die."

"Why can't I tolerate the sunlight?" he hissed.

The woman only sighed.

"Answer me!" he yelled at her.

"You won't be able to go out into the day anymore."

"W-what are y-you?" he stammered. "W-what did you do to m-me?"

"You, my dear captain, are a vampire," she stated. "I saved you from death."

"A vampire?" he scoffed.

"Yes. The monsters of myth are a reality. Now you will walk the night with me."

Zac slid down the wall and sunk his head into his knees. He was a vampire? A devil doomed to walk the night for eternity.

"You lie," he whispered.

"You lie to yourself. Your destiny has claimed you, captain."

Zac shook his head, threading his fingers through his hair and tugging. The sun, the blood, his death... Was this what he was now? A monster?

"*And what choice did you give me?*" He lunged across the room faster than he thought possible, grasping her around the neck, but she pushed him across the room, his shoulder punching a hole in the crude plaster before he fell to his knees. She'd thrown him like he weighed nothing at all.

"*Shh,*" she whispered in his ear, suddenly at his

side and placing her hand over his mouth. "Do not fear, I will teach you. You and I will rule the South. Don't think I didn't see you fight yesterday. You killed nine of them and three of their horses in minutes before they could fell you. We will do many great things together, Captain Degaud."

"My family," he whispered as she slid her hand away. "I— What..."

"You cannot go home," she said, a note of warning in her voice. "Your family will not understand. They will fear you."

He shook his head but understood it was futile to argue. The woman smiled again and drew him to his feet, placing her hand on his face.

"Who are you?" he whispered.

"I am Victoria."

***

Zac lost control too many times to count in his first weeks as a vampire. His hunger for human blood drove him mad, and Victoria didn't try to curb his frenzy. She was pleased with him.

He was disgusted at the monster he'd become but didn't know how to stop. Restraint was the one thing she'd neglected to teach him. Victoria had turned him into a monster, a cold-blooded killer and hunter. A vicious predator intent on one thing and one thing only. *Blood.*

She spent many hours teaching him to use his bloodlust to his advantage and use his new skills to hunt and kill. They were almost the same, apart from age, but there was one singular difference that stood out with glaring clarity.

She could walk in the sunlight, but she never explained why he would burn and she would not. He tried on many occasions to go outside but was driven back into the darkness every time.

He thought about his family often. They would've received word of his death weeks ago. Perhaps it was for the best, as Victoria kept telling him. He was now a vampire, and that was a secret he had to keep if he wanted to stay alive. Well, as alive as he could be.

The Civil War had ended only days after his death, and it was like a punch in the gut. He was so close to going home, so close... Instead, he spent his days holed up in darkness and his nights trying not to kill innocent women and children.

There would be no relief for him.

Tonight saw them in a new city. Petersburg and the aftermath of the war were far behind them. The hour was late, dawn was close, and many residents had already long retired for the evening. Only a few stragglers remained, hurrying home to be with their families or partake in more unsavoury deeds. Victoria slid her arm through his as they walked the darkened street. It wasn't he who led his lady down the sidewalk; it was all her. He was her puppet to play with. Her toy to shape. She was his guide and teacher in this unknown life he called death.

They walked the street of this new city, seeking the unfortunate. Stalking their prey. And they always found humans ripe for the picking. Tonight was no different.

Up ahead, a woman walked down the street alone, finely dressed, but reeking of something else. Excess. He felt Victoria's excitement, but didn't mention it.

"Her," she said. He didn't have to ask what she meant.

"She's a prostitute."

"So? She won't be missed."

He shrugged as he felt her disappear from his side. Exhaling, he walked forwards, altering his path to meet that of the woman's. As her gaze met his, he let a grin pull at his lips and she halted.

"Evenin', sir." She dipped into a slight curtsey.

Zac nodded his head, not trusting himself to speak.

"Oh?" she said. "Not fond of talking, are we?"

He shook his head, struggling with what Victoria was forcing him to do.

The woman gave him a knowing look. "Sir, the sun is set to rise within the hour. Come with me, I only have a short while. You..." she smiled suggestively, "you I will do for free."

He didn't protest when she took his arm, leading him from the street into the darkness of an alley, their footsteps echoing between the close walls. The woman looked back over her shoulder and opened a door set in the brickwork, revealing a flight of stairs.

Zac glanced into the shadows where his vampire eyes saw Victoria lingering, watching him with an air of approval.

"Do it," he heard her whisper and he turned, following the woman up the stairs.

Once on the landing, the room opened into a small, but lavishly furnished bedroom. Looking around, he saw no other entrances, only a window on the wall behind him with tightly closed drapes. As she lit a lamp on the dresser, he idly wondered how many men she brought here and if she was happy with how her life had turned out. She seemed to enjoy her occupation.

"Now," the woman purred, standing before him. "Where were we?"

As she reached behind herself and unlaced her corset, he could only see the pulsing vein in her neck. His gaze came up to meet hers as he felt the slow burn in his throat. Just the thought of her blood made him hungry and the more he dwelt on it, the more it seared.

Then, it was as if someone else was controlling his movements and the predator inside awoke. Stepping forwards, he reached around and grasped the woman's wrists and pulled her hard against him, burying his head into the crook of her neck.

"*Oh*," she exclaimed. "That's more like it."

He breathed deeply, inhaling the promising scent

of blood, his lips brushing against her skin. As his vision blurred into darkness, he knew it was too late. He wouldn't be able to stop himself now, nor did he want to.

He softly kissed her skin, her breath hitching as his hands lightly traced the outline of her arms, then burying into her hair. Gently tugging her head to the side, his teeth ached and he could draw it out no longer. Biting down into her jugular, he tore at her flesh viciously, her blood beginning to pour from the open wound.

The woman let out a shriek of horror, her frantic sobs grating on his nerves. He clapped a hand over her mouth to stifle the annoying sounds as he pulled the life from her in heaving gulps, the coppery tang of her blood overwhelming his senses until there was nothing else.

When she stilled, legs crumbling beneath her, he gently lowered her to the ground, cradling her body as he drank the last drops, her heart slowing and finally stopping. It was only then that he pulled away and looked at the corpse he held with black eyes and a bloodstained mouth.

Monster.

Zac knew Victoria was standing over him. As he looked up at her, she shook her head, a sly smile playing at her lips.

He'd killed before, but this time it was different.

This time there was no going back. He'd killed and finally... *he liked it.*

"Let her go, Zachary," she murmured, and he looked at the woman in his arms with sudden distaste. He stood sharply, dropping her lifeless body onto the floor. There was blood everywhere.

"What have you done to me?" he whispered in horror as his eyes cleared.

"I've done nothing but help you survive," she said.

"You've done nothing but make me kill."

Victoria snarled and grabbed him by the scruff of the neck and dragged him towards the window, flinging the curtains open wide. Pushing him into the dawn, his skin seared and he cried out at the sudden pain.

"Stop it," he sobbed, trying to control himself. If she held him there for much longer...

"Understand, Zachary," she hissed into his ear, "I'm the one with the power here."

"*Please.*"

Victoria hauled him into the shadows and he fell to his knees. The pungent smell of burnt flesh dissipated as his skin healed.

"This is what you are now," she said, looking down at him with disdain. "There's no going back. It would be such a waste if I had to let you go."

His eyes snapped up to meet hers. "You wouldn't."

"Oh, my dear, I would in a heartbeat."

Zac knew she would. She would kill him in an

instant if he were no longer useful, if he could no longer serve his purpose.

Victoria was every inch the monster she'd created in her own image. The monster she'd turned him into.

There would be no going back. *Ever.*

<hr>

Answers were the one thing Victoria wouldn't give Zac.

She was secretive about her reasons for turning him and would dodge his questions, sometimes slapping him across the face, splitting his lip against his teeth. She would tell him that they would be together for eternity, that they would do great things. What those things were didn't reveal themselves until weeks later, when they travelled to Louisiana.

Victoria found them a house in New Orleans, where she left him for days at a time, off on some undisclosed business. 'All in good time,' she would say when he enquired. He didn't dare leave the house at night for fear he would be recognised, having spent much time here when he'd first enlisted.

Zac became increasingly agitated at his confinement and Victoria finally agreed to keep him company. They were in the parlour that night when she received a guest. A tall, well-built man dressed in a fine waistcoat and jacket, stood in the doorway. Victoria bade Zac stay as she took their guest to the dining room.

He knew the man was a vampire; he wasn't trying to hide it at all. Casting his hearing out, he heard the door close behind them. Stepping out into the hallway, he moved towards the dining room and hesitated. The voices of the two vampires murmured on the other side. They hadn't noticed his approach. Leaning his back against the wall, he listened.

"When he is ready, he will be unstoppable," Victoria said. "He is still too new, too prone to the rage."

"There is another who has their sights on the South, Victoria," the man replied, his voice urgent.

"I know full well what we're up against. Zachary will bend to my will one way or another and he will be the cold-blooded killer I am shaping him to be," she said with pride. "You should see him, Alistair. Even when he loses control, he's beautiful to watch."

"If you're right, then together, we will be forever safe from them," the man named Alistair replied.

"That is the goal. After I let her escape in Paris..." She sighed. "If we win the South, we will have her. I know she's here."

"I hope you are right, Victoria... for all our sakes."

Finally understanding, he closed his eyes and took a deep breath to calm himself. Victoria had turned him to help her win the South for her own gain. He had been a captain who'd commanded respect... a respect that drove thirty-five men to their deaths unquestioned. Fighting and killing was second nature to him as a human. As a vampire, he would be capable of a much greater horror.

Victoria was using him.

When she finally came back to the parlour, closing the door behind her, she saw the hatred in Zac's eyes. Sitting beside him, she forced his face towards hers.

"What is it, my dear?" she asked.

He stood abruptly, wrenching himself free and paced over to the fireplace. "Tell me the truth, Victoria."

She smiled as she rose. "I have always been truthful to you."

"You're a masterful liar. Tell me the truth." When she didn't reply straight away, he spat, "You're training me to do your bidding."

"Not mine, Zachary. *Ours*."

He shook his head in disbelief. "I never wanted this!"

"Dear, Zachary." She caressed his cheek, attempting to calm him. "You will kill for us. It's the only thing you're good at. It's how we survive."

He let her go, his expression falling into resentment. Victoria stepped into him, resting her head against his chest, her arms circling his waist.

"I won't let you use me," he whispered into her hair. "I am not your puppet."

She smiled up at him and kissed his cheek. "Oh, but you are and forever will be."

She reached up and grasped his face as her

expression contorted into malice. She was too quick for him. She'd broken his neck before he could pull away, and he was dead before he hit the ground.

It was around midnight when he finally woke.

He sat upright, gasping for breath. Looking around, he realised he was alone. The house was empty.

"*Victoria!*" he roared but knew he would receive no answer.

Standing, he paced back and forth, rubbing his neck. Where could she be? He knew nothing of her dealings, other than what he'd overheard. Halting, he realised that Victoria would teach him a lesson for his defiance. The only thing she knew he cared about was his family.

She was... He heaved in a breath to calm himself. *Think, Zac.*

Ashburton was thirty miles to the northwest. His family's manor and plantation sat on the outskirts, closest to New Orleans, about eight miles from the centre of town. That made it approximately twenty-two miles. If he ran as fast as he could, he would be there in less than an hour.

He didn't think twice.

The street outside was empty as he burst from the house. He was across town in five minutes, moving so fast, the humans he passed thought a gust of wind had curiously buffeted them on an otherwise still and humid night.

Pushing himself harder and harder, not caring who saw him, Zac ran, hoping he would make it in time. Victoria would kill everyone he'd ever loved to ensure his obedience, to break the last shred of his humanity.

As he finally reached the plantations and turned up the long road that led to the main house, he smelt the blood. Unable to control himself, his eyes misted into black pools of nothingness, but he didn't stop. He couldn't.

Skidding to a halt at the top of the driveway, he heard the screams. Shaking his head to clear his thoughts, he listened for his parents and brother. He couldn't lose control now, not when their lives were at stake. Then he heard her musical laughter on the air, drifting from around the side of the house.

He ran towards the sound, coming to a complete stop at the doors to his father's study, an invisible barrier stopping him from entering. The floors and walls were splattered with blood and he couldn't get in. Willing it to be an unpleasant dream, he saw his mother and father on the floor, the life having ebbed away from them. The sickly scent of their blood hung in the air, threatening to take his sanity, but his grief was enough to hold him.

Unable to move, he whispered, "*No.*"

"Zac?" a familiar voice from across the room called.

"Samuel?" he cried, his head snapping up from the

gruesome sight before him, seeking out his little brother.

He stumbled from the shadows, his eyes flickering to the bodies of their parents and up to those of his older brother, whose eyes were eerily black. It was then he realised Victoria was behind him, staring over his shoulder into Zac's eyes, the bloodlust etched in her once pretty features. *They'd invited her in.*

Zac saw the blood in Sam's mouth as it dripped from his lips. Victoria had fed him her blood. She intended to turn him.

"No," Zac pleaded. "Not him, please not him."

She stood behind his brother, grinning maliciously. "This is what happens when I'm defied, Zachary."

Sam gasped as she snapped his spine, his legs crumbling beneath his weight. Then she bent down and snapped his neck before he could cry out.

"*No!*" Zac roared, lunging for Victoria, his eyes black with rage.

All the human occupants of the house were dead, and he crossed the threshold without hinderance.

She'd taken everything from him--his parents, his brother, his home. She'd even taken his death. He should've died in that pile of corpses and remained that way.

His hands grasped empty air as she disappeared, her laughter echoing from behind. Snarling deep in his throat, he swung around to find her on the verandah, just outside the opened French doors.

"Come and kill me, Zachary, or help your little brother change," she said with a sneer. "It's the only choice I will ever give you."

His gaze shifted to Sam's limp body. In this moment, he hated Victoria more than he ever thought possible. She'd forced him to make a hopeless decision. He would either have to kill his brother or turn him.

Unable to control himself, he rushed Victoria, wanting to tear her to pieces. If this was the one thing he was good at, then she would bear witness to it firsthand.

She ran, luring him into the surrounding forest, but all the training he'd had in the Army came as second nature out here. For once, he had an advantage over her.

He cornered her in a small gully where an old cave used to open up onto the lake. They were surrounded by rock, Victoria's back against a fallen boulder. Her eyes widened as if she finally comprehended the true nature of the monster she'd created.

His rage was all-consuming, all reason lost. Lunging for her, his hands grasped her neck and squeezed.

"How could you?" he heard himself say. "Murderer. *Murderer!*"

"You're a killer, Zachary," Victoria gasped, her fingernails raking at his hands. "And you're mine. I made you. *I made you!*"

"I'm not yours!" he spat at her, letting his rage overwhelm him. Feeling his fingers sink into her flesh, he tore her neck open, his fangs sinking into the open wound, tearing out anything they clasped hold of. With a roar, he tore her head clean off, casting it aside as her limp body fell to the ground, her blood pooling in the dirt.

He watched numbly as her body turned grey and withered. His chest heaved and he wiped his hands on his blood-soaked shirt.

Victoria was right. He *was* good at killing.

A piercing scream brought him back from the edge of his frenzy and his head snapped towards the manor.

Samuel!

Turning, he ran, needing to get to his brother before he did something he'd regret. He needed to explain to Sam, let him know his options. Give him the choice he'd never had.

Running up the long driveway, he saw his brother in front of the house, clutching a young woman to his chest, his head buried against her neck.

Zac couldn't smell her blood, he hadn't fed yet. He pushed himself to run faster than his vampire feet had ever taken him.

"*Sam!*" he yelled, but he was too late.

He helplessly watched as his brother sunk his newly grown fangs into the woman's neck. Stopping dead in his tracks, he could only watch his twenty-year-old little brother toss the woman aside as if she were nothing.

Sam looked confused as he stumbled down the driveway, blood dripping down his chin, the ground littered with the corpses of the massacred slaves and servants. Silent tears streamed down his cheeks as Zac fell to his knees.

"Zac..." Sam gasped, clutching his chest. The change was on him. "I couldn't help it. I—" He roared in pain and collapsed.

Sam writhed on the ground, Zac subduing his thrashing with strong hands. When he finally slipped into unconsciousness, Zac let his grasp slacken.

It was his fault. All of it was his fault. If he hadn't defied Victoria, then she would have never come here. His parents would be alive and Sam would be human.

As his vampire eyes saw the first hint of dawn colour the sky, Zac could only do the one thing that was left in his power.

Picking up his brother's limp body, he carried him down the driveway and away from their home for good.

CHAPTER 4

Zac had become a permanent fixture at *Max's* bar. He no longer cared about the scandalous gossip he was perpetuating as Ashburton's latest alcoholic train wreck. He just wanted everything to go the hell away, and the more alcohol he could consume, the better.

For the first time since setting foot in this stinking town, he'd had to compel the bar staff, otherwise they'd cut him off. He was turning into the worst kind of drunk.

The only kind of control Zac wanted was the numb, inebriated kind.

He sensed her concern from across the room before he heard her approach. Gabby sat at the bar beside him, worry set in her features, and he rolled his eyes.

"You're better," he said, still staring straight ahead, fingers clasped around his glass.

"Much," she replied, eyeing the drink in front of him. "Zac, I'm—"

"I know."

She was frowning at him. People frowned in his direction a lot lately. Why were they saying sorry to him? He hadn't had his heart torn out, but he may as well have. They'd all heard, all saw. She'd told him she loved him. She made him a better person, but he didn't know where that left him now. He snorted, closing his dry eyes.

"What are you doing?" Gabby asked as if she didn't already know.

"I'm just sitting here thinking about all the choices that I made to get to this point. The pathetic, lonely, homicidal maniac." Because it was true.

"You're not alone, Zac. You have Sam and Liz. Alex. And you have me," she told him.

"*Pfft.* Sam doesn't want to help me... he wants to *change* me."

She sighed, shaking her head. "Zac. You need to pull yourself out of this. Do you think it's what she would've wanted?"

Zac turned and glared at her. "Depressed or predator. Take your pick, Tabitha. Which is the lesser of two evils? Which has the lowest body count?"

"Don't," she whispered, edging away from him.

"I kill people, Gabby. It's what I do. It's who I am," he snarled. "I'm a vampire and I eat people. Shock. Horror."

"This isn't you." She shook her head. "You're better than that."

"Am I? Am I, really? What makes you think you even know me? I was a soldier, a trained killer. It's what I was good at. I enlisted in both World Wars and Vietnam because I wanted to kill. Oh, he's fallen off the wagon, everyone said. But I was just honouring my true nature, Gabby—a predator who needs to kill to survive." Venom dripped from his words. "Everyone wants me to be the good guy. I've never been the good guy. I can't do it. I wasn't good enough for Liz and wasn't good enough to save Aya. That's what being good gets you. *Nothing.*"

He looked over his shoulder towards the entrance, narrowing his eyes as he sensed who was coming... at who he guessed was coming. Gabby follows his gaze as the door banged open, letting in the late afternoon light and something else.

Arturius.

Zac glanced to Gabby, who nodded. She'd seen him that night in the clearing, his arm bloodied up to the elbow, Aya's heart clutched in his hand.

She grabbed Zac's arm as he went to stand, as a low growl formed deep in his throat. "Stop, Zac. Getting yourself killed is not the answer."

"If I die in the attempt of tearing that piece of shit apart, then so be it. It would be a benefit to the human race."

Arturius leaned against the bar a few stools down

and ordered a drink, glancing in Zac's direction. It was all the invitation Zac needed.

He walked up to the Roman and slammed his fist into the bar, glaring at the vampire who ruined everything.

For a moment, he acted as if Zac wasn't there, making him seethe even more. Finally turning, he looked him up and down and obviously found him wanting.

"*Ah.*" He grinned as the bartender placed his order in front of him. "You're the comatose one."

"What are you doing here?" he snarled at the Roman.

"Having a sunny southern holiday," he replied. "Tying up a few loose ends."

"Well, didn't you just put a big bow on it already," Zac said through his teeth. "What are you still doing here?"

Arturius seemed to find this amusing. "What makes you think it's my prerogative to tell you anything?"

Zac was a hairsbreadth away from losing it. "I'm having an existential crisis, Artie. You see, you killed the woman I love and that makes me mad. And what do you think happens when I get mad?"

Arturius laughed. "Are you trying to threaten me, Zachary? You have no hope in besting me."

"You don't think I know?" He glared at him, not

breaking eye contact. "I know a lot of things. Perhaps you ought to be the one who's worried."

"I know you have no idea how to kill me. And I also know Aeriaya gave you her blood, so if you haven't already seen what became of her kind, then you would know that there is no hope for you. The fact that you're alive right now is because I *choose* not to end you." He stood with a sigh, throwing some money onto the bar. "Don't push too hard, Zachary, or you might lose your head."

Zac lunged for the founder, but before he could raise his fist, he slammed into an invisible wall. Surprised, he tried again, but met the same resistance.

"Not in the bar." Gabby came up behind them. "If you're going to fight, take it into the forest where no one can see. I won't have innocent people put into danger by the likes of you two."

Arturius sneered at her, his eyes gliding up and down her body. "I'm always in need of a witch... especially a witch who was powerful enough to stand against Katrin." He gave her a knowing look.

Zac knew Arturius had been in the cemetery as he'd laid unconscious. Sam had told him how the Roman had stood over Aya's lifeless body like it was some kind of trophy. And he'd seen Gabby there. Would he come after her now that Aya was gone?

He didn't know what Arturius was looking for—he never understood everything that'd happened that night—but he seemed to think Gabby could tell him something.

The Roman sneered at her and gave a last warning glance to Zac before turning and leaving the bar, regrouping now that Gabby had come forwards to protect the town.

Zac turned and gave her a look. The fleeting note of panic that flickered in her eyes didn't escape his notice. He knew something was up. Fact was, he always knew, regardless if anyone told him or not.

He didn't know if it was the encounter with Arturius or the amount of alcohol he had consumed, but for the first time, he let it drop, not saying a single word. Maybe he was just mad she'd stopped him from hitting the Roman, or maybe he just didn't care.

"Go away, Gabby," he said, sitting back down.

And she was gone before he could change his mind.

***

It'd been almost two weeks since Gabby had gone to Memphis with the brothers to free Aya, who'd been captured by the founding vampire, Caius. And it'd been a week since she'd found out who Aya really was.

She was a Celestine. The beginning of magic. The race that founded the first witches and the caretakers of the earth. Creatures with power beyond reckoning.

Aya had dedicated herself to protecting the origins of power… and the legacy of her people.

The Celestine's secrets in the wrong hands could plunge the world into darkness.

Gabby didn't know exactly what Aya had become when Arturius had turned her, but with her help that night in the void, she'd become something close to what she once was.

Her kind had granted the first witches their power and had promptly become extinct at the hands of a woman of their own creation—Katrin. It was a tale that was as sad as it was twisted, and Gabby had to keep this secret or face the possibility of doing greater harm.

In her desire to help her new friend, she'd awaken powers inside herself she never dreamed she could possess… but it was a dream she wanted to take back. All she wanted was to understand and control her power, but she got the complete opposite.

The power she had coiled inside seemed endless and terrified her.

It'd been so easy when she stood in that yard in Memphis. She'd obliterated the three witches with nothing more than an absent flick of the wrist. They'd disintegrated, their ash flying away on the breeze like sand in a sandstorm. If she done nothing, they would've all died. Sam, Zac, Aya… they would've all died. Aya had told her after that she would've killed them, that those witches had given themselves over to evil, but it didn't make Gabby feel any better.

All that seemed like nothing now that Aya was gone. She could've helped her to understand. Magic was truly dead without her.

She now sat with Liz and Alex in the middle of the lounge room floor of her apartment, a pizza on one side, wine on the other, and the grimoire in her lap. As she told them about what'd happened in the bar earlier with Zac and Arturius, Liz's expression turned into sorrow and Alex's into thought.

Arturius had shown interest in Gabby and she was forced to admit she was worried he'd stuck around because of her, that the Roman wanted her magic.

"He's really..." She couldn't think of the right word.

"Scary?" Liz offered.

"Psychotic?" Alex countered, even though he hadn't been there that night in the cemetery.

Psychotic had nothing on it.

"Why would he want you?" Liz asked. "I mean, he must have others to do his dirty work..."

"He said he was always in need of a witch. I guess the more he has, the fewer people would oppose him," she replied, taking a large gulp of wine, not elaborating further.

She felt bad keeping Aya's secret from her oldest friends. Friends who'd helped her through one of the toughest times in her life—finding her grams—but she was bound.

What she didn't tell anyone was that ever since she'd linked to Aya in the void, she'd hardly been able to control herself. There was a growing darkness inside of her that wanted to get out. She didn't know how to stop whatever had triggered the growth. So, she stopped practicing altogether. Perhaps that's what Arturius had sensed in her.

"But you'd never do that," Alex exclaimed. "He's mad."

"Yeah, raving mad," Gabby scoffed. "I'd never help him."

"We have to do something," Alex declared. "He killed Aya, and God knows what he might do to you."

"That's what I was trying to figure out before you guys came over," she said and absently opened the grimoire.

Liz sat up straighter, her eyes lighting up with hope. "Do you have any ideas?"

"All spells have a workaround," Gabby said, leafing through the grimoire. "There's always a way to undo something that's been brought forth with power."

"Always?" Liz asked.

"Well, so far I haven't come across a reason for it not to be the case, but I guess there might be some spells that might be impossible to counter." She shrugged. "In the case of the founding vampires, they were made with the power of a witch. That power can be unraveled... or at least, in theory. With you and the brothers, that can't be undone as another vampire created you." She hesitated when she realised she was pressing on a nerve. Liz had never wanted to be a vampire, and like the brothers, it'd been forced on her.

"I kind of figured already," Liz told her.

"So, what do you think might undo the spell?" Alex asked, directing the conversation away.

"That's the problem," Gabby replied. "I would need to know what the spell was to find out for sure. And a spell like that is kind of bad news. It's dark, no go, kind of stuff."

"*Whoa*," Alex said, his eyes widening. "Like black magic?"

Gabby gave him a look. "*Dark* magic. It's not exactly a thing that's written anywhere, at least not in my grimoire. I hoped something might have been written about it. Now that I can read the pages I couldn't before, I thought I might find something."

"But there isn't anything, is there?" Liz asked, her voice betraying her disappointment.

"Yep. A big fat zero." She rolled her eyes. Gabby knew deep down that that kind of magic wouldn't be written anywhere. It was darkness that came from powerful emotions. Hate.

"How do you think we could find out?" Alex wondered out loud. "Could there be someone alive who knows about this kind of dark magic?"

"Maybe," Gabby replied with a shrug. "But it'd be dangerous."

"How dangerous?" Liz asked slowly.

"Crazy dangerous." Gabby shook her head. "That

kind of magic is what Aya would've killed a witch for." What she didn't say was that she was afraid she was turning to it without even wanting to… that she was the darkness.

"Well," Alex said, "there you have it."

"You need to tell Zac," Liz said. "He could be able to help."

"I don't think so, Liz. You didn't see him today. I've never seen him like that." She was very hesitant.

"He has a right to know," she told her.

"Maybe, but it might do more harm than good."

"Maybe we should leave it until we can find something more solid to go on," Alex said. "If it comes to nothing, then we would only be giving him false hope. That might be the thing that pushes him off the edge."

Liz nodded, her reluctance clear. "Perhaps I can talk to Sam about it."

"I'd rather just keep it between us," Gabby said. "The more people know about it, the more trouble it'll become. Besides, this is a witch thing. You're the only vampire who's coming close to this."

Liz nodded. "If that's what you want."

"I just need time to find out what I can the right way. The good way," she said firmly.

Alex winked. "Well, if you need help, just call. I don't know what we could dig up to help, but I can ask my sister."

Alex's sister, Isobel, was studying anthropology and

archaeology at Oxford University in the United Kingdom. It was possible she could dig up some old legends. Things that meant nothing to a historian might mean the world to a witch. Besides, she might unknowingly uncover something that could save all their lives—save them from Arturius and from her power.

Gabby topped off all their glasses with wine, emptying the bottle, thankful she had friends as wholeheartedly good as Liz and Alex. She hoped with everything she had that her power wouldn't overwhelm them all.

CHAPTER 5

As Aeriaya's eyes snapped open, she gasped for breath in heaving gulps.

Piece by piece, she became aware of her surroundings as her mind cleared. At first, she thought they'd moved her elsewhere, but she soon realised her vision had become sharper. The walls were more defined. The rise and fall of the dirt floor was more pronounced. The light spilling in from above sparkled like diamonds.

The clarity made her head ache. She sat up tentatively, her neck stiff.

Holding her hands in front of her face, she tilted them into the murky light. Her skin didn't shimmer anymore, it was dull and lifeless. Pulling at the strands of black hair that fell about her shoulders, she found it was her own. Her silver waves had changed to straight raven locks that hung to her waist. Then the most horrifying realisation came when she realised she couldn't feel the earth anymore. Desperately, she placed her hands onto the ground, but she was only greeted with silence.

She put her head to her knees and sobbed. What had Arturius done? He'd led her to believe that he loved her and that he was going to help her escape.

He'd betrayed her, but the more she dwelt on it, she realised that he had been using her from the beginning. He didn't want to help her; he wanted her family's secrets just like the witch Katrin and the other Romans. He'd been manipulating and preying on her emotions.

She jumped when she heard the bolts on the cell door pull back. Arturius strode in, pulling a young girl by the hair. She was sobbing, but placid. He was glad to see her awake, but she shrunk back against the wall, wary of what he was doing. She wouldn't fall for the same trick again.

"I've brought you a gift, love," he said, dragging the girl towards her. "I'm sure you're famished."

She drew a sharp breath as his eyes became black as night, his teeth elongating into sharp fangs. He leaned over the girl and bit into her neck and drank, a small rivulet of crimson blood running down her neck. Arturius gestured her forwards and she couldn't stop herself. The newly made vampire in her lusted for this unfamiliar sensation, a need for survival. Unsure, she looked from the girl's open neck to Arturius.

"Don't worry, she won't feel anything. I have

compelled her into complacency." He stroked her raven hair in wonder. "A little trick with your eyes to make others do what you wish, love."

When she still hesitated, he grasped the back of her head and pushed her into the flow of blood. Aeriaya didn't have any choice but to swallow and pain tore through her insides as the blood ran down her throat.

Falling to the ground, she clutched her knees to her chest and cried out, tears falling from her wide eyes. Arturius dragged the dead girl from the cell and locked the door, leaving her to complete the agonising change into vampire alone.

Jolted awake, Aeriaya was dragged to her feet. Arturius held her at the base of her neck, a hand wound painfully in her hair. He jerked her around to face Katrin, whose expression was laced with rage and annoyance.

Aeriaya sensed Katrin's power and tensed. It was one part of herself she hadn't lost in the change. *One part...*

Katrin grasped her face and turned it side to side, looking into her eyes. "I want her dead," she snarled at Arturius. "You had no place making her. If she got out, she would cause a lot of trouble."

"Yes, my lady." He inclined his head, his lips pursed.

Katrin pushed past him. "Clean up your mess, Arturius. I will not tell you again."

As the witch left them, he pushed Aeriaya to the ground with a curse.

Whimpering, she looked up at him, but Arturius only gazed at her like she was an annoyance. Saying nothing, he turned and walked from the cell, closing the door heavily behind him. She heard the bolts snap shut, then receding footsteps.

"Open the grate," she heard his voice drift down the hallway. Moments later, the capping on the ceiling above scraped back with an ear-piercing screech. She clasped her hands over her sensitive ears as the dull glow from the night sky inched its way inside. She couldn't hear the stars anymore and it only seemed to add to her despair.

Alone. She was so alone. Even her birthright had abandoned her.

"Will it do the job?" she heard a voice say.

"The sun will burn her to ash." She recognised Arturius' tenor.

So, he'd manipulated her and made her a vampire against her will to see what would happen. To see if she would betray her people. He'd been sorely disappointed.

Now she was to die in the most horrible way she

could imagine. There was little hope of escape now. The sun would rise, and she would burn.

Perhaps it was better this way. Her family could never accept her now that the creatures their magic had created had turned her. Katrin had betrayed them in the most unforgivable way and now she was also touched by the same corrupt malice.

Aeriaya curled up into a ball at the far side of the cell and awaited the sunrise. It was all she had left.

Aeriaya woke with a start, not understanding where she was. The cell was lit with the bright rays of the summer sun and she was brought back to reality. She was still in shadow, but the line separating light from dark was quickly approaching. She let out a gasp and squinted in the glare.

The time to die was almost here.

She inched back against the wall as the sunlight approached, terror rendering her senseless. Weeping, she curled her toes back into the last sliver of shadow —the sun was almost overhead, and she could escape her fate no longer.

Covering her head with her arms, she sobbed for her family. For what the vampires had done to her.

The rays of the midday sun warmed her exposed arms and she cried out... but nothing happened. The burning agony she was terrified of never came.

Raising her head, she squinted up at the grated opening above where the round circle of the sun was burning.

Should she be thankful for this mercy? That their vampirism hadn't affected her in the same way? Now she was terrified of what would happen when they came to check on her. What would they try next when they saw she was alive?

She couldn't escape, that much she knew. The sun had no power over her like it did the Romans.

She silently begged Arturius to come back so she could tear him to pieces. So she could see if she was as strong as they were. Her parents had taught her revenge was evil and to take another's life was the highest of all crimes, but Aeriaya no longer cared. They'd abandoned her to this fate, and she would do whatever she needed to do. It was all she had left.

She would become the monster that'd been forced upon her. She'd do it to end their corruption once and for all.

The stars were shining above when she finally heard footsteps approach. There was nowhere to hide in her cell, so she merely stood in the centre of the room with her hands clasped. Her head hung low, her long raven hair falling about her shoulders covered her face. She looked the epitome of submission.

The door opened with a loud groan. A figure stood in the doorway, his shadow looming across the floor, lit by the warm glow of the torches behind him. There was a sharp intake of breath that gave away that they had thought to find a pile of ash, not a living girl.

Aeriaya lifted her head and was surprised to see Titus, not Arturius as she'd expected.

No matter. He would die just the same.

He strode forwards and grabbed her hair, wrenching her head back cruelly. "You were meant to burn, witch," he spat. "We'll just have to find another way to kill you."

She felt his fangs rake along her exposed neck, and she shuddered.

He laughed and hissed into her ear, "I'm going to have so much fun with you, *whore*."

It was now or never. The door was open and Titus felt he was in control. She felt rage burn inside of her and she gave herself over to it. Her vision burned white around the edges as it consumed her, and she felt a tightness in her mouth as her fangs grew for the first time.

With impossible speed, she reached up and grasped his throat, hurling him across the room with a scream of rage. He collided with enough force to loosen the stones, and dust and rubble showered down on him as he hit the floor.

She clutched the back of her head where he had torn out a clump of her hair and as her hand came back wet, she smelt the intoxicating scent of blood as a true vampire for the first time. Looking over to Titus, she took a step towards him, but he was already back on his feet, his eyes black and snarling in anger.

Lunging for her, his arms closed on empty space. She was behind him, viciously kicking his legs out from underneath his bulky frame.

Falling face forward onto the putrid floor, he spluttered in surprise. Snarling, Aeriaya grasped one leg and twisted with all her strength. There was an audible crack as it broke and Titus screamed. Before he could retaliate, she clutched the other and snapped that, too. She knew enough to know that he'd heal, but he wouldn't be alive long enough to see it done. He was hobbled and unable to run.

She felt a semblance of her old power rise inside her and she reached out with her mind, grasping it. Straddling Titus, she placed her palm over the spot where she felt his erratic heartbeat, her outstretched arm and hand burning with blue fire. Grimacing with anger and pain, she dug her fingertips into his skin, all the while Titus writhed in agony, pleading with her to stop. She couldn't, even if she wanted to—the burning taste of revenge had consumed her. She plunged her hand into his chest cavity and pulverised his heart in the power of her grasp, the blue fire finishing the pieces she'd missed. He jerked, letting out a strangled cry of pain, then stilled.

She stood slowly as Titus' body turned grey and began to desiccate, the blood and magic sustaining his life drying up. What was left of him covered her arms and dress and she absently licked the back of her hand. Her eyes were white, shining in the semi-darkness like marble.

Listening to the sounds of the surrounding castle, she heard movement far above. There were too many layers of stone for anyone to have heard Titus' screams.

She flew from the dungeon and was in the courtyard in a second. A few men were in the stable mucking out stalls, the putrid stench of horse manure and stale hay flaring her nostrils. The men were too busy to notice her. Before anyone could come into the yard, she scaled the outer wall and disappeared into the surrounding forest.

Aeriaya wasn't prepared for the overload on her senses as she ran through the trees. Where once she would have felt safe in familiar territory, she was in a whole new world. Her vampire eyes saw things she had never beheld, and her vampire ears heard sounds her earth sense had never uncovered. Disorientated, she stumbled and rolled down an embankment, coming to rest in a muddy ditch. She squeezed her eyes closed and clasped her hands over her ears to dull the onslaught. She couldn't focus on anything... she was lost.

Aeriaya didn't know how long she lay in the ditch wanting to die. When she raised her head, the moon still hung low, casting its silvery light across the field. As she became accustomed to her heightened senses, she tentatively uncovered her ears. There was still night left, so she had to be careful. The Romans would've discovered Titus's body by now and would be searching for her.

Crawling out of the ditch, she surveyed the land. She didn't know how she knew, but she was certain she was alone. Thinking about her family, she realised she had to see if they were safe. They would certainly try to kill her for what she'd become, but she had to see them safe. They were still her family, despite abandoning her. They were too important to leave to a bloody fate. They were the last.

She walked for what felt like hours, trying to remember where her home lay in the forest. If she was still herself, her power would have led her home, but now all she had were her eyes.

Finally coming across familiar territory, she approached the place that was once her home and felt a disruption in the air. *Something was wrong.* Then she caught the tang of blood in the warm night air.

Aeriaya blinked, then looked up.

Grant and Lance, the two boys who helped tend the house, were hanging by their feet from the trees, their bodies covered with bloody gashes, guts and insides hanging level with their dangling hands. Blood dripped in rivulets down their arms and fingers, pooling beneath them.

She stifled a horrified sob at the sight. Alarmed, she turned to the house. The bodies served as a warning to what she'd find within. Her mother and father... Her dear brother...

Inching open the front door, she caught the scent of blood. She ran down the hallway, unable to hold herself back and cried out in horror as she beheld her parents' room.

Everything was covered in blood. The walls and floors were splattered with it. The rugs and curtains were stained. It seeped into the joins in the floorboards. There was no surface it didn't touch.

Slowly approaching the bed, Aeriaya knew she would find their mutilated bodies. She covered her mouth and nose to stop the stench of their blood overtaking her senses. They'd been laid side by side with their hands clasped, put back together by some sadistic Roman. What was left of their opalescent skin had lost its lustre, their silver hair matted with blood and pieces of each other's flesh.

She stared at their faces, their eyes open and vacant, and no hint of the warmth she once knew. Now, only cold death had them.

Numbly, she stepped backwards, careful not to slip in the pooled blood.

She ran down the hallway to her brother's room, her bare feet slapping against the wooden floor, and wrenched the door open. She already knew what she would find. One glimpse confirmed it.

Collapsing to her knees, Aeriaya cried out in

anguish, her head in her hands. Everyone was dead, mutilated. The ultimate desecration and betrayal...

She could bear it no more. Bursting out of the front door, she ran through the forest, her vampire feet taking her farther and faster than she'd ever been.

The Romans had come looking for her. They were no longer concerned with her family's secrets, content to kill them to send her a message. Finally, when she could run no more, she collapsed in a clearing, howling in agony.

Aeriaya stood just within the tree line, watching the Roman's castle. It was bathed in the pink glow of the rising sun. The sky was crisp and clear... it would be a fine summer's day. A fine day for revenge.

She nestled into the bushes and waited for the light to grow, when they would be weaker. She cast her mind about like she used to, feeling for the presence of the forest about her. She felt nothing of the earth, but she knew the Romans were inside and angry. They couldn't leave to search for her, they were trapped in the shadows until nightfall.

As the sun rose higher into early morning, she emerged from her vantage point and made her way towards the Roman's castle. The waiting had only amplified her thirst for revenge and her vision burned white-hot with it. The closer she came to the outer walls, the better she could sense the life inside them.

Aeriaya walked through the main gate in a daze—it'd been left open. The castle grounds were abandoned, the stables devoid of any life. The horses and their keepers had left, the disarray evidence they'd fled in a hurry. She walked inside, towards the great hall, where she felt the presence of two Romans. There were dismembered bodies at irregular intervals in the hallways, slumped here and there against the walls.

They were angry enough over her escape to have eaten their compelled help. Glancing warily at the bodies, she decided that she'd come this far and there was no turning back now.

Standing under the stone arch and staring into the hall, she saw a man and a woman seated at the long table bickering with each other—she knew them as Marcus and Octavia.

The woman stood with a hiss as she caught her attention.

Marcus appeared in front of Aeriaya and grasped her by the throat, lifting her from the ground.

"You came back," he snarled. "You're either crazy or stupid."

"I'd say she's crazy," Octavia stated. "Arturius' blood mixed with hers? That fool ruined *everything*."

Aeriaya said nothing.

Marcus growled with rage and threw her clear across the room. She slammed into the wall, several ribs cracking as she landed on the floor, but the pain hardly registered.

Ignoring the throbbing in her side, Aeriaya rose to her full height. As Marcus lunged for her again, she collided with him, wedging her shoulder against his chest. The momentum sent him hurtling over her shoulder. He slammed upside down against the wall, landing face-first against the stone floor.

Octavia darted forwards but was thrown back onto the table, splitting it in half.

Before either of the Romans could rise, Aeriaya's fist punctured Marcus' chest, the blue fire that'd killed Titus burning the Roman from the inside out. He screamed in agony as he turned grey, his eyes bulging with the force of his death rattle.

When he'd let go of his last breath, Aeriaya pulled her hand free and he fell heavily to the ground, violently convulsing before becoming still.

"*No!*" Octavia screamed, falling to her knees beside what was left of Marcus. The second it took for the vampire to gather her grief was all it took for her to be thrown across the room again.

Before the vampire could stand, she was held against the wall with an iron grip. Pulling the dagger from Octavia's belt, Aeriaya plunged it viciously into her stomach.

As the Roman struggled, the dagger twisted deeper, tormenting her to madness, and she spat blood all over Aeriaya's face in defiance.

Disregarding the blood, she screamed, "*Where are they!*"

Octavia laughed, blood running from her mouth and dripping down her chin. "They're not here, *witch*. But they will come for you once they find out what you've done. And they will make it *slow*."

"Not if I find them first," she snarled, the blue fire searing down her arm into the dagger. Octavia's scream chilled her blood as she turned a sickly grey, her eyes sinking back into her skull, finally turning to ash as the life left her.

Aeriaya let the dagger go and Octavia's body slumped to the floor.

Regarding the two desiccated Romans for a moment, she weighed her options. Finally, she strolled from the castle into the yard.

Across the way, she saw a stone pit where a fire still burned. Grabbing two torches, she lit them in the unattended flame. With her fast vampire feet, she darted through the castle, lighting every piece of fabric and furniture she could find. Last, she set the stables ablaze and even the main gate as she left.

Turning, she walked. The sun had set before she stopped at the base of a hill that rose from the green fields. She climbed, her emotions numb.

When she could ascend no more, she sat upon the hilltop, watching the fierce glow of the still burning castle on the horizon. Arturius and his two brothers were still alive somewhere out there, and so was the witch Katrin. They would hunt her to the ends of the Earth... and the end of time if need be.

She rubbed her bloodstained palm against her heart and winced. The anguish at the loss of herself and the brutal murder of her family and friends was beginning to sink in. She felt a blind hatred for the monster she'd become.

What was she going to do now?

CHAPTER 6

Sam worried about a lot of things lately. Ever since Zac had woken up, he'd had to look over both their shoulders. Arturius was still lurking doing God knew what, Zac was a hairsbreadth away from snapping, and he hadn't a clue what to do about any of it. The Roman had no reason to stay after he'd ambushed Aya, but he lingered, enjoying prodding his brother closer to the edge.

Liz had told him in confidence that Gabby said there was always a loophole, a way around a spell, but so far, they hadn't found a loophole for the one that'd created the Romans. Hell, they didn't even know what the spell was. It was entirely possible that it'd died along with Aya and Katrin.

Alex had gone to call his sister, Isobel. Apparently, she was an expert in this kind of thing—ancient legends. But Sam thought it wasn't worth the bother. If the founders were smart—and they were if Arturius was anything to go bu—they would've erased every mention of them and the witches with ruthless accuracy. Then there was Aya, the most secretive of all.

Sam stood by his bedroom window and looked down at his brother, who was sitting on the bench in the overgrown garden with his back to the house. His shoulders were hunched and he looked absolutely defeated.

Sam had no idea what to do. He'd never seen this kind of reaction in Zac before, not even the lure of revenge and violence could draw him out. It was as if he'd just given up... and Zac never gave up.

"Just give him some time." Liz was behind him, gazing through the window. "He'll be okay."

Sam sighed, turning to embrace her. "I don't know, Liz. I don't know if he's coming back this time."

"I can go talk to him."

"Yeah," he whispered. "Nothing I say seems to get through to him. Maybe he'll listen to you."

She smiled, nodding as she crossed the room. He had no idea what she was going to say, but she'd better say something.

Zac stared across the yard, watching the distant grass blow back and forth in the slight breeze.

What was he meant to do now? What was he going to do before all this happened? He had no idea.

If you don't know, then you could do anything. Her words echoed in his memory and he pushed them aside.

Zac wasn't sure what it was about the garden that she'd liked. She'd sit here for hours, doing whatever it was that she did. The longer he sat there, the farther away she seemed. He saw how at ease the silver-haired woman from his dream had been in the forest. His thoughts wandered to that night when they'd gone to the silo near Memphis to free her from Caius. She'd apologised to him, hallucinating that he was her long-dead brother. She was sorry she couldn't save him.

There was no understanding it at the time, but now...? He'd seen her slaughtered family through her memories and felt her pain.

If Zac learned one thing in the Army, it was how to whittle. Weighing the stake he held in his hand, he found it well-balanced, perfect for the job. It would be so easy to plunge it through his heart and stop the pain. He could die like he was meant to in 1865. While it wasn't a bullet, it was close enough.

If he learned one thing about being a vampire, it was how to kill one. He placed the stake between his ribs at an angle—the fastest way to his heart with no annoying bone to slow it down. It would only hurt for a second, then he could rest. He took a few sharp breaths through his teeth, the point of the stake pressing through the cotton of his shirt into flesh, drawing a few beads of blood. It would only take a second.

Suddenly, he was pushed backwards off the bench onto the ground, the stake torn from his grasp. He stared up at the sky, blinking in the sunlight. His face was cast in shadow as Liz stood above him, her expression dripping with anger.

"What the hell, Zac!"

He sat up stiffly, perching on the bench again, elbows resting on his knees. Liz crouched in front of him, but he stared over her shoulder into the empty space.

"What do you think you're doing?" She grabbed his wrists, staring up at him, horrified.

He didn't know what to say, so he just shrugged.

"Don't do this. I know it hurts," she pleaded. "We need you, Zac."

"I don't know why," he said, focusing on her face for the first time. "I've never been well adjusted."

"Zac," she whispered, placing a gentle hand on his cheek. "Give it some time. We're here for you. You're not alone in this."

Glaring at her, he abruptly pulled away. "Has anyone you loved died? A grandparent, a friend?"

"Sure, my grandparents have all passed..." she began.

"Well, then think of how much it hurt to lose them, then multiply that by a billion. Even then, you wouldn't be close."

Liz stared at him for a moment, then sat beside him and took his hand.

When he didn't pull away, she said, "Don't. Just don't do that again, okay?" She was crying.

"Fine," he spat then stood. "I won't do myself in, but I'm not promising I won't let anyone else."

He stalked across the yard and was gone so fast, whatever Liz was going to say died on the breeze behind him.

***

Gabby had no desire to work, but still sat at her desk staring blankly at the monitor that displayed an endless stream of emails.

Her thoughts kept coming back to her predicament, despite trying to work through the massive to-do list she'd compiled.

The thing inside of her was clamouring to get out.

"Gabby!" The excited squeal of the real estate's receptionist, Bianca, filtered through the office, breaking through her melancholy.

Before Gabby could get up and see what all the fuss was about, she caught sight of Bianca running down the hallway with a bunch of flowers. Not just any flowers... *red roses*.

"Looks like you've got a secret admirer," Bianca trilled, setting them on Gabby's desk.

"Why do you say secret?" she asked.

"You haven't got a boyfriend and if you had a date, you would've told me about it."

Gabby laughed. "How do you know me so well?"

"Woman's intuition." Bianca smiled and walked back out to reception.

Picking up the flowers, Gabby sighed. Five red roses, all the colour of blood.

They were a message that only she would know the significance of. Five was a scared witch's number. The five points of a pentagram. The five elements. The five founding witches.

Their abnormally deep red colour was a dead giveaway, *and* the fact the thorns had been left on the stems. They could only have come from one person.

Opening the card, she snorted as she read the message. *Love, Arturius.* Ugh.

She leaned back in her chair and rubbed her temples. Why the hell was that freak still hanging around? And why was he sending her flowers? She had to find a way to end him before it was too late. Whatever kind of game he thought he was playing, he could just play it by himself.

"Gabrielle."

Jumping at the sound of a familiar and unwelcomed voice, she turned to find Arturius leaning against the partition around her desk.

"What the hell," she cursed, flinging the card into the trash.

His eyes narrowed slightly at the gesture, but his lips curved into a grin. "Do you like the flowers?"

"No, I don't."

Ignoring her tone, he lightly stroked the stem of one rose. "I know how you witches are with your numbers."

"I'm not a traditional witch, Arturius. I wasn't brought up that way."

"No, you weren't, were you?" he mused. "You thought you were normal."

"How did you get in here?"

"You know how." He stared at her with cool eyes.

Snorting, she knew he'd compelled everyone in the office to ignore his presence. She wished she could just ignore him. "Whatever you're trying to do, forget about it. Your flattery won't get you anywhere with me."

Arturius laughed and sat on the edge of her desk. "You're so spirited, Gabrielle. That's what I like about you."

"Eat shit, Arturius."

He smirked at her blatant, childish insult. "There's a prime example."

"I'm not going to help you."

"You don't even know why I'm here, love." He leaned closer, making her inch backwards.

"And I don't want to know," she replied with a sneer. "Aya was a friend. A friend that you killed in cold blood. Why would I ever listen to you?"

Arturius scoffed, "You think she was your *friend*?

She may have revealed her true self to you, Gabrielle, but that was only out of necessity. Do you think she would've done it voluntarily?"

She glared at the Roman, knowing he was probably right, but Aya had tried to help her in her own way. She'd been limited in the information she could let go of. She'd attempted to push her into going to see her grandmother, and Gabby wondered if she knew that their meeting would result in her finding her true powers. Knowing Aya now, that was entirely possible.

"Don't be so naïve, love. A creature of power should never have been turned. It was my mistake to correct. And wouldn't you know?" He held out his hands, palms up. "I'm a man of my word."

"Go away, Arturius."

To her annoyance, he ignored her. "I have access to something you want."

"And what might that be...?" she asked.

"Control."

She couldn't help it when her eyes widened slightly. How did he know?

"C'mon, Gabrielle," he said with a laugh. "Give me a little credit. A witch with a power as natural and deep as yours needs help controlling it. You've been fumbling around in the *dark* and you know it."

She pursed her lips, waiting to see what else he was going to say.

"I'm offering my help."

"I don't believe you."

"Believe what you want, Gabrielle. My intentions are noble."

"You have something I want." She cocked her head to the side. "So what do you want in return?"

Arturius smirked and glanced at his watch. "Time flies, Gabrielle. Think about my offer. You'll know where to find me when you come around."

Zac wasn't sure how he found himself here of all places.

Perched on the embankment that ran down to the mouth of the cave, he played with a stick, frowning at the boulder that blocked the entrance. His entire existence seemed like an endless joke and the joke was on him.

He'd dreamed of Aya—not once, but twice—her horrible end playing out in front of his eyes. Dropping the stick, he clutched his head in his hands and sobbed. She had never spoke about her past to any of them and he now knew why. There was no doubt the other dream he had was about her as well. He wished above all else that he could hold her in his arms and comfort her, but she was dead and gone.

She'd told them her blood was poison to anyone who drank it. Was this the reason? Those who drank it would learn her secrets? See her memories? He couldn't believe it, he refused to. It was too far-fetched.

Aeriaya, Aya. Who was she?

He was so engrossed in his melancholy that he didn't hear the approach he should have been aware of minutes before. A branch snapped behind him and he was on his feet in an instant, turning towards the forest. His breath caught at the sight of a familiar figure leaning against a tree.

"Morgan?"

"Hello, Zac," the woman replied, a grin on her face. Tall, blonde, and flawless, she looked like she'd stepped right out of a 1940s wartime propaganda poster. Her clothes were different, but she was exactly as he remembered her.

And she was the last vampire he'd ever expect to see out here of all places, in the middle of nowhere.

"What are you doing here?" he asked.

"Looking for you, of course." She grinned, walking towards him.

He sighed. "You haven't changed one bit."

"Except maybe the uniform." She embraced him, her familiar form strangely comforting.

He forced a smile. "Nurse Knowles."

"Man, you look strung out." She pulled back and laughed. "I can see nothing's changed with you."

"I'm a hard case, you know that." He shook his head. "How did you find me?"

"When word reached me of the bloody demise of a werewolf pack down in Louisiana, I had to come and see for myself. And lo-and-behold." She gestured to him.

Zac snorted, turning away.

"I've been thinking about you a lot lately," she said, standing beside him. "Wondering how you were doing."

"I was doing fine."

"Was?" She tilted her head to the side. "Does it have anything to do with that huge old rock you're staring at?"

He grimaced, glancing back towards the cave. "Yeah."

When he didn't continue, Morgan nudged him with an elbow. "And...?"

"It's a long story."

"Then give me the *Reader's Digest* version."

Zac ran a hand over his face and shrugged. "I killed Victoria here. And Aya is buried in the cave."

"Who's Aya?" Morgan asked, her brow furrowing.

"The love of my pathetic afterlife."

She sighed, turning her face away for a moment. When she looked at him again, she smiled wryly. "So, this is where you killed the psycho bitch who turned you?"

"Ironic, huh?"

She shook her head. "An unfortunate association."

Zac sighed, his head dipping. "I was going to die this morning."

"What do you mean?" Morgan grabbed his arm, turning him around to face her.

"I don't think I was really going to do it." He looked at her, his expression empty. "Not really."

"You were going to kill yourself?" She was horrified and rightly so.

"I thought about it."

She raised her hand, running a thumb across his cheek, brushing away a tear that'd escaped from the corner of his eye. "You must have loved her very much," she whispered.

"I do." He held her hand against his face, closing his eyes. "That's the problem."

"Come." Morgan coaxed him to sit beside her.

"I... we're in a lot of trouble." He grimaced as he sat heavily beside her. "If you're going to stick around, you might be pulled into it, whether you want to or not."

"So be it."

"Just warning you."

"Wait, *we're* in a lot of trouble? Who else is here?"

"My brother and some friends."

"Your brother Sam?"

"Yes." He had told her a lot about Sam back when they'd first met, but he'd told no one about Morgan. She'd been a part of his life that needed to stay buried.

"Does he know what you went through during the war?" she asked carefully.

"Which one?"

"*Zac.*" She pursed her lips.

"No, he doesn't know anything, and I want it to stay that way. He trusted me, Morgan. If he knew how bad it really was, it would tear him up. I've put him through enough lately without dragging up old shit. I never told him about me and you."

"Well, you know I've got your back." She placed an arm across his back. "What's been going on? Can I help?"

"Morgan, it's been seventy years."

"Who's counting?" She shrugged. "I've been here a handful of minutes and it already feels like old times. The perks of being a vampire."

He rubbed his eyes. "It's bad. I can't ask you to help us."

"Out with it, Degaud."

He couldn't help but smile at her forceful use of his surname. It reminded him of the war, the Army. She'd been a breath of fresh air, right when he needed it, but she couldn't know all of it. He wouldn't tell her all of it. The less she knew, the better. "A few months ago, I got into a fight with an old vampire."

"How old?"

"Five hundred at least," he replied. "I killed him, but somehow caught the attention of an ancient and powerful witch. She was plotting to kill me, and we had no idea how to stop her, so we found a vampire who was willing to help us. One that was hunted by the same witch."

"Who was the vampire?" Morgan asked when he paused.

"Aya."

"Oh," she said, her arm dropping away.

"She helped us above and beyond what was asked of her. She helped me." He glanced away, knowing that Morgan would get it. "The thing she didn't tell us right away was that she was mixed up with the founding vampires."

"The first vampires?" she asked, a note of hesitation in her voice.

"Yeah. Two thousand year old assholes." He scuffed his boot into the dirt, shaking his head. "She helped us take out the witch and one of the founders, but..."

"They killed her, didn't they?" she asked quietly.

"Yes."

"I'm sorry, Zac." Morgan wrapped her arms around him, her head resting against his shoulder.

"He's still here, Morgan," he said seriously, his arm snaking around her back. "Arturius. We're not sure what he wants, but I'm sure it has something to do with our friend Gabby."

"Gabby? Is she a vampire, too?"

He grimaced at the notion. "No, she's a witch."

Morgan whistled, knowing it was a huge deal that a vampire and a witch were best buddies.

"I have no idea what to do," Zac said with a frown. "I can't... I can't stop thinking about her." It was his fault that Aya had died. If he hadn't been cursed by that hag Katrin, then she would still be here. Hell, if he had kept his big mouth shut the day Alistair had walked into *Max's* bar, he wouldn't have met her but she would still be alive.

"It's okay, Zac. I'm here to help you. I managed it the last time, right?" Morgan grinned, trying to pull him out of his depression.

"I know."

The last time Zac had lost hold of his humanity, he could no longer tell friend from foe. He'd regressed into a predator. Victoria would've been proud of her creation. This was much different than that, but if he wasn't careful, he could just as easily go back down the same road.

And death would be the only thing he was capable of.

CHAPTER 7

P*aris, France*
August 1944

Zac had been a vampire for eighty years and he still couldn't control himself all the time.

War was familiar to him. Fighting for a cause, killing in the name of king and country, that was him through and through. This time he was fighting with Britain against the oppression of the Nazi regime and their stranglehold on Europe. Hitler had to go, and it seemed like a noble cause to lose himself in.

But the battlefield was different this time. The American Civil War had been brutal—it was a war between brothers. World War I had been nothing but a massacre that'd fed his bloodlust. This was—that'd become known as World War II—would either be his end or his saving grace.

He would learn control here. He had to.

Zac had fared well up until the British had finally deployed to Normandy. Long ago, his family had immigrated to America from Reims in Northern France. Perhaps this time, he would see it.

Two months of hard fighting on enemy soil had seen tens of thousands of lives lost, but the Allies were set to win back much of the north from German control. Paris was next on the list to be liberated.

It was the evening after a bloody fight on the approach to the French capital that Zac felt his control slip. He stood in the middle of the village green in a small hamlet they'd been tasked to neutralise. Standing there in the wake of the carnage, he realised he was alone. Everyone was dead. Even with all his speed and strength, everyone had still perished.

The bodies of men, British and German alike, were strewn across the square, torn to shreds by machine gun fire. The air was clogged with the smell of dirty blood and gunpowder and it made Zac gag. As he felt the familiar burn in his throat, he hightailed it out of there as fast as he could.

When he finally rendezvoused with a neighbouring unit and gave his report to the CO, he'd had enough. The best thing for everyone, including himself, was to get the hell out of there. He was so hungry, he would tear through the entire unit to sate it.

Standing to attention before the commanding officer, he gave his report as calmly as he could.

"Twenty Germans dead, fourteen British. They ambushed us as we entered the village. They came from behind and in front, machine guns were stationed on rooftops and cleverly camouflaged, sir."

"Any civilian casualties?"

"Zero. The village was empty, sir."

The CO frowned and wrote something on the map on his desk. A minute passed before he looked up at Zac. "And how did you manage to escape, soldier?"

"They sent me to neutralise the guns, sir. I was the best covert they had. When I realised I was the last one left, I commandeered one of their points and took out the remaining hostiles, sir." That was mostly the truth. He had torn the last few apart with his bare hands, but he couldn't tell the CO that.

"Dismissed, Degaud," the CO said curtly. "Report to Major Lewis in the morning for reassignment."

Zac didn't want reassignment; he wanted out of there. There was only one thing left to do.

"Permission to speak freely, sir?"

The CO looked at him curiously and nodded sharply.

"I'm sorry, sir, but I have to go. If anyone stops me, they'll die. You will discharge me from service as wounded. If anyone enquires, I've been sent back to London with the other casualties. I will leave this camp unchallenged. Do you understand?" He didn't want any trouble on the road. If he was stopped, it'd become messy *fast*.

The CO looked at him, slack jawed, his expression vacant as he absorbed Zac's command. He nodded his understanding as the compulsion took hold. "Dismissed, lieutenant. Safe journey home."

Zac wasn't challenged as he left the camp. The sentries didn't even see him pass in the darkness. He wasn't sure where he was going, but he ran into the night regardless.

The countryside passed by in a blur and he was hardly aware of anyone or anything. He had to run to clear his head and he didn't care what direction he went in. If any enemy activity was around, he saw nothing.

It was some time before he realised the city limits surrounded him. Paris. No sane person wearing a British military uniform would come here, especially since the Germans occupied Paris.

Zac found himself deep in the city, in the area he knew to be Montmartre. He stood on Rue d'Orsel and stared up at the *Basilique du Sacre-Coeur*, hardly believing that his vampire feet had taken him so far so quickly.

The basilica was shrouded in silver moonlight, making the grey stone appear haunted. The streets were empty, the threat of imminent invasion had scared everyone indoors and into bunkers—all save for a few brave souls who lingered around the *Moulin Rouge* and the whorehouses that littered the side streets.

Gestapo officers, soldiers, and sympathetic locals hurried back and forth as he lingered in the shadows, pondering his next move until the familiar clink of metal drew his attention to the opposite end of the street.

A German patrol was advancing on his position, boots thumping on the flagstones as they scanned windows and doorways. It would've been smarter to retreat and avoid confrontation entirely, but he was hungry and his wits were gone.

There were only five soldiers and one officer, gestapo. They had to be looking for someone or something—there was no reason for the officer to be out in the night with regular infantry. *Well,* Zac thought, *whatever they're doing, I'll save that one for last.*

Stepping from the shadows into the moonlight, he tilted his head and listened, waiting to see what they would do. Five rifles and one revolver were cocked and aimed directly at him.

"Halt!" the gestapo officer cried.

Zac didn't move as they came forward, their guns never dropping. One soldier came forward and patted him down, checking for any concealed weapons.

"*löschen,*" he said, stepping back.

"British," the officer said in English, his thick accent making the word sound strange. "What are you doing out here? Reconnaissance, secret mission? Eh?"

When Zac didn't reply, he gestured for his men to take him. As an arm reached out to grab his, he twisted, darting behind the soldier to his left. His comrades fired, but the bullets only hit their friend, the spray of blood staining his shirt. Zac grabbed the dying man from behind and snapped his neck, letting the limp body fall to the ground.

"Actually, I'm American," he snarled.

Time seemed to slow as he felt his eyes mist into blackness at the promise of more blood. Wide-eyed, the remaining soldiers all took a step backwards. The gestapo officer looked horrified, like he was about to piss his pants.

"Who wants to go first?" Zac asked, his voice thick with anticipation.

Bullets ripped through the material of his jacket, grazing the skin of his arms, and embedding into his stomach, but he kept coming. Wrenching a rifle away from one man, Zac stabbed it backwards, the bayonet impaling the soldier behind him. As the blade was still slicing, his hands came up and grasped the helmeted head of the man in front and twisted. The audible snap hardly registered as he turned for the remainder of his prey, who were running in the opposite direction.

Before the soldiers could reach the end of the street, Zac was in front of them, plunging his hands into their chests. Tearing away, he let their hearts fall to the ground beside their dead owners.

The gestapo officer skidded to a halt, dropping his revolver with a clatter. Twenty seconds had passed since the man had given the order to take him and all his men were dead.

Zac felt the warm, sticky blood drip down his fingers and onto the ground as he stepped forwards. This was the part he would enjoy the most.

The officer pleaded for his life. Zac let out a laugh as he pushed the man against the wall of a closed café, his hand tight around the German's neck. The stench of blood was driving him mad.

"Do you show mercy to those you kill?" Zac seethed as the man begged for mercy. His grip tightened around his neck and he choked. "Because I don't."

The man screamed as Zac lunged, his fangs tearing into the officer's jugular. His blood tasted foul, like fear, murder, and cowardice. He groaned as it filled his veins. This was what he wanted.

As the man's heart stopped beating, he let him drop and staggered backwards, wiping his face with the back of his hand.

Two minutes. It'd only taken him two minutes to slaughter six armed men. Six trained soldiers. This was exactly the thing he was trying to overcome. How had he let himself do this? He could've saved someone tonight, someone the gestapo was looking for, but how did that make him any better than them?

Those soldiers were just ordinary people following orders, just like the British he fought with. Did they believe the cause of their leaders? Did they want to be here, fighting? Did they ask for this? Did they enjoy it?

Slaughter and murder walked hand in hand. Maybe no one was clean.

Not wanting to be near the stench of his own failure, he fled into the darkness, backtracking across the city towards the hidden British units. He couldn't be found here. Challenge would see nothing but death. He wouldn't be able to stop himself.

Zac limped through a field on the outskirts of Paris, blood running from the gunshot wounds in his stomach. Stumbling against a stone fence, he knelt in the dirt and grimaced. Digging his fingers into his own flesh, he pulled the annoying bullets out and waited for the wounds to heal. As he sat there, hidden from the road, he heard something approach.

Peering over the fence, he caught sight of a convoy in the distance, travelling down another major road, but he wasn't alone.

Movement in the darkness gave him reason to pause. It was a group of six men, who he guessed had been sent out to scout the surrounding countryside. He hovered in the tree line, watching their progress. He caught a familiar scent in the air as they came closer. These men had been fighting. Gunpowder, sweat, and blood filled his head—the scent of war.

The scene he had fled back in Paris filled his mind and he stumbled backwards. A hairsbreadth separated him from losing it again and if he did, these men would die. He didn't have the strength to stop anymore.

"Who goes there?" An unmistakable British accent came from the shadows, but Zac could only smell the man's blood. At some point he'd been injured, but it didn't matter if it was only a scrape. In his state, he could smell the slightest drop.

Before he realised what he was doing, Zac stood in the middle of the unlit road staring down the six soldiers. They came to a sudden stop, rifles aimed at the unknown assailant that'd magically appeared in front of them.

"Stop!" the lead soldier cried, but Zac kept walking forwards, the order landing on deaf ears.

The crack of a single gunshot rang out across the silent countryside and Zac hissed as he felt the bullet lodge in his chest. He dropped to one knee in surprise and dug the bullet out with shaking fingers. The horrified gazes of the British soldiers were on him as he tore the annoying piece of metal from his flesh and tossed it to the side.

A growl came deep from his chest as he stood, eyes black and fangs bared. The sound of six rifles cocking didn't stop his advance. The smell of their fear egged him on, a game made specifically for his darkest urges.

Then he was directly in front of the lead soldier, a sergeant. He wrenched the rifle from the man's grasp and before he could stop himself, he swung the butt directly at the soldier's head and the man's skull splintered with a sickening crunch.

As the sergeant fell to the ground, the remaining soldiers stumbled backwards, their eyes wide with fear and hearts hammering in their chests.

The stench of blood from the soldier's caved skull was everywhere. Zac knew it was too late as he felt his fangs grow in completely. The soldiers would run, but it would be pointless.

Zac scarcely comprehended what he was doing as his fangs tore into flesh, the animal inside of him taking over. The remaining five men had fallen before they could fire another shot, their blood staining his face and hands, the taste of it on his tongue.

Stumbling backwards as he realised what he'd done *again*, he fell into the mud at the side of the road and sobbed. Rolling onto his back, he held his breath to stop the stench of blood from taking him again.

Monster.

He couldn't tell friend from foe and it made him sick. He couldn't go on like this. He *wouldn't* go on like this.

Zac didn't know how long he lay there wanting to die. He was so out of it he didn't realise that someone was looking down at him.

A woman.

He first thought she was an angel come to take him away, her blonde hair sparkling in the moonlight.

What must he look like? Covered in blood, lying in a ditch at the side of the road, six mutilated soldiers from his own side scattered across the asphalt. Had she come to take him to Hell?

Strong hands hauled him into a sitting position and somehow, he knew the woman was like him. Why did she care? He was a stranger to her, a psychotic killer. He was all the bad things about being a vampire.

He realised then that she was a nurse. He took in her uniform and couldn't fathom it. "How can you—" he began, but the words died in his throat. The moment he spoke, the burning came back and he choked.

"How can I stand the blood?" she asked as he grasped his forehead, rubbing his temples with bloodstained hands.

Zac nodded, his eyes wide.

"Practice." She grinned lopsidedly. "What's your name, soldier?"

"Degaud," he rasped.

"Well, Lieutenant Degaud," she had spied the insignia on his jacket, "first things first... let's get you out of the mud."

"Why?" he whispered but stumbled to his feet.

"I can't really leave you out here like this," she said, gesturing to his stained clothing. "And you're kind of in the midst of a rampage."

Zac knew she was right. If she left him, God knows

what he would do next. He didn't have a choice but to follow her, though she hadn't given him the option.

The woman led him to an abandoned barn in a field some way from the major roadways. It was decayed and falling down but served as a good hiding place for the time being. It seemed she had used this place before. The ground was trampled and the scent of freshly turned hay filled the air. There were hidden things here in forgotten corners.

She saw him looking, though she said nothing. He was positive that she knew he'd worked it out. A vampire saw much more than a human would. What worried him was why she had been here before if she was a nurse with the British Army.

When she noticed his confused look, she said, "I sometimes bring Resistance here. If things get too close in Paris and they need to hide for a night, I help get them out."

She was a vampire that moonlighted as a nurse for the British Army *and* the French Resistance? What the hell was she?

She took out a bottle of wine that had been hidden under a pile of hay and handed it to him. A bundle followed, containing clean civilian clothes that were probably meant for some future political refugee. "Best you get out of those clothes, you stink of blood."

He took a long draught of the wine, the alcohol soothing his burning throat. Taking the clothes, he went into one of the old stalls and peeled off his wet, dirty uniform. A basin of water was pushed under the door and he washed the dirt and blood away.

"Will anyone miss you?"

"What?" He jumped at her sudden question and pulled on the dark grey shirt from the bundle.

"Your CO," she explained.

"No."

"I hope you had enough sense to compel him and not rip his face off," she scolded.

"I'm not a total imbecile," he spat.

"Calm down." She held her hands up when he peered at her over the stall door. "I was just asking."

Zac snorted and pulled his boots back on, throwing his wet coat over the wall. When he came out, the woman was perched on an old bale of hay, looking at him.

"I'm going to help you," she declared.

"Why?" He had it in him already that he was a lost cause.

"Because I can, and I was in the right place at the right time." She didn't seem too put off by the circumstances of his downward spiral. Handing him the bottle of wine, she smiled and gestured for him to sit.

"Who are you?"

"Nurse Knowles," she said. "Morgan Knowles."

"How do you do it? Resist?"

"I was a nurse before," she replied. "I guess the

calm carried over when I was made. It has never bothered me."

"You're lucky," he whispered and swallowed a mouthful of the wine.

"I wouldn't call it lucky, lieutenant. I don't know about you, but I didn't particularly want to be a vampire. It kind of grew on me, though."

"How?"

"My, aren't you forward?"

Zac frowned. He guessed he wasn't in any position to ask questions. He coughed and wiped his brow, realising the burning in his throat was subsiding.

"I'm only kidding, soldier," she said with a smile. "If it pleases you, I'll tell you the sordid tale. It might keep your mind off things."

Morgan told him she'd been turned five years ago. She had been working at Great Ormond Street Hospital in London at the time. As she left one evening, she was attacked from behind. The assailant was human, just out to get off on the high of killing an innocent woman. He stabbed her multiple times and left her to bleed out in a gutter. If she'd been found by a human, she said she would've died. Her wounds had been fatal.

A vampire happened upon her intending to help, but was too late to do much of anything, but believing there was hope, the vampire still tried. But she'd died with their blood in her system and thus, became a vampire.

An unfortunate turn of events, she called it, but who was she to complain? She was gifted with a second chance, no matter how twisted, and she used it to help others.

Her saviour was named William and he was new himself. New to a vampire was a few decades old, so when he'd said he was fifty years dead, he hadn't understood why she thought it was old. He stuck with her for a while and taught her how to look after herself and she soon returned to her old life at the hospital, unable to let her human calling go. Then she was called up to join the war effort and William disappeared as vampires often did.

"And now I'm here," she said. "I could hardly let my skills go to waste. To have this strength and do nothing? I couldn't turn away."

He knew from her expectant look that she wanted him to tell her about his own turning, but he said nothing.

Morgan sighed. "Get some sleep, Lieutenant Degaud. I'll still be here when you wake."

When morning finally came, Zac was surprised to see Morgan out in the sunlight.

"Britain is an ancient land," she said when he stood next to her. "Witches are two a penny if you know where to look."

He grunted, looking out across the fields. His attitude still stunk.

"I said I was going to help you," Morgan scolded him, placing her hands on her hips. "And if that means going through the basics, then so be it."

"What, now?" he protested.

"No time like the present." She took his arm and led him across the field.

A small flock of sheep were grazing at one end, the crispness of the early morning caused them to huddle together for warmth.

"Your problem is that you don't know when to stop." She pointed to the sheep. "Go get one."

"A sheep?" he asked, an eyebrow rising.

"Don't worry about looking like an imbecile in front of me. I've seen it all."

So that was that, then.

They worked like this for several days until he didn't feel the desire to feed at the slightest scent of fresh blood. It took some work and many dead sheep, unfortunately. Some farmer was going to be furious at the mysterious loss of his livestock. When Zac could let the sheep walk away, bleeding but alive, he felt a lot better. His control seemed to be coming back, piece by piece, and with Morgan's help, it'd never been this fast. She really did have a gift for healing lost causes.

One evening they hid in the barn and talked late into the night. Morgan told him about her human life growing up in Britain. She was born in a small village in Surrey and had always hoped she would become a nurse. She told him about her work after she'd been turned and about what she'd been doing with the army in France.

Using her new skills to help the Resistance, she helped free prisoners, extract informants, and smuggle them out of the country and into Allied territory, sometimes through blockades and trenches. Thus, her real identity was a carefully guarded secret. The French had even given her a codename, but she never told him what it was.

In turn, Zac told her much about his brother Sam and their travels as vampires. Eighty years was a lifetime and they had wandered far. He told her about his time in the American Civil War and World War I. He even caved into her sweetness and told her how he'd turned and what'd happened to his family—the massacre and Victoria's abrupt end.

She had a way with words that drew him in. His shoulders felt lighter than they had in a long time.

Morgan understood it all and didn't judge him for any of it.

"You're too good for me," he told her one evening. In their barn in the middle of the French countryside, the war and his struggles seemed so far away.

"Lieutenant Degaud," she murmured, placing her small hands on his face. "If I have learned anything about you in the past week, it's that you're more than a monster. You're a good man."

"How do you know?" he whispered, sliding a hand onto her waist.

"I can see it in your eyes when you speak about your brother. And when you speak about the person you want to be. There's a fire inside of you."

He couldn't help shivering as she leaned forwards, her lips brushing against his. "Zac," he whispered. "Call me Zac."

Her hand dropped to his shirt and she pulled him close, his lips colliding with hers. When he kissed her, he only felt his body respond, not his heart or his mind. He didn't love her... it wasn't like that. They were a comfort to each other. Nothing more would ever come of it.

Her hands slipped inside his shirt and he pushed her back into the hay, pulling off her dress.

Comfort. That's all it was.

The sound of a bird rustling around in the barn roof woke him just as the sun was rising. Morgan was curled against him, naked, her back pressing into his chest. She was sound asleep... dead to the world.

Not wanting to disturb her, he didn't move. When she finally stirred, he ran a hand along the curve of her waist, pulling her hips back against him.

"You know I can't stay forever," he said, burying his face into her hair.

"I know."

"I have to go find my brother soon. He'll be worried."

"Where is he?"

"America," he replied. "Louisiana. He talked about going to New Orleans. I hope to find him there."

She sat up and dressed, the sadness in her face so fleeting, he barely noticed it before she turned away.

"Morgan—"

"We need to go back to civilisation," she cut him off before he could explain. "I have things to do. Missions. Reports. It won't be long before I'm missed."

"Of course, I—"

"But you need to pass the final test before you go."

Zac knew she meant human blood. The control he'd learned over the past week would mean nothing unless he could hold back with a human.

Sighing, he dressed, aware of Morgan's eyes on him. She'd changed. He shouldn't have...

"We'll go to Calais," she said, interrupting his thoughts. "From there, it will be easier to get back to London. I'm sure you'll find passage back to America from there, war or not."

"Morgan." He had her in his arms before she could turn away. "I'm sorry."

"It's okay, Zac," she whispered into his chest. "I always knew you had to go sometime. Just not so soon."

"Now?" he asked.

"Of course. Time is precious in war."

He let his arms drop and without another word, she led him outside and back to the road.

They hitched rides with Army convoys travelling north during the day and ran during the night. By sunrise the next morning, they were in Calais. News had already reached the town that Paris had been liberated and was now in the hands of the Allies.

It seemed too soon, but as they explored the city, they walked past a makeshift army hospital where casualties were lined up in the hundreds. Everything from gunshot wounds to amputations were laid out and bleeding.

Morgan pushed him backwards.

"I'm so sorry, Zac. I didn't know." She tried to hold him back as he registered what they'd stumbled upon.

Human blood was more potent than that of any animal. Its rich coppery scent hit him like a ton of bricks, and he turned away sharply, fighting to keep himself in check.

"Zac," Morgan cried, knowing that the slightest trace of blood would set him off.

Blinking hard, he felt the burn in his throat subside. "It's okay," he rasped. "I won't."

Thankfully, she pulled him down the street, away from the tent hospital, the sea breeze pulling the scent away.

They found themselves at the pier where many

British and American war and supply ships were docked. Men were running up and down the gangplanks, and crates and trucks were everywhere, unloading supplies bound for the front, and many of the supply frigates were being loaded with the wounded for their trip home.

Zac knew this was his ticket back to America.

"I need to go." Zac sounded almost desperate. He wanted to see Sam so much.

"Are you sure you can handle it? I mean, back there..." She gestured back towards the tent hospital.

"Yes. I've come back before. This feels the same."

She said nothing and they walked the length of the dock, the crowd of people jostling them as they searched for a departing vessel. They found one, a passenger liner that'd been drafted into the Merchant Navy and repainted grey, preparing to weigh anchor.

Morgan smiled sadly as they stood at the end of the dock. "Well then. Safe journey, soldier."

"Thank you, Morgan. For everything." Zac took her in his arms and kissed the top of her head. She shrugged away from him and gestured for him to go. He had to go now or wait God knows how long for another ship to gain clearance to leave.

As Zac walked along the gangplank and onto the ship, he turned and leaned against the railing, watching as Morgan disappeared into the bustling crowd. It didn't feel right, leaving her so soon. They'd become friends in the brief time he'd known her and he felt like he'd used her, only taking... never giving to her once.

As the ship pulled away from the dock, he knew it was too late to go back. If he jumped, thousands of people would see. Besides, she was already gone.

He hoped one day they'd cross paths. He'd tell her then that he was sorry.

CHAPTER 8

Zac walked towards the manor with Morgan, feeling a lot better. It was a huge turnaround from that morning when he'd been prepared to die. He still wanted Aya more than anything, but he no longer felt powerless.

"Wow," Morgan breathed, breaking the silence. "It's beautiful out here."

"Is it your first time in the South?" he asked. He was kind of surprised, knowing how old she was.

"Yes," she replied with a nod. "I mean, it's stinking hot, but the swamp, the forest... It's kind of magical."

"I bet that's what the settlers thought."

"Were your parents..."

He shook his head. "No. My grandparents came out from France a while after New Orleans was founded."

"Did you ever see where they were from? I mean, when you were over there for the war?"

"No."

He was relieved when Morgan didn't push him to explain. She knew all about it.

They approached the driveway side by side, her familiar presence calming. He had always been jealous of her. She was calm, level-headed, caring, and had the control he craved. Morgan had purpose and he'd just lost his to a two-thousand year-old vampire. He desperately needed direction before his grip on his humanity vanished again.

As they turned up the long driveway towards the front of the manor, Morgan whistled. "Lieutenant Degaud, I had no idea," she said with a delighted laugh.

"That I was stinking rich?" He chuckled, feeling better than he had in days.

The willows lining the gravelled drive dipped low and Morgan ran her hands through the fronds, a strange look on her face. She smiled when she caught Zac looking at her and disappeared behind the curtain of leaves.

He hesitated, wondering if he should follow or just continue up to the house, but she came back out laughing. "Just look at things from another perspective, Degaud." She tugged on his arm and pulled him through the branches. "See, isn't that better?"

The air was cooler in the shade and the dimmed light was calming. Morgan shook her head and took his arm. They walked towards the manor and if he closed his eyes, Zac could almost imagine it was 1863 again.

His parents had hosted a ball the night before he left for Virginia. He forgot what it was for but walking arm in arm with a lady brought back the memory like it was yesterday.

Carriages had lined the road, filling the air with the sound of hooves on gravel, carrying finely dressed men and women come to social climb. Businessmen from New Orleans, property barons, plantation owners. His parents were obsessed with it and that's why it'd cut them so deep when he joined the Confederate forces. His father had wanted him to take it all over, to help their status rise even further, but it just made him feel sick.

Zac sighed. He could almost see the bright moonlit night, the perfumed smell of the wisteria on the warm air, the glow of the gas lamps. The music that filtered through the open doors and windows. The sick feeling in his stomach that'd occupied him all night—he was leaving for Petersburg the following morning. It was a feeling he wouldn't understand until much later. He wouldn't see this again—the house, his family. This place would never be alive again. He was going to his death.

"Zac?"

He jumped as Morgan's voice pulled him back.

"Where did you go just then?" She frowned at him, her head tilted to the side, waiting to see what he'd say.

"Nowhere." He dropped her arm and scowled. They were standing before the front door and now he'd have to go inside and come clean to Sam. He turned to Morgan. "Stay here."

"I can come in eventually, right?" she asked.

"Yes, of course. I just want to explain to Sam first."

"It's okay, Zac. I get it. Just let me know when I can come meet him."

"Sure."

"I'll be right here." She winked as he walked inside.

Closing the door behind him, he knew Sam was in the parlour. He could feel him lingering there. What was he going to say? *Hey, so in the forties I kind of went psychopathic and I was saved by a vampire posing as a nurse?* Perhaps he should be less sarcastic.

"Zac." Sam stood as he came through the doorway, a concerned look plastered on his face. "Liz said—"

"Stop." Zac held his hand up. He didn't really want to be told off for trying to off himself.

"What's going on?"

He took a half empty bottle of whisky from the shelf and sat down on the sofa. "Look, I'm sorry about this morning, okay? It won't happen again."

Sam didn't look convinced but nodded anyway. "Something's happened, hasn't it?"

"Nothing *bad*."

Zac sighed and took a draught of the alcohol before placing it heavily on the chipped coffee table. Sam had ripped shreds off him when he found the damage he'd inflicted with his knife the day Aya had brought him back from his last uncontrollable adventure. The table was antique.

"Well," he continued, "depends on how you want to look at it."

"Shit, Zac."

"Yeah, yeah." He waved a hand at his little brother.

"Just tell me. With what you pulled this morning, it'll be hard to top that."

He leaned back onto the sofa and grimaced. "We have a visitor."

Sam narrowed his eyes. "What kind of visitor?"

"One from my sordid past."

"Care to elaborate further?"

"Her name is Morgan." He rolled his eyes when he caught the look on Sam's face. "It's not like that. I don't have a woman in every port, you know."

"If you say so..."

Zac let his expression drop and ran his hands over his face. "Back in the forties when I went... I went to war. I was desperate. I couldn't take it anymore. Always feeling..." He couldn't say it. He always felt hungry. Not hungry for blood like a human is hungry for food; he was hungry for violence. "Morgan pulled me back from the edge."

Sam was silent as he digested this little gem of his pathetic past. "How bad did it get before she found you?"

"It wasn't pretty, Sam." He couldn't bear to tell him

the truth, it would break his heart, but he knew he had to come clean.

"How bad, Zac?"

He grimaced.

"Zac?"

He rubbed his temples. "*Bad*. When she found me, I'd just slaughtered twelve men. Friend, foe, it didn't matter." He let his head drop into his hands. "I don't know when I would've stopped. It was a miracle Morgan came along when she did."

"Where were you when she found you?"

"Somewhere in the countryside outside of Paris. I don't know."

"What was she doing out there?"

"She was a nurse with the British Army. She also moonlighted with the French Resistance. It was right before Paris was taken back from the Germans. She helped get a lot of people out during the occupation. She had a safe house nearby, I guess she was in residence."

Sam looked at him for a moment, waiting for him to crack. When he didn't, he said, "Look, I'm not happy you didn't tell me, Zac. I want to help you. I can't do that if you're not forthcoming."

"Sam, just leave it. It's the past. Done. Whatever." *Please, just let it go.*

"What is she doing here now?"

"She told me she heard about the werewolves and

came looking... for me." Before Sam could jump to conclusions he said, "It's not like that."

"I wasn't going to say anything."

"Whatever," he said sullenly.

"We don't know her."

"But I do," Zac said. "Sam, she saved my pathetic life."

Sam looked like he was going to disagree, but he threw his hands in the air. "Okay. Just be careful what you tell her. If she so much as puts any of us in danger..."

"Need to know," Zac told him. "I'll make sure of it."

Zac would've liked to have said Sam took to Morgan like a duck to water, but he was wary of her intentions. After all, she'd just appeared out of thin air looking for his big brother right at the moment he'd tried to stake himself.

They'd stood in the parlour, eyeing each other with something akin to jealousy. They both wanted to protect Zac in their own way, and it annoyed the hell out of him. He didn't want to be coddled like the psycho everyone thought he was.

He'd told Morgan she couldn't stay at the manor. The only room they had spare was Aya's. She'd left in good spirits, but he suspected it was a show for his benefit. He'd be annoyed, too. Most of the next day he spent staring into space until Sam dragged him out to take his mind off things.

Relief came in the form of alcohol and *Max's* was the perfect place to partake in it. Gabby and Liz had ambushed Morgan the moment she came in, drilling her for information. It seemed the mystery woman from Zac's past was too much temptation for them.

"I was a nurse," Morgan explained. "I remained one after... you know."

"Wow," Liz exclaimed. "That would've taken some guts."

Morgan laughed. "Some would say I was lucky. Blood never bothered me before. I knew some nurses who were prone to fainting when they first started out. I never had a problem with it, so I always assumed that's why it carried over."

"So, you still practice now?" Gabby asked, trying to sound casual about it.

"Not right now. It's harder these days to blend into the system. In the forties, it was much simpler. For one, there was a war going on and they didn't care where you came from. The only thing they wanted to know was if you were capable."

"Couldn't you use compulsion?"

Morgan grimaced. "Yeah, but I'd rather not. I never liked doing that."

"Except when you get cornered by the gestapo," Zac interrupted, earning him a few raised eyebrows.

Morgan laughed. "Then it comes in handy."

"What do you mean?" Liz asked, leaning heavily on the table.

The girls were smitten with Morgan, especially Liz. Another female vampire, and one with such an exciting history had put stars in her eyes.

"I was with the Resistance."

"The French Resistance?" Gabby asked, her eyebrows raising.

"Yes."

"Is that how you two met?" *Damnit, why did Gabby have to ask that question?*

Zac stood with a snort and strode over towards the bar to get away from the inevitable awkwardness that was about to descend on them. Everyone knew how unhinged he could be, but the last thing he wanted was for it to be rubbed in his face. He heard the conversation come to an abrupt halt behind him and he rolled his eyes.

"So, you and Zac...?" he heard Liz say after a moment.

"Oh," Morgan sounded surprised. "It was never like that."

He sat heavily on a stool by the bar and gestured for another drink, anything to stop himself from hearing them. He'd already relived it once today, he didn't need to go back so soon.

He didn't bother looking up when Morgan sat next to him a moment later. He was tired of being coddled and asked if he was okay. He was far from it, but he didn't need his hand held. Not by anyone. *Never.*

"They're being nice, I hope," he said to be polite.

"Yes, they're nice enough." He didn't miss the implied meaning in her words. How couldn't she know that they were giving her the third degree?

"It's just a weird time for everyone..."

"I understand, Zac. I'm the outsider. Trust is a hot commodity around here." She nudged him with her elbow.

"You're taking it rather well." He glanced at her warily, spinning the ice around in his glass.

"Should I be taking it badly?"

"No, I—"

"Drop it, Degaud."

He sighed. "Consider it dropped."

Zac had thought coming out to the bar tonight was an awful idea, Morgan or not. His mood swings were giving him whiplash, and he didn't care to think about Sam or the others.

"Why does Sam work in the gardens?" Morgan asked, breaking into his thoughts yet again.

"I don't know," he replied. "I always assumed it was part of the ruse."

"Have you ever asked him if he likes it?"

"No. I'm selfish like that."

"Maybe you should."

"Why?"

"Because it's nice."

"Why do I need to be nice?"

"Because he's your brother?" Morgan rolled her eyes at him. "C'mon. Let's go back."

She offered him a hand and he scowled at it.

"It's not going to trigger the apocalypse," she said with a laugh. "*C'mon.*"

"*Fine.*" He took her hand and she led him back to the table.

Sitting in a chair next to Sam, Zac ignored the all too familiar worried look his little brother typically wore.

When the girls moved off towards the bar with empty glasses, he turned to Sam, thinking about what Morgan had said to him. "Why do you work in the gardens?" he asked awkwardly.

Sam gave him a confused look. "What kind of question is that?"

"Morgan is trying to make me a better person."

"After one day?"

He shrugged.

"Just be who you are," Sam told him.

"An asshole?"

"Yeah. An asshole."

"I don't know what to do, Sam. About any of it," he said quietly, conscious of Morgan, who was busy chatting with Gabby and Liz.

"I don't think it's about being a better person," Sam said with a frown. "You've been through a hell of a lot. It'll take time. Just give it time."

Zac grunted and downed the rest of his drink. Time was all he had left.

"I'm going to stay at Liz's tonight," Sam said, looking over his shoulder towards Morgan. "Will you be okay?"

Zac groaned, catching his brother's glance. "It's not like that, Sam. Aya has been gone a week. I'm an ass, but even I'm not that heartless."

"Sorry, I just—"

"I'll never love anyone else," he whispered, looking away. "That's the last I want to hear about it."

Sam thumped him on the shoulder, making him look back up. "I know. Later, bro."

"Later."

The night was clear and bright, the moon full when Zac left the bar and it reminded him of her. He'd followed her that first night, wanting answers. Instead, he almost found his death. This time he was alone, the stars she seemed to love shone endlessly above him. He'd do anything to see her again. To touch her. To feel her lips against his.

The sound of the door closing behind him snapped him out of his memory and Morgan was beside him, smiling.

"Care for a walk?" she asked.

Zac wasn't ready to go back to the manor yet. It'd

be dark and empty. Ironically, that was exactly how he felt. He nodded and Morgan took his arm, leading him across the street and into the gardens.

"I can understand why Sam likes this place," she murmured. "It's pretty."

"Yeah." He tried to sound upbeat about it, but he didn't really care.

"Your friends seem lovely."

"They're okay."

"Zac," Morgan scolded him. "They've got your back. You're lucky."

"I know," he said as he looked up at the sky again.

She elbowed him, bringing him back to earth. "You scared me yesterday."

He shrugged. "I didn't mean to. I wasn't thinking."

Morgan stopped underneath a low hanging willow and he jerked away slightly as she placed a hand on his face. He stared at her as she traced the edge of his jaw with her fingertips, her expression undecipherable. He didn't dare move for fear of doing the wrong thing. Instead, he watched her gaze take him in. They seemed to become closer, the world disappearing around them. Zac pushed his troubled thoughts to the back of his mind.

They'd spent a week together decades ago, but it'd been so full of emotion, it was hard to shake the memory of her. Sometimes Zac wished his memory was still human... it'd been easier to forget.

Morgan pressed up against him, her familiar form

comforting, and as she brushed her lips against his, he let out a shaky breath. Her arms snaked around his neck and pulled his body into hers. He was frozen to the spot, unable to turn away, even though he knew it was wrong. Then her lips were against his, fingers wound into his messy hair and his longing came back... but it was a longing for another woman.

Groaning deep in his chest, he felt himself kiss her back, her tongue melding with his. As he ran his hands down her back, her breath hitched in her throat and it was enough to snap him out of it. Tearing away from her, he gasped for air and blinked hard.

Zac didn't dare look Morgan in the eye—he knew exactly what he would find. He'd done it again, but this time he knew she had feelings for him. Why else come all the way to a backwards-nowhere town in the South?

He was an asshole and this time, he was sorry. It was a goddamn miracle he cared at all.

When he didn't move, Morgan sat heavily on the bench. He wanted to die this morning and now Morgan was kissing him. He was on an emotional roller coaster of the worst kind.

"I'm sorry," he whispered, knowing she could hear him even with his back turned. "I can't."

"I shouldn't have left you that day in Calais." She was looking at her hands and he tried to ignore her humiliation.

He sat next to her. "Morgan..."

"It's the truth. I just let you go and it's what, been

seventy years? I'm not stupid to think that you hadn't moved on... or weren't even there in the first place."

Zac took her hands and she stilled. He hesitated, trying to think of something to say. The *right* thing to say.

He felt her gaze burn into him but he couldn't bring himself to look up.

Zac had been trying to avoid it ever since she'd found him by the cave. The day he left Morgan in Calais in 1945, he knew that he'd overstepped a boundary by the way she'd shoved him onto that ship. She'd developed feelings for him, and he'd handled it in a less than gentlemanly way. Hell, he'd just sailed away into the sunset, never to see her again... after all she had done for him.

Now decades later, she sat next to him and he suspected that time had done nothing to change her perspective. He hoped to God that she hadn't held a flame for him all that time. He couldn't give her what she wanted.

Aya was dead, but his heart would be forever hers.

"I'm sorry."

"For what?"

"For leaving so soon after—"

"Forget it, Zac. It's been a long time."

"I feel like I used you."

"Yeah, you did." When he finally looked up at her, his expression was surprised. "But you needed to. It was a survival thing. I get it."

"I still feel like shit about it."

"Don't." Morgan stood abruptly, looking across the garden.

"I'm sorry."

"For God's sake, stop being sorry," she snapped. He watched her as she wrestled with her thoughts, her teeth grinding. Would she forgive him in time? Or was that it?

He stood and took a step towards her, but she jerked away. "Goodnight, Zac."

He opened his mouth to say something, anything, but she'd already disappeared into the night.

CHAPTER 9

Zac found himself outside, but the air was full of a different kind of moisture. It'd been raining, the air crisp and cold, full of fog, but it wasn't the mists of the swamp.

The dirt track he stood on was slick with mud and slush, and dirty snow lay in patches amongst the grass and trees on either side. Wherever he was, it was a long way from home.

The muffled sound of an approaching horse broke the silence, and he stood to the side of the track and awaited its approach. When it finally came into sight, he gasped in surprise as he recognised the woman who rode it.

Aya was a small figure compared to the huge black horse on which she sat, but it couldn't be anyone else, not with those otherworldly blue eyes.

The horse snorted and gusts of vapour clouded from its nostrils and hung in the still morning air.

As she reined the horse in beneath a tree, she took out a heavy length of rope and fastened it to a thick branch that hung low across the track. He took a few steps towards her, realising what she was about to do, but either she was ignoring him or was oblivious to his presence.

With the noose firmly around her neck, she turned and slapped the horse hard on the rump. It shrieked and bolted forwards in surprise. Wrenched from the saddle by the noose, he heard the snap as her neck partially broke, her eyes wide as she gasped for air.

He ran forward with a cry of horror and tried to clutch her legs and lift her to stop the noose from strangling her, but his arms passed through air.

"No!" he cried in frustration.

He had to sit there and watch her choke to death as her body gently swung from side to side, the rope creaking against the branch, tears streaking his face. He didn't dare look to see if she still lived.

It seemed like an age had passed before she suddenly gasped for air. Zac looked up and stifled a sob. As she'd healed, the bones in her neck had fused at an odd angle, but the rasp of air was a sign that her windpipe wasn't faring so well.

Her hands grasped at the noose above her as she lifted herself up. It seemed she realised this tactic wasn't working as she clawed her way up to the branch and tore the rope free. Landing heavily on the ground, she tossed the rope to one side. It was useless.

Then, she grasped her head and twisted, correcting her mistake…

A sharp scream broke the heavy silence. Turning, Zac found himself in the centre of a small village. He looked around, trying to find where she would appear, but there was chaos all around and no one paid him any attention.

The village was under attack. The screams of women and children pierced the smokey air as they ran from an unknown enemy. The assault came from the north, the clash of steel mingling with their terror as whoever was trying to protect them fought back.

Flaming projectiles pierced thatched roofs and burst into flame, smoke clogging the air so it was hard to see, even for his vampire eyes.

Then he saw her.

The battle raged all around as she stood still, waiting. The apparent enemy—their faces painted with a kind of natural blue paint—fought against the inhabitants of the village who he recognised as Romans. This must be what Arturius called the frontier lands—Britain, two thousand years ago.

Zac knew he wasn't really there, but he moved forwards regardless, eyes wide. She couldn't be serious? They would cut her down in cold blood.

One of the blue-painted men ran towards her, a blood-curdling scream tearing apart the air as his sword came down, tearing her chest open.

Time seemed to slow as she fell and Zac's heart

stopped. The man's crude sword followed her, and as her body collided with the ground, he impaled her through the stomach, the cruelest wound anyone could inflict on another. Then he pulled the blade free and slit her throat for good measure, revealing his true disposition. This wild man deserved to die, and he did moments later when a Roman soldier cut him down with a swift, clean stab to the heart. A more efficient death than he deserved.

She never made a sound as they murdered her. No scream or sob escaped her lips. Just the bubbling of blood as her body tried to draw in air through a torn trachea.

Kneeling next to her as the battle continued to rage around them, he fought back his emotions as the growing pool of her blood stained the ground darker and darker. He knew the exact moment she died, but as with before, her body didn't desiccate.

The battle simmered around him as he waited for her to wake, the only sound remaining was the crackling of flame as the houses burnt to the ground. When night fell, she sat up, gasping, her eyes wide. The air smelt of charred wood and blood, and she dropped her head into her hands and sobbed.

When she dissolved, he knew the dream was taking him somewhere else. The putrid stench of burning flesh made him gag, and he placed an arm across his nose and mouth to block the overwhelming scent. Knowing what he would see when he turned around didn't stop him from doing it anyway.

She was lashed to a pyre that was well and truly alight, her flesh already cooking and charring. A mob had gathered and were yelling things in an unknown language. From their demeanour, he assumed they were less than pleased with her. They'd accused her of being a witch, demon, or evil spirit, but it didn't really matter. She wanted to die. So far, she hadn't been able to.

When the flames finally died down, a few men who'd been with the mob took down her charred, disfigured body and dumped it into a ditch at the edge of the small village. They left, not bothering to bury her, content to let her corpse be desecrated further by any wild animals who were hungry enough to drag her away.

Vampires couldn't survive fire. He always knew she was more, but not this...

He sat on the edge of the ditch and tried his best not to look at what was left of her. It was well within her power to escape such a fate, so why did she feel she had to let them do this to her? She would come back, her body would heal itself, but perhaps she didn't understand. As far as he knew, she was one of the first turned vampires. This must be a time where she was very new in all senses of the word. How would she know the mechanics of being a vampire? She was on her own.

His heart broke all over again when she opened her eyes, still horribly burnt and disfigured. The pain she would be in... But she made no sound at all, the disappointment in her eyes crystal clear.

When the dream shifted again, he did all he could to will himself awake. He couldn't see another, it was too much. He felt like he was going mad. Was he being punished? What kind of cruel joke was this? He couldn't fathom how many times she must have tried and failed.

He was in a dark barn of some sort or maybe a stable, the sound of a struggle pulling his attention to the darkest corner. She had a man up against the wall, the coppery tang of blood thick on the air. She pulled back, gasping, the man pleading for his life in some unknown language.

Her hands were covered in blood and it ran from her mouth, staining the front of her dress. The man stumbled backwards at the sight of her, eyes wide with fear. He was yelling a word at her that sounded a lot like vampire. She was yelling back at him, goading him on and pointing at her chest. Was she asking him to stake her?

She picked up the crude hoe the man had dropped and snapped the end off with ease. Thrusting the jagged piece of wood at him, she said something that he didn't understand. The man nodded and grasped the makeshift stake in his shaking hands.

He realised then that she'd asked the farmer to free her.

When the man drove the stake into her heart, she gasped and fell backwards into the hay. He stood over her as the man backed away, fleeing the stable. Her eyes had glazed over the moment the life left her, but he knew she would come back from this, too. Sam had staked Caius, and he had desiccated and still revived.

But Aya didn't. She didn't change at all.

Zac jolted awake, gasping for breath. Sam stood above him, shaking his shoulder.

"Zac, what the hell?" He sounded panicked.

"What?" He grimaced, rubbing his eyes. He had fallen asleep on the sofa, and the morning sun was flooding through the windows.

"You were yelling in your sleep." His little brother was prodding him for more information.

Sitting up, Zac held his head in his hands and drew in a sharp breath, thrown off by the latest set of dreams. It was like a cruel joke that he had to sit by and watch as she tried to end herself over and over, powerless to save her each time. He wanted to protect her, but when it mattered, he couldn't.

"It's nothing," he whispered.

Sam frowned at his brother. "Something's bothering you."

Zac ran his fingers over the stubble on his chin and sighed. There was no use hiding it from him any longer. "I've been dreaming."

"Dreaming?" Sam's eyebrows shot up in surprise. "Since when?"

"Since..." His voice caught in his throat. "Her blood."

Sam said nothing for a while, waiting for him to pull himself together.

Drawing a deep breath, Zac told his brother about the dreams Aya's blood had given him, the horrible insight to her painful beginnings. He told him about the creature she'd been before... silver-haired and beautiful, at home in the forest. The day she'd been abducted by the Roman Regulus and delivered to Katrin. How Arturius manipulated and turned her into the thing she'd hated the most. Then her escape from the prison the Romans had made for her and their subsequent murder of her entire family. Finally, the horrible ways she'd tried to end her life.

Sam remained silent throughout, allowing Zac to let it all out.

"Things that should end a vampire for good... She came back from so many."

"A heart?" Sam was suddenly panicked. "Do you think?"

"How could she come back from a torn-out heart? From what I saw, she never tried that." He was tired from the massive info-dump that the dreams had placed on him—emotionally drained beyond belief. "Vampires still need a heart to move blood around. No moving blood means no healing. She's not a founder. She was turned."

Sam looked doubtful but nodded his agreement. "All the dreams were about her?"

"Yes." He sighed, his head in his hands again. "They were like memories, vivid memories."

Sam was silent, not knowing what to say.

"I don't even think most of them were real," Zac whispered.

"What makes you say that?" Sam asked. They sounded real enough to him.

"After thousands of years, memories would twist. Even memories after a hundred years fade..." Zac said wryly. "I can attest to that."

"You do have a point, but this might be useful in dealing with Arturius," he said.

Zac shook his head. "She used her ability the same way she used it on Caius. There was nothing different. It was... instinctual."

Zac had been a shadow of himself for the past two weeks. After seeing her die over and over, something had changed in him, brought him back. Even when he was on the edge, he never backed down from a fight. What the hell had he been thinking? He was a Class-A jerk, but what else was new?

"Arturius," Zac began. "He's still here. Why?"

"Gabby," Sam told him. "He's been to see her."

He snarled and clenched his fists. Aya wouldn't let it stand, so why should he?

"We need to work together," Sam said, picking up on his internal turmoil. "All of us. It's the only way we can fend him off and end him for good."

"I know, brother."

"Can we count on you, Zac?" Sam asked.

"Yeah." He looked up at his little brother. "Yeah, you can."

***

Her world was falling into pieces around her, but Gabby still went to work. It seemed to be the only thing in her life she had control over and right now, she needed it like she needed air to breathe.

She'd kept a tight rein over her magic, bottling it deep inside, too afraid to tap into it, not even to meditate or light a measly candle. The moment she loosened her grip was the moment it would all crumble around her.

She pressed the heel of her palm against her gut and grimaced. It felt like she had stomach acid.

"Have you thought about my offer, Gabrielle?"

She jumped, her heart skipping a beat. Her hand came up to her chest and she scowled at Arturius, who had appeared out of thin air beside her. "Do you have to do that?"

"Have you thought about my offer?" he repeated, sitting on the chair opposite her.

"Yes," she spat but didn't elaborate.

"And?" He was going to make her say it.

"My answer is no."

"Don't be so hasty, Gabrielle." He played with the papers on her desk. "I'm sure you have some questions."

"Oh, I have loads of them." She rolled her eyes and snatched a folder from his hands.

He smirked at her sharp gesture. "What do you want to know?"

She looked at him with contempt, throwing the folder into a drawer. "Like you'll tell me the truth anyway," she scoffed.

"Complete transparency, dear. I'll tell you what you want to know." He leaned forwards, elbows on his knees and narrowed his eyes at her. "As long as it's something I want to tell you."

Gabby snorted. "Figures."

"Well," he chuckled, "have at it."

"Why are you such an asshole?"

Arturius laughed, throwing his head back. "Oh, Gabrielle. That's the spirit."

"You didn't answer my question."

"Because I have no shame, dear. No shame at all." His chin came to rest on his hand and he stroked his scar with the tip of his finger. "That was an easy one. Ask something more interesting."

Gabby hesitated, not knowing how far she could push the Roman. Her magic wouldn't stop him if he decided to kill her, but she took a gamble and pushed. "Why did you kill Aya?"

He snorted, his eyes becoming dark. "I made a mistake and I fixed it."

"What do you mean? What mistake?"

"One of her kind should never have been turned. You're lucky you only knew her now. When she was new, she was never good at controlling herself. Her strength was unparalleled."

Gabby understood now. "She was unstable."

She'd felt Aya's power when they'd confronted Katrin, or what was left of it. She'd been powerful beyond anything Gabby could fathom and paired with the predatory instincts of a vampire—a creature that felt everything tenfold over a human—it was a disaster waiting to happen.

But Aya had learned control. That much was clear when she'd saved Zac from the werewolf pack. When Sam had told Gabby about that the other day, it was just another piece of the puzzle. Now it'd all fallen into place.

"We've done some terrible things in our time," Arturius said, "but so did she."

"At least she learned to control herself. No thanks to you."

"Control is only part of the equation, Gabrielle. She may have killed in the name of revenge, or whatever cause she believed in, but she still killed. I know you understand what I mean."

Gabby gritted her teeth and tried to stop herself from taking the bait.

Her reaction caused a smirk to tug at his lips. "How did it feel when you killed Caius' witches?"

"Eat shit, Arturius."

"Always with the shit-eating," he said with a laugh. "You modern witches are a colourful lot. That's what I like most about you."

"Why won't you just leave me alone?" She tried to hold back the tears threatening to form in her eyes. Dammed if she would let Arturius see them.

"Because you need to admit something to yourself, dear."

She rolled her eyes, willing him to go away. "And what's that?"

"That when you obliterated those three women, *you liked it.*"

"*Go and die,*" she spat, standing up sharply.

Arturius grabbed her arm as she went to stalk away, pulling her back into his hard chest. He wrapped an arm around her waist and lowered his lips to her ear. "You need help, Gabrielle. Your power will consume you. Even now, I can feel it building inside of you." His hand came to rest on her stomach. "Let me help you before you hurt someone else. Before you hurt Alex. Before you hurt Liz. Before you hurt your *family.*"

His mouth was at her ear, murmuring his poisonous words. Whispering to her like a lover and cradling her stomach like she was pregnant with their child.

She felt sick as she wrenched herself away. "Stop trying to manipulate me, Arturius. You don't want to help me. You want to use me. Don't think for one second that I'm that naïve. I will never come to you. *Ever*."

He sneered at her, amusement sparkling in his chestnut eyes. Not wanting to stay a moment longer, Gabby turned on her heel and stormed out, pushing away the feeling of dread that'd sank into her bones. Arturius couldn't persuade her to come willingly, and the only other thing she knew he would try was to take her by force.

And that scared the hell out of her.

CHAPTER 10

Morgan had been wandering around Ashburton all morning looking for Zac.

She'd said a lot of things last night. Things that needed to be said, but the more she thought about it, she knew she'd gone about it the wrong way. She knew she had feelings for him all this time, but she hadn't realised just how strong they were until she laid eyes on him again. When she saw him in the forest—much like she had found him all that time ago—she knew what was in her heart hadn't been a fantasy.

It was impulsive and a little silly, but she couldn't help herself. She kissed him and it'd felt good. *Amazing.* When he'd kissed her back, she knew he must feel it too, but it was too soon. The woman he'd been in love with had just died. It would take time, something she had plenty of, but she still had to apologise.

She snorted and shook her head. Morgan Knowles bowed to no man. Well, maybe only to Zachary Degaud.

So far, she hadn't found him anywhere. The gardens were a last resort since she'd been everywhere else. She'd almost given up on finding him when she saw Sam in the distance, digging up a flowerbed.

He looked up at her as she approached and nodded curtly. "Morgan."

"Hi, Sam." She hesitated, knowing that he didn't trust her...yet.

"Did you want something?" He wiped his hands on his pants, smearing them with dirt and waited.

"I'm looking for Zac but can't seem to find him anywhere." She tried to keep the tone in her voice light, but from the look on Sam's face, she wasn't doing a very good job of it.

His eyebrow rose and he shrugged, sitting on the grass. "If he's not at the manor, he's either in the forest or at the bar."

"At this hour?" she exclaimed as she sat next to him.

"They know him, if you know what I mean."

"Thanks." She went to stand again, but Sam grasped her arm, pulling her back down.

"What's going on?" His tone was strained.

"I wanted to apologise," she told him. "I said some things I shouldn't have."

"Like what?"

"Like none of your business," she huffed, turning red.

Sam ignored the blush in her cheeks, even though it was quite the effort for a vampire. "I understand what you did for him, Morgan, but this time it's different. He's not on a bender, he's got a broken heart. You and I both know how much it took for him to get one. If you care for him, don't push it."

"Of course, I care for him," she hissed, turning away. "We were only together for little over a week, but that's all it takes with Zac. I don't think he's even aware of his effect on people."

Sam snorted. "Oh, he's aware."

"Then perhaps that's to his detriment." She picked up on his tone, knowing that Zac must use it to his advantage in other ways.

Sam tilted his head, waiting for her to explain.

"In terms of this..." she gestured between them, "being a vampire."

Sam seemed to struggle with himself for a moment, his expression softening. "Zac and I were as close as brothers could hope to be before. When we were human, he was..." he struggled to find the word, "good. He always did the right thing by me and for lack of a better word, he was kind. Cocky as hell, but kind. I'll never understand what he went through in the beginning, but he hasn't been the same since."

She was suddenly apprehensive. Sam obviously cared a great deal for his brother and was trying to make a point. "And you think this Aya had something to do with making him remember?"

He nodded. "He was different around her. Better. She challenged him in a way no one ever had, and when he needed it the most."

Morgan grimaced and looked away.

Sam frowned at her reaction. "Sometimes I think he's trying to be the man he was before. Sometimes I think he doesn't want to be anything other than a vampire."

"Sounds like he has a choice to make."

"Look, Zac's in an awful place right now. There're things he doesn't even tell me, and I don't even know how forthcoming he was with Aya. I don't know what he'll do and that's the problem."

"You mean with Arturius?"

"Especially with Arturius." He sighed, resting his head on his knees. "It was only the other day Liz caught him with a stake. All I'm saying is to back off for a bit. The last thing he needs—or any of us needs—is for him to go off again."

"Sam," Morgan began, "I know there's a lot of things I don't know, but as you said, I care for him in my own way. I'm not going to abandon him just because things are a little tough. That means you and your friends, too. I'll be here if you need me. If Zac wants me to go, then I'll go. I just need time to figure out what to do next."

Sam just looked at her, his expression guarded. Sighing, she decided to listen to him. After all, he knew Zac the best, and if he thought keeping clear for a while would be better for them all, then she would give him a day or two. Trust went both ways and she wanted Sam's if she was to win Zac's heart again.

"He's one of a kind," she said with a shrug, breaking the silence.

"Don't I know it," Sam replied, the sarcasm dripping from his voice.

Ever since Arturius had cornered her in the office, Gabby had been looking over her shoulder expecting him to appear yet again.

She remembered the covetous look he'd given her when she stopped Zac from hitting him that day in *Max's* and it freaked her out. And when he appeared at her office... *twice*? That was just too much. A two-thousand-year-old vampire had to have some twisted card up his sleeve and she had to be ready when he went to play it.

Problem was, Arturius could do anything and she wasn't sure she was ready for it.

She'd been stuck back late that day, and the sun had just sunk below the horizon, the eerie remnants of twilight fading into the silver glow cast by the moon. Since she lived a few blocks from the office, she usually walked the short distance so she didn't see the point of owning a car. Until now, that was.

As Gabby locked up the office and made her way through the sleepy Ashburton streets, she cast out her senses, searching for anything out of place. She was still terrified of using her power but let a little trickle through the barriers she'd placed around it. *So far, so good.*

It wasn't long before the risk paid off.

Someone was watching her, waiting. She could feel it.

Walking faster, she had to get home and inside as soon as possible. Once she was there, no vampire other than Liz and the brothers were invited in. She'd be safe until she could call Sam. If she was jumped before then, she could use her powers to buy some time and make a run for it... but even that felt like a last resort.

Gabby let out a surprised yelp as she came around the corner and almost ran headlong into a man standing on the sidewalk in front of her. As she recognised the vampire, she stumbled back a few more steps in fear. *Arturius.*

She eyeballed him, willing his brain to explode, giving him a million tiny blood clots all at once, but nothing happened. He just stood there smiling maniacally at her. She thought it was the barriers she'd placed inside of her mind, but from the satisfied look on his face, she knew he was shielded from her power. It wouldn't help her now, controlled or not.

Arturius laughed. "Something wrong?"

Dumbfounded, she edged backwards and her voice wavered as she said, "Come closer and I'll scream. Do you really want an audience for this?"

His eyebrow rose as she turned and ran.

"You can scream as much as you want, Gabrielle," Arturius yelled after her. "The whole neighbourhood has been compelled. They won't lift a finger to help you."

Gabby looked across the street where warm light filtered through the lounge room windows of the Johnson's place. Inside, they were gathered around the television. They didn't notice her screams.

She turned and saw old Mr. Price tinkering around in his garage. She yelled out to him for help, but he went about his task without the slightest inkling she was there.

Arturius appeared in front of her. "You can't run forever."

She staggered backwards and sobbed, trying to get away from him, but she only stumbled back into his solid chest, his arms circling her waist. She twisted around to face him and beat helplessly against his chest, her power useless.

"*Shh*," he soothed, stroking her hair. "You're too pretty to cry, Gabrielle."

Suddenly, the Roman's eyes widened and his look

of satisfaction slackened. A wooden stake protruded from his chest, a breath away from her face.

Gabby sobbed in disbelief as Arturius fell to the ground, gasping for breath as his skin turned grey. Then he was still.

Looking up, she saw Alex staring down at her, her shock echoed on his face.

"Are you all right?" he asked after a moment.

Gabby could only nod as he embraced her, and she cried into his chest.

"Come inside," he murmured into her hair. "Get some things together and come to my place. He can't come into the house. You'll be safe there for now."

She watched as Alex dragged Arturius' temporarily dead body from the road and dumped him in the neighbour's bushes. Now that he was dead, the compulsion he'd placed on the neighbourhood would've been broken. The last thing they could afford to happen was someone coming along and find a mummified vampire in the street.

Alex helped Gabby into her apartment, doing his best to hide his trembling hands. He'd staked a vampire, and not just any vampire. *Arturius.*

As Gabby stumbled into her bedroom and began pulling things into a bag with shaking hands, he took out his cell phone. He dialled Sam's number as she fumbled through drawers, adrenaline seeming to be the only thing keeping her from collapsing.

Sam answered after a few rings. "Alex, what's up?"

"Arturius just attacked Gabby." Best to just come out with it.

Silence, then Sam asked quietly, "Are you both okay?"

"Yeah, I staked him before he could grab her." His voice wavered a little, still in shock at what he'd done.

"Seriously?"

"Sam, he compelled the entire neighbourhood," he told him.

There was another silence from the other end of the phone for a moment.

"Well, at least now we know what he's capable of," Sam drawled.

"If I hadn't come along when I did, I don't know what would've happened to her," Alex said looking over his shoulder to where Gabby had moved onto the bathroom. She was rifling through the drawers noisily, throwing more things into her already overflowing bag.

"Where's Arturius now?"

"I didn't know what to do with him, so I dragged him off the street and into some bushes. He'll wake up pretty angry, I guess."

"Where did you get a stake from?" Sam sounded a little impressed.

"Well, with all the vampires running around this

town lately, I thought I should have something to protect myself with, especially since if I'm only a feeble human."

"Pretty gutsy, Alex. Staking a founding vampire." Sam whistled. "How's Gabby? Do you need me to come over?"

"She's pretty shaken. I'm taking her to my place for now. As far as I know, Arturius doesn't know where I live, so she should be safe for the time being. You can come over if you want, but he can't get in."

"I'll come as soon as I can," he promised. "I just have to check up on Zac."

"I understand."

"Please keep this from him for now," Sam continued. "It would be bad for us all if he found out. He'd go kamikaze on us and we've only just got him back on track."

"Right, okay," Alex said uncomfortably. "We're leaving now."

As he hung up, Gabby was standing there looking up at him with wide, fearful eyes. Now, more than ever, he wished Aya was still alive. She'd know what to do.

Remembering what she'd told him when she and Sam had rescued him from that first vampire, he sniffed. *You're the first human who has liked me for who I was and not what I was.* God, he wished she was here.

Alex didn't have any hope of helping them defeat Katrin—he was only a regular human being with no supernatural powers or immortality—but with this, at least he could do something. Even if it was only offering a place where vampires couldn't enter, a temporary safe house.

"C'mon," he said, placing an arm around Gabby's shoulders, "let's get you home."

CHAPTER 11

The next evening, one witch, three vampires, and one human, assembled at the Degaud Manor, determined to work out a plan to thwart Arturius.

The constant bullshit was wearing Zac down. The sooner the Roman was gone, the better they'd all be. Without an immediate threat, perhaps they could search for a way to end him for good and who knew how long that would take. But he knew he wouldn't rest until he had avenged Aya's death. It had taken a tragedy for him to find a purpose and wasn't that just a kick in the guts?

"What about Morgan?" Sam asked him. "Is she coming?"

"This isn't for her," Zac replied. "She's a good person, but this is our problem. Besides, I don't think Aya would've wanted her secrets handed out to just anyone."

"She spent thousands of years doing whatever it took to keep them," Gabby agreed.

"Exactly. So far, Morgan's just hanging around town, trying to figure out her next move. She has to choose herself if she wants to stay and help us, but I won't have her knowing everything."

From the look in Sam's eyes, Zac knew his brother thought it was a good idea. The more people who knew, the more danger everyone was in. Aya's past was a secret for a reason. Whatever that reason was, she'd killed for it. That was enough for him to keep Morgan out of it.

"There has to be a way," Liz said. "Nothing can live forever. We can die, so can he."

"Short of severing his head from his shoulders and encasing him in concrete, I wouldn't have a clue," Zac said sarcastically.

"Then why don't you do that?" Gabby asked.

Zac shook his head. "There's always the chance someone could chisel him out, isn't there?"

"What about the dreams?" Sam asked.

Not wanting to discuss it, Zac sighed. "What about them? They reveal nothing we don't already know."

"What dreams?" Liz sat up, confused. No one paid her question any attention.

"I've been doing a little research on them," Alex said, sitting forward.

Zac groaned. "You told Alex?"

"I told Alex because his sister might be able

to help," Sam said, an unmistakable note of warning in his voice. "She's studying in Oxford and has access to a lot of stuff we don't."

"They're not even real," he said, disregarding the notion.

"There's no way of knowing what is and what isn't," Sam said. "Any information is worth it when we have nothing else to go on."

"I only told Isobel the bare minimum," Alex interjected. "I said a friend here was studying some ancient myths for a thesis and asked if she could find some references."

"Did she find anything?" Sam asked eagerly.

"Well, something in one dream kind of stuck with me," Alex said quietly, as if he was wary of his friends' reactions. "I asked her if she knew anything about the vampire myth and the origins of witchcraft."

Zac rolled his eyes. "Get to the point."

Alex glared at him and continued, "She's been studying the history of the Britons, otherwise known as the Celts, and from what I understand, the myths and legends were set around the time Aya was turned and the Founders were created. There was a story about a deity who was thought to be fae."

Zac snorted. "A fairy?"

"Not exactly..." Gabby told him. "More like an elemental spirit."

"The story was a reference to a deity called Aericura, one name you said Arturius gave Aya," Alex continued, referring to the email on his cell. "Basically, it says Aericura was taken from the forest by some deities from the underworld and corrupted. The thing that is strange about this is that the deities are described as something very similar to a vampire. Then the same reference appeared in a medieval manuscript in 605 A.D. Aericura, the raven-haired star, her purity taken by the blood of devils. Isobel said both were vague references, which is why it interested her as nothing else was really recorded other than the modern representation."

Sam's brows furrowed. "What's the modern version?"

"She was worshipped as a goddess of blossoming, fertility... She was also believed to be a guardian in battle," Gabby said a little uncomfortably, shifting on either foot. "Vague at best."

Zac narrowed his eyes at her. She was holding something back, it was written all over her face. "I seriously doubt that the answers we're looking for are the kind that were written down."

"I agree," Sam said, nodding. "If the founding vampires or witches found their secrets written down for anyone to read, they'd stop at nothing to destroy any trace of it. Vague is exactly what we're looking for."

"There's a bunch of other goddesses worshipped around that time that are related." Alex had been Googling on his phone. "Aerten, Agrona... All goddesses related to war and the heavens. There's an Irish goddess that sounds like her—the Morrigan. Known as the Phantom Queen, reigning over war and strife, she appears as a crow or wolf."

"Sounds like Aya," Zac said.

"You think these were all identities she took at one time or another?" Sam asked, resting his elbows on his knees.

"That's what Isobel seemed to think. They all sounded like the same person and it's what she's researching for her thesis. She didn't exactly say why she thought it, though. I haven't had a chance to call her back. I assume she was trying to find proof."

"So, you're saying your sister is researching Aya for her *thesis*?" Zac asked.

Alex shrugged.

Silence fell on the room as they all thought this over. It would be folly to think Aya hadn't meddled in people's lives in different guises as she went about avenging her family's memory. The length of time she'd walked the Earth was unfathomable to Zac. In terms of vampirism, he was a baby.

"What exactly did she do to kill Caius?" Liz spoke up, breaking into their thoughts.

"It was strange..." Sam frowned, trying to remember. "It was like she generated some kind of blue fire that burned the life from him."

"Is it some kind of witch's power?" Alex asked.

"No," Gabby said, "that's not anything I can do."

"In my dream, the Romans called her Celestine," Zac said, a faraway look on his face. He sensed Gabby's sudden uneasiness and frowned, remembering the other day at *Max's*. Arturius had implied she'd known more than she was letting on and being content with his melancholy, he'd let it drop and promptly forgotten. When his gaze flickered to the witch, her face flushed red and she glanced away.

Suddenly angry, he snarled, "What do you know, Gabby?"

Gabby cowered, seemingly unable to speak.

"What does Arturius want with you?" Zac seethed, determined to get it out of her.

Sam grabbed the back of his shirt. "Lay off, Zac."

"No, she knows what he's after. It's written all over her face." He wrenched himself free from his brother's grip.

"I can't tell you!" she cried as he grasped her arms. "Something terrible will happen!"

"Gabby—" he began, the warning plain in his voice.

"*I can't.*"

Zac backed off, glaring at her. "I think it's okay." He tapped his temple and rolled his eyes. "If the dreams are mostly true, then I've seen just about everything. It just hasn't been spelt out phonetically for my puny little mind."

"He's right, Gabby," Sam murmured. "He's told me

and nothing's happened. If something was going to happen, it already would have. Right?"

She glanced from Sam to Zac. Taking a deep breath, she said, "He wants to know the secrets of power."

"And Aya knew something about it." Zac sighed, remembering the dream where Arturius was trying to get the same information from Aya. "And they think you do, too."

"I don't know anything," she sobbed. "I don't understand any of it, so how could I?"

"It's okay." Alex placed an arm around her shoulders to comfort her.

"He approached me the other day," she began.

"Gabby..." Zac started, his voice low. "We can't help you if you don't tell us what's going on."

"He didn't *do* anything," she told him. "He tried to suck me in with empty promises. Nothing he could offer will turn me to his side."

Alex held her close. "Regardless of what he wants, he won't get it here. We need to get rid of him. For what he did to Aya... and before he tries to take you."

"We need to find a weakness," Liz said, biting her nails. "Should we see what we could trick out of him?"

Sam seemed pleased at Liz's sudden intuition. "Could be worth a shot. At the very least, it could buy us some time."

"Then I'll go," Zac declared. When Sam went to disagree, he cut him off. "Arturius is arrogant. When you piss off arrogant people, they tend to let go of information they otherwise wouldn't. And you'd have to agree, I have a talent for pissing people off." Their silence was all the permission he needed.

"There's always a loophole," Gabby said out of nowhere.

"Gabby..." Alex began and gave Liz a wary look.

"What do you mean?" Zac asked. They weren't telling him the entire story, that much he knew. Was it to save his temper? Or was it something else?

"When casting a spell, there's always a way to undo it or at least counteract." She shrugged. "If we could figure out what Katrin used to make the Romans, then we might find a way to undo it."

"There could be another way to kill him for good?"

"Perhaps. But maybe Aya's ability was the loophole," she said. "I can try to find out, but I wouldn't get your hopes up."

"Gabby's right," Sam agreed. "If we can get him to leave all together, that would be our best bet. We shouldn't count on there being another way."

"Understood," Zac said, already wanting to go and search for the Roman.

When he rose, Liz said, "Be careful, Zac."

Grinning lopsidedly for the first time in weeks, he said, "Advice noted."

165

Zac knew if he hung around *Max's* bar long enough, Arturius was bound to show his face sooner or later, but when Morgan sat beside him, he suddenly wanted her to go away.

"I feel like I've hardly had time with you since I got here," she said as she gestured to the bartender.

"I'm sorry," Zac said. "It's not the greatest time."

"No." She laughed as the bartender handed her a drink.

"We've never really had a lot of time, have we?"

She shrugged. "I guess we've always been needed elsewhere."

"You're too nice, Morgan. We both know my mind has been elsewhere. Then and now," he said, laying it out.

She shook her head and sipped from her glass. It was a while before she spoke again, and he wondered if he'd annoyed her.

"You're hiding something from me." She frowned and looked away. "I can tell."

"Morgan…" He rubbed his temples, grimacing. "I can't tell you everything."

"Why not?"

"They're not my secrets to tell."

"Because they're *her* secrets?"

He sighed and drained his glass. He'd been trying to avoid it ever since she'd found him by the cave.

"Yes," he said after a moment, "her secrets." Zac didn't have to look at her to know that his suspicions were true. "Morgan, get out of here." He tried to cover the sudden awkwardness between them. "I'm waiting for Arturius. If something happens, I can't protect you."

"No." She shook her head. "I said I would help you."

He took her hand. "Please."

Morgan gazed at him, her expression conflicted. Abruptly, she dropped his hand and stood, downing the last of her drink.

"Morgan..." he groaned, reaching for her.

"I get it," she said angrily, stepping backwards before shrugging and walking from the bar, the door closing heavily behind her.

Zac resumed his favourite position—glass in hand, the epitome of a boozehound. He would have to apologise to her later. He was a major asshole at the best of times, but she didn't deserve that. He'd make it up to her later after he goaded Arturius on a bit.

It wasn't long before the Roman sat next to him, finally taking the bait, but he wouldn't find the same down-and-out vampire he had the last time.

"What are you still doing here, Arthur?" Zac sneered, using the name he'd found in his father's book.

"You know exactly why I'm still here," he replied, giving him a little credit.

"Gabby?" he guessed.

"Where is she, Zachary?" he snarled.

He shrugged.

"Don't play games with me," the founder spat. "Wherever you've hidden her, I will find her eventually. You're only stalling the inevitable."

"Well, you can't have her," he replied. "Off limits, Artie."

Arturius cocked his head to the side. "There is no such thing as limits where I am concerned. I take what I want, when I want."

"You're so full of yourself," Zac prodded him. "Don't you ever tire of living? Ever just want to lie down and die?"

The Roman was arrogant but didn't fire up. Instead, he hit where it hurt. "Happen you know a little English rose by the name of Victoria?"

Zac stiffened at the mention of her name. His maker had never elaborated the reasons she had for her attempts at claiming the South for vampires. The only thing he'd ever overheard was that she was trying to gain favour with someone. Who that was, he never knew.

Arturius smirked at his reaction. "Thought so."

But now he knew. She was trying to win favour with the Romans by using him.

"Victoria was my brother's pet," Arturius continued almost resentfully. "Regulus always has these grand schemes. Shame none of them worked when they mattered the most."

Zac shook his head. "Why are you telling me this?"

"We heard about you before her head was torn off." Arturius looked at him with disdain. "Honestly, I don't know what she saw in you. Perhaps I'm biased by the ages where men fought with swords and bare hands and didn't hide behind their automatic weapons. As a man, I fought the savages of the frontier lands with naught but a flimsy blade. Do you know how I got this?" He traced the scar that ran down his forehead to jaw over his left eye. "A Briton tried to hack my skull open with an axe," he said with a sneer. "And you know what happened to him? I ripped his heart out with my bare human hands." He laughed, sitting back onto the barstool. "Very effective, wouldn't you agree?"

Zac sneered at the founder. "If I live to be two thousand, do you suppose I will be as mental as you?"

"Zachary, if you hadn't jumped the fence, I might have liked you. You could have been great. Such a waste…"

"I would never have fought for you," he spat. "Never. I'd rather watch you die. Speaking of dying… How about it?"

"Try all you like, Zac. The only thing that can kill me is dead," Arturius said smugly, thumping him on the shoulder. "My family are now true immortals."

Zac didn't believe him one bit. From what Gabby had said, there was always a way to undo a spell. Aya had obviously been turned after the founders and she could kill them. That meant there was a loophole, another way. How had she done it? They just had to find how, and perhaps they could replicate it.

That's it. How hadn't he thought of it before? Perhaps Gabby could replicate it.

"Now," Arturius said. "How about we talk like men, Zachary? I'd like to begin by stating one specific term."

"Which is?" *This ought to be good.*

"I want the human."

He frowned. "What human?"

"*The gardener.*"

Alex? Zac's eyebrows rose. What did Alex have to do with anything?

Arturius snorted. "He didn't tell you?"

"Tell me what?"

The Roman's eyes darkened and he leaned close. "No mortal stakes me and gets away with it."

CHAPTER 12

Aya's eyes snapped open.

So, she'd died again. This was her rebirth.

The secret she'd kept for two thousand years. She was the one true immortal. Last of her kind, yet the only one of her kind. In all that time, no one had tasted her blood and lived to remember it...until Zac lay dying in that clearing.

Aya's body began to awaken and she writhed in the pain that was returning along with her senses. Her heart was racing... *her heart!* It'd been torn from her body.

Clawing at her chest, she found it intact, the muscles still knitting themselves together. She was still raw, but her heart had grown back.

She curled up into a ball as the searing heat of her muscles reaching out to each other overwhelmed all her other senses. She was hardly aware she was screaming as her insides began to fuse together, the blood flowing more freely in her newly grown veins. Tears streamed down her face as she gave herself to the onslaught of agony. This was the part she hated the most.

When she finally came to, she found herself in the cave at the edge of the manor grounds. Who had put her here? Perhaps Sam and Zac had made this her tomb. *Zac…*

She tried to stand, but slipped and fell onto the rocky ground, cutting her hands and knees. Cursing, she crawled towards the cave entrance. She was weak, but without blood, she wouldn't gain her former strength and the wound wouldn't heal completely. Using the cave wall, she stood and made her way through the dark passageway.

Coming to the rock that blocked the entrance, she cursed. The effort it took to move it almost wore her out right there and then.

Outside, it was early morning. The sun was still below the tree line in the distance, but the sky glowed. The light hurt her eyes and burned against her sensitive skin. Looking around, the grounds seemed suddenly unfamiliar. Had they changed somehow? How long had she been unconscious?

Disoriented, Aya could only put one foot in front of the other and hope she found her way.

The only thing Alex hated more than early mornings was *extremely* early mornings. The sun had only just broken the horizon and he was already halfway into town. His tools rattled in the tray as he went over bump after bump on the old road.

He'd gone to the lumberyard on the outskirts of New Orleans to pick up some supplies and was running ahead of time. At least with an early start, he would finish the last of the build at Mrs. Greene's café, scary Roman vampires or not.

He had Liz to thank for suggesting starting something on the side of his job at the gardens and hooking him up with her boss. This was his best work by far. If this went down well, then the real estate company would be begging him to take on their contract. That meant building and landscaping. Regular work meant regular money, and he was fond of money.

Catching sight of someone walking on the road ahead, Alex cursed. He was slowing down to give them a piece of his mind when he noticed it was a woman, and she was walking all strange like she was drunk. No, she must be hurt—it was way too early for anyone to be drunk... unless it was from the night before.

That was beside the point. It was dangerous to be out walking on a backroad, especially one that had a high-speed limit and with such little light. Someone might run her over.

Chivalry set in and he pulled his truck over. He

jumped out and called, "Miss? Miss, are you okay? Do you need help? *Miss*?"

Her long back hair was all messed up, her jeans torn, and her jacket had a huge hole in the back. Alex jogged to catch her. She was still stumbling along as if she hadn't heard him. It looked like he'd have to take her to a hospital or call the cops, maybe both.

He reached out and touched her shoulder and she stopped, turning slightly. He started as he saw two piercing blue eyes peering at him through a tangle of hair.

"*Aya*?" Alex exclaimed. "Aya? We all thought you were dead! Hell, are you okay? What are you doing out here?"

Aya stared at him for a moment and her expression softened with a hint of recognition. "Alex?" Her voice was a ragged whisper.

"Yes, it's me, Alex. We've got to get you to the brothers' place. Shit, you're all messed up..." And he had to race forwards to catch her as she passed out.

He held her in his arms, noticing the raw-looking skin on her chest through the hole in her shirt. Hadn't Sam mentioned her heart was ripped out? Yet, here she was. Since when could vampires grow back vital organs? He knew they couldn't, but Aya was different, that much he understood.

Opening the passenger side door, he gently placed her in the front seat of his truck and buckled the seatbelt around her. Jumping in the driver's seat, he spun the tires in the dirt as he accelerated back onto the road. Grabbing his phone from his pocket, and breaking about a billion laws, he clumsily dialled Sam's number.

***

Zac stared out the window into nothingness.

"They're only dreams, Sam. It's not like we can verify them." He was tired of talking about it. It was all they had done for the past few days. He couldn't even get anything out of Arturius, and Gabby thought his idea that she could replicate Aya's ability was foolish. She'd even scolded him for being angry that she hadn't told him about Alex staking Arturius.

If they didn't tell him things, then what the hell could he do? They were right back at the square one.

The sun was burning his face as he loosened his will around the sunlight spell on his body.

Sam pushed him away from the window into the shadows. "Don't mess around with your spell, Zac. And no, it's not about verification. Aya wanted no one to taste her blood because it would do this. She said her blood acted like poison."

Zac's eyes looked as if they were about to cloud over. Sam held up his hand defensively as he approached.

"They're true dreams, Zac. She gave you her blood to save you because she was in love with you." Zac grabbed the front of his shirt and they were face to face. "Arturius is the one you want. Save your anger for him."

Zac breathed deeply, trying to sate his rage. He wanted to rip something apart, something living. He needed to feel warm living blood through his fingers.

Then Morgan was pulling him off Sam, standing between them, her hand on his chest. She'd appeared out of thin air and he was grateful she'd chosen to come looking at that moment.

"Snap out of it, Zac," she said, glaring at him from under her lashes.

Clutching his head in his trembling hands as his eyes settled, he said what he'd been thinking every day for the past two weeks, "I failed her. I should have died... Not her."

He didn't understand the look on Morgan's face, but her hand dropped away and she glanced at Sam, who grasped both of his shoulders and stated, "You did not fail. Know that we will avenge her."

He glanced from his brother to Morgan, ashamed that she had found him slipping back into his old ways.

"I'm with you," she said, sensing the uncertainty in his gaze. "Whatever it takes."

The moment was broken as Sam's cell rang. Pulling it from his back pocket, he saw it was Alex. Sliding his finger across the screen, he put it up to his ear and said, "Alex..." His expression morphed into confusion. "Slow down, slow down. What's happened?" His eyes widened. "Come to the house. Now."

Zac grabbed his brother's shoulder, his composure returning. "What's happened?"

Sam looked at him with an expression laced with confusion and disbelief. "Aya is alive."

Alex slammed on the brakes as he came up the driveway to the brothers' house. Sam burst out of the front door as he jumped from the cab with Zac not far behind. Morgan lingered in the doorway, unsure, a sick look of disbelief plastered on her face, but Alex didn't give her a second thought.

"Take her to my room," Zac said as Sam picked Aya's limp form from the passenger side. Her arm flopped to one side and her shoulder lay exposed. The muscle had fused together, but her skin was raw and had begun to bleed.

"Holy shit, Zac," Sam said. "Her heart has grown back."

They exchanged a concerned look and Alex realised it was the same as Zac's dreams. Sam had mentioned she'd tried... He followed the vampires into the house, watching as Sam bounded up the stairs two at a time.

Morgan stood beside him, her eyes wide.

"So that happened, huh?" she drawled.

Aya opened her eyes, blinking to clear the fog that threatened to take her again.

The pain in her chest was overwhelming and involuntarily, she cried out, her back arching. She felt hands hold her down on a bed... Bed? She'd lost all sense of time and place... but she could smell the blood. She knew it was her own, but she needed blood or she would fall back to the abyss. She would be trapped in the black sea of primordial nothingness for eternity if she didn't feed.

She struggled against the hands and the pain and opened her eyes wide in an effort for clarity.

And there she beheld Zac. Zac, who she'd saved. The only one who had ever tasted her blood and lived to tell the tale. His eyes were wide with surprise and worry, but she couldn't tell what he was feeling... what he'd seen.

"Aya," he was speaking to her, "what do you need? *Please.*"

Blood, she wanted to say, but nothing came out of her mouth. She collapsed back into the bed, almost spent. Zac sat beside her, cradling her weak body against his chest.

Her head nestled against his shoulder.

Her lips against the skin of his neck.

"Drink, Aya. I trust you."

He understood.

When she'd drunk his blood in the silo, it'd awakened her power stronger than ever before. There was no way of knowing what would happen if she did again. For the first time in two thousand years, she felt genuinely afraid.

When she didn't respond, Zac stroked her hair with his free hand and whispered ever so slightly, "Please, let me save you."

He sighed in relief as he felt her teeth sink into him. Looking at his brother, who hovered by the side of the bed, he gestured for him to leave. Sam backed into the hallway and closed the door behind him.

Once Aya had drunk her fill, he laid her down and pulled a blanket over her, all the while not taking his gaze away, afraid she'd disappear again.

As her eyes grew heavy, he caressed her face, his heart hammering in his chest. Soon she was sound asleep as her body continued to heal itself.

Taking a washcloth from the adjoining bathroom, he wiped the blood from her face and his neck, the wound having already closed over. Then he kicked off his boots and lay on the bed beside her.

He took in her sleeping form and considered all the things he'd dreamed over the past two weeks. He regretted not going to check on her after seeing her regenerate from other, more horrific wounds. He should've, but the grief at her loss was too much. He didn't believe.

And now here she was, asleep beside him.

For the first time, he understood who she was and why she'd pushed him away.

Her entire life had been about avenging her family and coming to terms with what she'd become. There had been nothing else for her.

Exhausted from the loss of blood, he brushed the hair from her face and pressed his lips to her forehead. No longer able to fight the fatigue that washed over him, he closed his eyes and before he knew it, he was fast asleep.

And for the first time in two weeks, his sleep was dreamless.

It was dark outside when Aya finally woke.

The curtains were still open and the pale silver light from the moon shone over the room.

Turning her head, she was surprised to see Zac asleep beside her, the music of his blood dulled. Taking in his sleeping form, her lips pulled into a smile, but it quickly turned into a frown. Her blood would've given him dreams and what those dreams were made her afraid.

What would he think of her now that he knew the monster she'd become?

Maybe he would understand, a small voice told her. *Because he's struggled too...*

Careful not to disturb him, she wearily made her way to the bathroom. Closing the door and turning on the light, she peeled off her torn and bloodied T-shirt, stripping to her bra. She surveyed her chest where the wound had been, fingers tentatively testing the newly grown skin. It was completely healed.

She scoffed at the irony. How many hearts was this? Three or four? She could scarcely remember.

Still feeling a little weak, Aya held onto the marble countertop and took a few deep breaths. She'd drunk Zac's blood again, and in hindsight, perhaps she shouldn't have. The fact it called to her was a warning. It was unknown territory, and there was no way of knowing what it might do to her if she overdosed on it. She'd drank so much, but there was no taking it back now.

Aya took in her reflection. Her hair was tangled and wild, but her eyes sparkled. Her pale skin felt sensitive and as she ran a hand across her cheek, a trail of colour followed her fingertips—like she used to be, like shimmering pearl, translucent.

Startled and suddenly light-headed, she fell backwards, knocking the bowl of soap onto the tiled floor with a crash.

Curling up in the corner, she was vaguely aware Zac had burst in and was scooping her up in his arms. He placed her back in bed and covered her shivering form with a blanket. Drawing her close, he rubbed her arms as if to warm her up.

"It's okay," he murmured.

"Zac," Aya whispered into his chest. "What have you done to me?"

He frowned, but her eyes were closed tightly, and he kissed her forehead. She shuddered at the contact and sighed.

"I saved you... just like you saved me," he whispered. "I'm sorry."

"For what?"

"For not coming to get you once..." he began.

Aya wasn't sure she was ready to hear what memories her blood had given him, but she could have a good guess as to what. Instead, she changed the subject. "What happened? Who killed me?"

"Arturius."

She froze. Of course, it would be him.

"I'm sorry, Aya," Zac went on. "It was my fault. If I hadn't been cursed, I..." He closed his eyes and sighed sadly. "We've been trying to find a way to kill him."

Aya wasn't sure if they were crazy or brave. "Zac, Arturius is a founder."

"We had to try. And we still will," he told her.

She squeezed her eyes shut as if she was in pain. "How long since..." she whispered, changing the subject yet again.

He drew her close. "About two weeks. I thought you were gone forever."

Her eyes filled with tears and he brushed them away with his thumb. He looked in wonder as her skin shone where he'd touched, but she looked away.

"Why are you still here?" she asked. "Why did you help me?"

Zac frowned. "What do you mean? Of course, I'm still here."

"What did you see?" Her voice was hesitant.

"You mean the dreams?" When she nodded, he said, "I saw you. As you were before. I saw what the Romans did to you. What Arturius did to you. Your escape. Then..." He wasn't sure how to phrase her many suicide attempts. It was obvious he wasn't happy about remembering those dreams.

"You saw how many times this has happened to me." She was distant again. "I've kept this secret for my entire existence. No one knows I can regenerate. I loathed what I'd become and had to end it any way I could. But I couldn't, no matter how hard I tried, I still woke up. The one true immortal."

Zac remained silent but held her closer.

"Why are you still here? Why are you helping me? You saw the disgusting things I inflicted on myself... Things that should never happen to any human. I did them to myself!" She tried to push him away.

"Aya, I love you. Nothing will ever change that," he said for the first time.

She turned her head away, not daring to hope.

He grasped her face, forcing her to look at

him. "We have both done horrible things in our past, but the future is ours to change. You can trust me to keep your secret. And without a doubt, you can trust Sam and Alex. Liz and Gabby, too. You're part of our family now."

She squeezed her eyes shut at the mention of family. "My family was slaughtered in their sleep. Anyone who comes close to me inevitably suffers the same fate. I can't... I can't do that to you."

"Aya, we all know the danger we're in. As with Katrin and Caius, we all understand what's at stake," Zac reassured her. "And we will fight Arturius and anyone else who threatens the ones we love." He pressed his lips against hers and she felt herself give into him. His touch melted everything away and only her love for him remained.

Aya scarcely hoped to believe what he said was true.

As if he sensed her holding back, he said, "I've waited a long time for you, Aya. One hundred and seventy years. I'm not going to let you go so easily."

CHAPTER 13

"How is she?" Sam asked as Zac shuffled into the parlour, rubbing his eyes.

"Drained, delirious." He sat on the sofa, his expression troubled.

"I think it's to be expected after resurrecting," Sam reasoned, sitting in the chair opposite. "That's got to take it out of her."

"All those dreams…" Zac said. "They were all true. Who she was before, what she became after… Arturius' betrayal. Her family."

The brothers sat in silence for a while, as if trying to digest what they'd already suspected was true. The last thing Aya would want was for them to sit there and pity her. What happened in the past couldn't be changed, it was what it was. A memory.

"All the more reason to go after Arturius," Sam said with finality.

"Oh, there's more." Zac sat forwards, elbows resting

on his knees. "There were *six* Romans. Aya killed three of them when she was turned. And we witnessed Caius' ass kicking. Arturius and his brother, Regulus, are the last remaining founders."

Sam cocked his head to the side. "And you want to go after him as well?"

"She'll never rest easy until they're all gone. And after everything that's happened, I intend to see it done."

"I don't doubt it." His brother smiled, shaking his head.

"Sure, she's got her problems, but the last thing we should do is sit here and feel sorry for something that happened two thousand years ago. We need to get rid of the threat entirely. Then perhaps we can live a peaceful life. That was the point of coming back here after all."

"I've never met a vampire who didn't have issues," Sam said. "And Morgan?"

"I can't ask her to do more than she already has. If she wants to stay, then it's her choice. I've been upfront with our situation."

"How much does she know?"

"The bare minimum. Nothing about the dreams or Aya's past." It wasn't his secret to tell and he worried what she would make of Aya's resurrection. How was he going to explain that?

Suddenly, they knew they were being watched. Turning, they saw Aya standing in the doorway, gazing at them curiously. She'd gone into her room and changed into fresh clothes and her long, raven hair had been brushed, but what gave the brothers reason to pause were her eyes. The depth of them seemed endless, like the entire universe lived inside her.

Zac stood hastily, whatever he was going to say dissolving in his throat. All he could see was her.

"It's the eyes, isn't it?" she asked.

Zac nodded. "What…"

"I know," she told them, tilting her head to the side. "I can't fathom it, either. I assume it has something to do with you."

"Me?" Zac sat hastily as she perched beside him on the sofa, his gaze fixated on her eyes.

She peered at him curiously. "It would seem your blood has woken something in me that I thought was lost."

"Your…"

She sighed. "Spirit. Powers. Magic. Whatever you want to call it."

Zac glanced at Sam. "Is that why it makes that sound? The… singing?"

"I don't know." She dropped her gaze and wrung her hands, suddenly nervous. Glancing up at them, she said, "I have a lot of explaining to do."

Sam seemed uncomfortable and went to stand. "I'll leave you two alone."

"No, Sam. You can stay. I assume Zac told you about the dreams." Aya curled her legs beneath her.

"You have as much right to hear what I have to say, given you're mixed up in this as much as I am. For that, I'm sorry. I never intended for you all to be put into the firing line. Once Katrin was gone, the others would have been my problem alone, but..."

"Aya," Sam grasped her hand, "you became one of us a long time ago. The things you've done for all of us, well, it's the least we can do. You don't need to apologise."

She smiled tiredly, pulling her hand back. "I have a lot to say."

"We've got time to hear it," Zac told her.

She sighed, trying to find the right place to begin. "I've been known by many names. Not all nice. People have worshipped the idea of what I was and what I became. The good and evil."

"Aericura, the raven-haired star..." Zac whispered absently.

Aya's eyes widened in surprise. "Yes, that's one name I was known by. Not the one I was given when I was born, but close enough."

Zac took her hand. "What *is* your name?"

"I was born, Aeriaya. She is dead." Her words signalled a finality, her eyes dark.

"I dreamed about you in the forest," he whispered. "You were in a clearing, surrounded by moss-covered trees and the ground was white, covered with small flowers... You shone like pearl and your hair was silver."

Aya was suddenly shy. He saw her cheeks turn pink as she blushed. He reached up and cupped her face in his hand, making her look at him.

"That girl is who I was before," she whispered sadly.

"Who was she?"

"I was never human," she said, looking hesitantly at Sam as Zac's hand dropped away. "I was the last daughter of my kind. We were called the Celestines. Those from the stars and the earth. We came from the fabric of the universe."

"That's why you were called the star..." Sam said, leaning forwards.

Aya nodded. "My family gave the first witches their power. They created their kind as you now know them. We were the source of the power behind nature. Of life. I had the strongest earth sense of all. I could feel the trees growing, flowers unfurling. At night, the stars would sing to me, their light would dance on my shoulders... an echo of where my family came from. I could feel the earth right down to the core.

"It was our purpose to keep the balance of nature, to ensure it was green and fertile and strong for those who lived on it. To protect our home away from the stars. But by the time I was born, we had dwindled to a mere few. My family was the last..." Her voice caught in her throat and she stifled a sob, determined to keep her emotions in check. "Katrin was one of the five founding witches. They were given their powers in trust to help keep the balance of the earth in the event of our absence. Katrin betrayed the faith that was placed in her and created the first vampires out of spite and a lust for power over us.

"She easily found willing victims for her scheme. There was war all over Britain, between tribes and from invasion from abroad. She found them from the ranks of the invading Roman armies. They were hungry for power and easily seduced by the lure of wealth, strength, and immortality. They would pay the price one way or another." Aya shivered as she remembered the day she was snatched in the forest. "Caius and Arturius, you know. Arturius turned me once they realised I was no good to them. My family wasn't coming to save me; rather than submit to Katrin, they left me to my fate. I hated them at the time for abandoning me, but now I understand they did it to protect the whole." She halted, then said, "He... he turned me just to see what would happen. He didn't understand the monster he would create."

"*Son of a bitch*." Zac glowered, though he'd been silent throughout her story until now.

"Katrin was desperate to learn the secrets of the Celestines," she spat. "With those secrets, she sought to control the Earth itself and everything on it."

"Do you know why she created vampires?" Sam asked, as much for himself as anyone.

"Vampires were created as a weapon and a way to learn what we wouldn't give. Celestines were most connected with their power at night—the stars could be used as a conduit to their sense of self. My sense of self. Hence, why vampires can only walk in the night. As you know, blood was one way Katrin could coerce information from us. She learned much from me while I was imprisoned, but none of it made sense. She could never learn what she needed that way. It had to be given freely."

"So, when they took your blood by force, their dreams were a garbled mess?" Sam shook his head.

Aya nodded. "The Romans were useless, but I doubt it was the only reason Katrin created them, but she's no longer in the position to give us any answers."

The brothers were silent, finally realising the gravity and the extent of what they'd avoided by helping her banish Katrin's spirit. It sounded like the ultimate cliché, but she'd truly tried to take over the world and it seemed Arturius wanted to continue on regardless.

"The Romans I killed that first day were Titus, Marcus, and Octavia," she went on. "I killed Titus when I escaped. I tore Marcus and Octavia apart when I returned for revenge. There is also Regulus, who is alive somewhere."

"I saw them in the dreams," Zac whispered. "Arturius we will deal with. Do you have any idea where Regulus might be?"

"It's a big, wide world, Zac. He could be anywhere. Sure as hell he knows that Caius and Katrin are dead.

I've hidden from them for two thousand years, undoing their work wherever I can. I'm not concerned that he'll find me once we corner Arturius."

Zac was miles away. "Maybe Arturius is doing his dirty work..."

Aya shook her head. "I don't know, but he was always the runt of the litter. He and Regulus never got on."

"I think we should concentrate on Arturius," Sam said, not betraying his reaction to her story. "He is the more pressing. While he is here, Gabby won't be safe."

"Gabby?" Aya sat up straighter on the sofa at the mention of her name.

"Yes," Sam replied. "Arturius has made some attempts to get her to turn to his side... He tried to take her a few nights ago. I suspect because of what she knows about you."

"From when we banished Katrin," she groaned. "Where is she now?"

"She's staying with Alex for the time being," Sam replied. "Arturius doesn't know where he lives yet and certainly cannot get into the house. For now, she's safe."

"Not for long." She worried her bottom lip. "Arturius is smart, Sam. He's been hunting me for so long, it's like second nature to him. He's come close many times. The only reason I haven't killed him is because he's protected himself with magic. If he hasn't already found her, he will at any moment."

"I'll check on them," Sam said. "I'll give you two some time."

Aya didn't speak for a long time after he'd left. Zac sat with her, grasping her hand like she was going to disappear as he watched thoughts tumble about her mind. She'd relived some of the most painful memories of her existence today, memories she'd buried for thousands of years. It must take some getting used to. Remembering.

When she was finally able to speak, she whispered, "I know what you're thinking."

"What?"

"The fact I grew my heart back," she replied. "How I can come back from being hung, drawn, and quartered. How I can survive being burned alive. Having my head chopped off."

He scoffed, "Decapitation? Are you serious?"

"I didn't do that one at the time, but I did get my head lopped off by some British king in the Middle Ages. You should've seen the look on his face when I bent over and picked it up."

"Hell," he hissed. "Do I want to know the logistics of that?"

"Not really. It hurt like hell, by the way."

"I'm sure it did," he said, rubbing his neck. "I can't understand how it's possible."

"How does anything work? Your existence and Gabby's is the result of magic for lack of a better word. It's that simple."

"You can't die because of magic."

"The ultimate conundrum," she said. "The source of magic turned into a creature made of magic. I'm a black hole that can't be cancelled out."

"And when everything's gone?" He wasn't sure he wanted to think about the end of time.

"Who knows?" She shrugged. "I don't really have a choice in the matter. Unless a solution to my consistent resurrections is found."

"That's dangerous information." Zac's eyes darkened. "Are you sure that's something you want to know?"

Her blue eyes were suddenly cold. "Maybe one day I'll want peace."

"You want—"

"One day, I do."

Zac's eyes searched hers, willing her to come back. She was the one true immortal, she'd said. She couldn't die—he'd seen it in his dreams and with his own eyes. Suddenly, he was overcome with sadness and he knew that Aya wanted to die. Maybe not today, or in a hundred years... but eventually, she wanted to go back to the earth. He wasn't sure what to say to reassure her. Maybe his love wouldn't be enough in the end.

Finally, she said, "Don't be mad at Gabby. She was bound to secrecy by a law older than us all. I don't know what would've happened if she'd broken it." She smiled faintly. "In a way, we are sisters. It was my mother who gifted her line with their power, along with a piece of herself. A piece of my family lives on in all witches. Misuse is a betrayal."

Zac nodded, understanding completely. "When you pulled Caius' life force from his body... that was..."

"A gift from my Celestine side." She shook her head. "If there is another way to kill a Roman, then I don't know it. As far as it's known, I'm the only one who has a chance. Zac, they mustn't know I'm alive. Until I can kill Arturius, no one must know."

"I'll speak to the others. I'll explain everything." He knew it pained her to talk about her past like this. He didn't want her to dwell on it for longer than necessary.

They needed a course of action and fast. The remaining Romans would die, and he would follow her into the bowels of hell if that's what it took.

CHAPTER 14

"Aya is alive?" Gabby exclaimed when Alex came home.

He'd been rather late to work the day before and spent a lot of time apologising profusely to Mrs. Greene. Thankfully, she had understood when he said a friend had taken ill that morning. It had pushed their schedule slightly behind. He'd planned to put all the finishing touches on today and had to stay late to compensate and work all the following day to make up for it.

"Yeah." He was still shocked by it as well. "I was driving into town and she was on the side of the road. I almost didn't recognise her until she turned around. Her heart had just grown back."

"Oh, my God." Gabby's hand flew to her mouth.

He fidgeted. "You know we have to keep this a secret, right?"

"Yes, of course," she reassured him. "Is she okay? I mean, that's kind of—"

"Full on," Alex finished for her. "Sam seemed to think so. She'll probably need to rest a few days, but I don't think they even know how it works, either."

Gabby seemed to contemplate this for a while, then she said, "Maybe now we can get rid of Arturius."

"Here's hoping," Alex said uncertainly.

"Would you ever take it back?' Gabby asked, her voice quiet.

"What?"

"Knowing all of this. What we all are?"

He laughed. "It's not exactly a picnic having a two-thousand-year-old vampire messing with your friends, but I wouldn't change it for the world. I used to be normal. Now I feel part of something, you know?"

Gabby curled her legs beneath her on the sofa and smiled. "You really like Aya, don't you?"

Alex shook his head and grinned. "She might be all scary and tough, but she's a good person. She knows what's right."

"You're very similar in that way." Alex frowned and she quickly added, "Knowing what's right. However, you're the least scary person I know."

There was a sharp knock at the door before he could reply. Naturally, he went to stand and go answer it, but hesitated at the last second, looking at Gabby.

She placed a finger to her lips to silence him.

When he mouthed *Arturius*, she nodded, her eyes betraying her fear.

"I know you're there," Arturius' gruff voice called through the door. "I can hear your hearts beating."

Damn, he worked fast.

Alex had no idea how he'd found them. They had almost two days of peace and he supposed it'd been generous. Sam had said he'd spent thousands of years hunting Aya, so maybe it shouldn't be such a surprise. Arturius was good at this kind of thing.

"Don't make it harder for yourself, Gabrielle," the Roman called out through the door. "Do you want your human friend to die? Because it can be arranged quite easily."

Alex strode to the door and wrenched it open. Coming face to face with Arturius for the first time scared the hell out of him. He couldn't show any fear or he'd be done.

"Go away," he spat, eyeballing the two-thousand-year-old vampire.

The Roman raised his hand to grab Alex around the throat but couldn't pass through the door. It was like he'd hit a pane of glass.

Arturius' face contorted into anger and he punched the air in front of him. Alex took a step back, even though he had no hope of touching him while he was still inside.

"You're not welcome here," he declared, not backing down.

"I don't want your welcome," the Roman growled at him. "I want your witch."

"Well, you can't have her." He slammed the door closed in the vampire's face.

"It's only fair that I kill you, human." The Roman banged a fist against the door. "After all, you staked me in cold blood. Eye for an eye."

Alex looked at Gabby, who was standing inside the lounge room, peering around the corner into the hall. What the hell were they going to do? They couldn't stay inside for the rest of their lives. A vampire had all the time in the world to wait them out.

But apparently, Arturius had a short attention span. When the front window blew in, Gabby screamed, the tinkling of glass raining about the lounge room. Alex pulled her into the hallway not a moment too soon.

"That was a warning..." his voice came from outside. "You would do well to heed it."

Alex stared in shock at the large rock that lay in the middle of his lounge. What the hell had he gotten himself into?

He scoffed, running his hands over his face. *Keep your head screwed on, Alex,* he thought. *Gabby's life is on the line.*

"He's gone," Gabby whispered, breaking his shocked perusal of his front windows. "But he'll be back."

Alex walked into the lounge and surveyed the

damage with a groan. The window had shattered with so much force, shards of glass had embedded themselves into the far wall and much of the furniture was shredded.

"Zac was right," he said, wrenching a piece of glass from the sofa, trying not to slice his hand open. "He's an arrogant bastard. And showy, too."

"What are we going to do?" Gabby asked quietly. "My power won't work on him."

"I'll call Sam. Maybe you-know-who might be able to help," he said, wary that someone might still be listening.

Aya supposedly being dead was their one weapon against the Romans. If Arturius found out, then it was all over before it even began.

***

Aya sat cross-legged in the middle of the garden, the overgrown grass rustling in the cool breeze of twilight. Zac was beside her, their knees touching.

He'd said nothing for a long time, content to wait for her, playing with a long blade of grass. It'd been a hell of a long day, but the load she'd been carrying around on her shoulders all this time felt lighter. Strangely, it was relieving.

She remembered glimpsing a blonde-haired woman at the manor when Sam carried her inside, someone she'd never seen before.

"Who is she?" she asked. Zac looked at her confused. "The blonde woman."

"Morgan," he said with a sigh and he seemed conflicted.

"So, I didn't hallucinate her then."

"No."

"Who is she to you?"

Zac was silent for a moment, frowning. "I met Morgan about seventy years ago. It was 1944 and I was in France. I was a soldier in the British Army. It was during World War II. She'd been turned a few years before and was there for much the same reason I was. We became friends of a sort, and when I could no longer tell friend from foe, she helped me back on the wagon. After the war ended, we lost contact and I never saw her again. Not until a week ago."

"She just turned up?" That sounded suspicious.

"She came looking for me."

"And?"

He sighed. "She's not working with anyone. I believe her when she said she only came to see me."

Aya frowned, unable to let go of her suspicion. This was a game she was all too familiar with, and randomly showing up when so much was going on was a glaring red flag. It would take a lot more than Zac vouching for the vampire for her to believe any of it. She would get to the bottom of Morgan's miraculous appearance any way she could.

"Did you tell Sam about her?" she asked, fishing for clues.

"No." He looked away. "Not at first."

"Why?"

Zac ran his hands over his face and grimaced. "Because that part of my life was awful. I didn't want him to know anything about it. He trusted me to keep my head straight when I left him, and I betrayed him. I didn't want him to know."

She placed a hand over his before letting it drop away. "Is she staying?"

"I don't know," he replied with a shake of his head. "As far as I'm concerned, she's welcome for now."

Aya exhaled, not trying to hide her annoyance. "How much does she know?"

"She knows about Arturius—I owed her that much. She walked into a shit storm, Aya. I had to."

"And she knows about me," Aya mused sullenly.

"Not everything. Only that you were dead and now you're not."

"Only?" Aya was annoyed. Their whole existence balanced on the fact that Arturius believed she was dead and gone.

"She doesn't know the circumstances, Aya. As far as she knows, you could be a founder yourself."

"I'm still not comfortable with it."

"Don't compel her. At least, not yet," he reasoned.

She didn't like his tone of voice. "What was she to you?"

"A companion, nothing more."

She snorted and looked back across the garden to the forest. The day was almost gone and the stars were beginning to shine. Feeling their song on her shoulders, she closed her eyes and exhaled. In her wildest dreams she never thought she'd see the day she would hear the stars sing to her again.

"What about Arturius? What was he to you?" Her head snapped up at Zac's question.

"I never loved Arturius," she said, knowing he meant the time when the Roman had spoken of his love for her—Zac had seen it in his dreams. "I didn't know the meaning of the word then, not really."

She felt Zac's gaze on her face. "And now?"

"Two thousand years is a lot of time to garner knowledge of such things," she said wryly. "I'm still learning. I don't think love is something anyone will ever truly understand."

She was sure Zac wouldn't complain about that. He would understand all too well dealing with emotions he couldn't control. It was much more difficult as a vampire. He obviously still had trouble with it, that much was obvious when he disappeared after that fight with Sam a few weeks ago.

When she closed her eyes, trying to hear the sounds that were coming back to her, he asked, "What does it sound like?"

She gave him a sidelong glance, her gaze curious.

"My blood," he prodded.

"I don't know if I can find the right words," she replied, trying to think. It was the strangest sensation. To hear someone. "It sounds like starlight." He looked at her curiously. There was much he wouldn't understand fully, but at least he wanted to try. She laughed nervously. "But you wouldn't know what that sounds like, either."

"Can you hear it all the time?" He dropped the piece of grass.

"Yes," she told him. "But I can block it out if I want to." *But not when your blood is pooling all over coffee tables.* "I need to find Arturius." She needed to change the subject. "This needs to end."

"What do you propose?"

"We are equally matched, apart from one thing—he doesn't know how I killed the others, only that I can. Once I have him, that's it." That much was clear from the memories Zac would have seen through his dreams. Once she touched a founder with her power, there was no going back. "But he will be protected, and we have to be ready for it."

"Protected by witches? Like Caius was?"

Aya nodded. "Though I'm betting he'll become lax. He thinks he's untouchable now."

"Are you sure you're up for this?" Zac asked concerned.

"I have to be," she replied. "There is no other option. I owe it to Gabby, you, Sam, Liz, Alex, and my family. I can't go back." She felt his gaze as she stared across the garden.

"Whatever you decide, we'll be behind you."

"Would you let me drink your blood?" she asked quietly. "I don't think I could summon enough power without it."

He smiled wickedly at her. "Of course. It kinda turns me on..."

Laughing, Aya slapped him playfully. It was hard for her to ask, never having relied on anyone before. Usually, she would've just taken it and gone. The whole notion of this mismatched family she found herself a part of was strange to her. How was she meant to act? How was she to move forwards?

"What do you think it is about me that helps you?" Zac asked, interrupting her train of thought.

"I have no idea, but if we get through this, we ought to find out."

He pressed his forehead against hers, his hand caressing the small of her back. She pulled away, turning her face from him, unsure.

Placing a hand on her arm, he said, "Why do you keep fighting me, Aya?"

She frowned. "I don't know how to do this..."

"Do what?"

"This. Together with you. Be a part of a family." She shook her head. "I don't know. I understand what it means to other people. I've helped enough. But me?

I've spent two thousand years keeping people away. Keeping them from the truth."

"You just have to trust us, like we trust you," Zac said, placing his hand over her heart. "And trust this. When I'm with you, just trust this."

"When did you become so nice." She sighed, resting her head against his shoulder.

"I only bring it out for you." He smiled, running a hand through her long black hair.

They sat like this for some time, Aya content to just have Zac beside her. It was such a comforting sensation to lean against another. It was alien to her, and she was still full of uncertainty. She wanted to trust him so much, but it would take time. She loved him, that much was certain.

"Perhaps this is what Sam wanted when he tried to change me," Zac murmured into her hair.

"And what's that?" she asked, pulling back to look at him.

Smiling, he leaned down to kiss her. "He wanted me to love."

***

Turned out, Sam was already on his way over, so when Alex called, it was only a few minutes until the vampire turned up on the front porch, surveying the damage Arturius had inflicted on the front windows.

Alex opened the door to let him in, but he

hesitated. "You need to invite me in." Sam grimaced, hovering just outside the door.

"Oh, shit." Alex frowned, remembering that he'd told Sam to basically go jump after he found out that he was a vampire. "Sorry. C'mon in."

Sam stepped inside and whistled when he saw the state of the lounge. "Bastard really did a number on the house, didn't he?"

Gabby was hovering in the opposite doorway, just inside the kitchen. "I'm just worried he'll come back."

"It'll be okay," Sam said. "He can't get inside the house and now we have Aya back, we can deal with him once and for all."

"How is she?" Alex asked. He hadn't seen her since he had found her on the side of the road.

"She's shaken, but apparently, it's happened to her before."

"You're not serious?" Alex scoffed and caught Sam's grimace. "*You're serious.*"

Sam turned towards the window, not wanting to dwell on the subject further. "We better get something to cover the windows. I'll help you fix it in the morning. I know a good glazier."

There was a loud pounding on the door, and they all tensed. Sam held up a hand and wrenched the door open, knowing who was on the other side.

"Haven't you done enough damage for one night, Arturius?"

The founder was standing on the porch, his

expression full of malice. "On the contrary... I think I've done too little." Sneering, Arturius pulled a gun from his back pocket and fired at Sam at point-blank range.

Gabby screamed as he fell back onto the floor. A trail of blood ran down his forehead from the bullet hole in his temple, his eyes wide open and blank.

Alex looked up at Arturius, who wasn't alone. A well-built man stood with him, a glazed look on his face—a compelled human.

As the man boldly walked inside, Alex held Gabby behind him and hissed, "*Run.*"

As Alex went to take a swing, the man ducked and pushed him against the wall, going after Gabby. Arturius leaned against the invisible wall that held him outside and laughed, confident he wasn't going home empty-handed.

Ignoring him, Alex pulled a baseball bat from the hall closet and circled around the lounge room towards the kitchen where he heard Gabby's sob. The human seemed to be immune to her power, and whatever she tried didn't stop his advance.

Peering around the doorjamb, Alex saw she'd drawn a knife from the block on the counter, her hand shaking. The poor guy had no choice in what he was doing. Alex recognised him from *Max's*... he might even work there.

Gabby dodged the man's lunge and darted into the dining room. Edging through the kitchen, he couldn't get a clear shot to knock the guy out. Gabby caught his eye as he ducked back behind the archway and a moment later, ran past him.

The guy didn't see Alex hiding in the kitchen and rushed into his perfectly aimed swing. As the bat collided with his head, the man fell backwards with a thump, out cold.

"Nice try, Arturius!" he yelled, his heart thumping in his chest.

The Roman's roar of annoyance sent shivers down his spine. That was twice they'd angered him tonight.

Pulling a roll of duct tape from his toolbox, Alex bound the man's hands behind his back and his ankles together. For good measure, he taped his mouth shut. The poor guy had been compelled and until someone could reverse it, it was better to restrain him.

"He's gone again," Gabby said, edging her way back to the front door where Sam's inert body lay. Crouching beside him, she surveyed the wound in his forehead.

"Is he dead?" Alex fell to his knees beside her.

"Yes, but he'll come back." She wiped away tears. "He's not desiccated. When a vampire truly dies, they turn a grey colour—they mummify."

"Umm, *gross*."

"We need to pull the bullet out or he won't revive anytime soon," she went on.

Alex looked at the hole the bullet had punctured in Sam's skull. There was no way they were pulling that out with their fingers. "Will needle-nose pliers do?" He wasn't even sure what he was suggesting.

"I guess."

"Do we need to sterilise them?" Why the hell was he even asking?

"No."

He grabbed the pliers from the junk draw in the kitchen and said, "Do you want to do the honours?" Once he saw the horrified expression on her face, he shrugged. "I guess I'll do it then."

Looking at the wound, he wasn't sure if he should be gentle or not. Sam would heal properly if he wasn't, wouldn't he?

Sam's eyes were still wide open and blank and Alex shivered.

"Could you close his eyes?" he asked Gabby. "It's kind of creepy."

Gabby ran her hand over the vampire's face and he sighed, readying himself. As he eased the pliers into his friend's head, he felt sick to the stomach and almost threw up as he felt metal graze on bone. Once he was past the skull, he felt the tip of the bullet and tried to grasp it.

"I can't get it." He grimaced. He was going to puke any second.

"Don't be so gentle," Gabby whispered, trying not to look. "You won't hurt him. He'll heal."

"Okay." He dug a little deeper.

Finally, he was able to grasp the bullet and with an

audible sucking sound, pulled it out. Blood pooled in the wound and ran down Sam's face as Alex threw the pliers to the side.

"Hell," Gabby hissed.

"Whoa," he exclaimed. "That was intense. How long until he wakes up?"

"It could be a few hours," she told him. "We'd better call Zac."

Alex, who'd let his dislike of the vampire drop some time ago, offered to do the honours. He wondered how this new development would go down.

***

"Are you going to invite me in, Alex?" Zac grimaced as he stood on the front porch, hands grasping either side of the doorframe. Aya had just sauntered straight inside, much to Alex's surprise.

"Aren't you worried Arturius will see you?" He was ignoring Zac on purpose, talking to Aya, who was looking much brighter than when he'd seen her last.

"No," she said. "I know he's not here. He won't try again tonight."

"You seem certain about that."

"I know him very well." She smiled. "Twice fooled, shame on you. Thrice fooled, never."

Alex frowned. "I think it goes a little differently than that."

"Probably," she told him, looking into the lounge.

Gabby bounded down the stairs then, and to Aya's surprise, threw her arms around her in a relieved hug. "Aya, I'm so glad you're here."

She laughed uneasily. "Um, okay?"

"Will someone invite me the hell in?" Zac's exasperated voice came from outside.

Alex tried to hide a grin despite their dire situation. "Come inside, you grumpy bastard."

He stepped through the door and went straight up the stairs to where he knew Sam was still lying semi-dead in Alex's spare bedroom. The wound had almost closed over, which meant he'd wake up any moment. Liz was sitting beside the bed and had obviously been there for some time.

"We need to get you out of here," Zac said to Gabby, who'd followed him and Aya. "Daylight won't stop him. First thing, get out of town until we can do something about it."

"What happened to the human?" Aya asked, cocking her head to the side.

"He's downstairs in the kitchen. I gaffer taped him to a chair," Alex replied.

"I'll take care of it," she said and disappeared.

Gabby scowled, obviously not happy with the turn events had taken.

"I will go with you, so you're not alone," Liz said when she noticed her discomfort. "We can go to your grandmothers. I called her on the way here."

"Liz!" Gabby exclaimed. "You had no right to drag her into this."

"She offered her help, Gabby. Sophia can help shield you until this is over. The both of you together... That's epic."

"But Arturius—"

"First thing," Zac interrupted, "get out of town and stay out of town. Let us do the rest."

CHAPTER 15

The early morning was bright and clear as Gabby, Alex, and Liz packed the truck for the drive to Sophia's.

None of them had gotten much sleep after the previous night and had finally conceded, packing up a duffle bag for each of them and deciding to go just after dawn. The sooner they were gone, the safer they would be.

Sam was furious when he awoke, but Zac and Aya had taken him back to the manor to work out their next move. He'd been reluctant to leave them alone, but they were safe in Alex's house for the time being. Gabby agreed with Aya when she said Arturius would back off.

As they stood in the driveway loading the truck, Liz tensed and looked towards the end of the street.

"What is it?" Gabby asked, but she already knew the answer. She felt it coming, too.

"Alex, get in the truck," Liz snarled, but it was too late.

As they were looking down the street, a man had crept up behind Gabby, but Alex, for all his humanity, was faster. He staked the vampire right through the heart and pushed him backwards into the garden.

The gun the assailant had been holding clattered to the ground and the sight of it sent a wave of terror through all of them.

"C'mon," Alex said, hurrying them to get in the truck.

Gabby gasped as she caught sight of three menacing figures standing on the sidewalk. Three vampires were advancing on them, intent on disabling any threat to themselves or their target. The man to the left raised a handgun and fired without hesitation.

They had no time to get out of the way.

Alex grunted in surprise and clutched his stomach, eyes wide. Liz went to grab his shoulder to steady him, but he was on his back, white as a ghost. *They'd shot him.*

Standing over him, she picked up the gun the first vampire had dropped and raised it with a roar of fury. With her vampire sight, she had no trouble aiming for the sweet spot, right in the heart.

She'd shot the three of them before they had a chance to aim. They were right in assuming they were vampires, all three bodies desiccated in moments.

"Gabby, get in the truck and drive." She took charge

as she lifted Alex into the tray as gently as she could manage.

The witch didn't protest, the engine roaring to life a moment later. Arturius was nowhere in sight and she didn't know what that meant, but they wouldn't be sticking around to find out.

Looking down at Alex, she cried out in horror. His blood was everywhere, seeping out of a wound that was much worse than she'd first thought.

She breathed in and her hands trembled as she tried to control herself before the smell of it took over. She had to save his life before it was too late.

As the truck bounced over the speed bump at the end of the street, Alex groaned, barely conscious.

"It's okay," she told him. "It's going to be okay. I'm going to save you."

Straddling him so she could hold his body still, she pulled his T-shirt up and felt for the wound with her hand. He'd been able to pull out the bullet in Sam's head with pliers, so she should be able to do this, vampire or no vampire.

Her finger found the hole in his stomach and without thinking too much about it, she stuck her thumb and forefinger in. She felt the little piece of metal almost immediately.

Alex screamed in pain, trying to thrash against her.

"I'm sorry," she sobbed, holding him down. *Hold on, Alex.*"

It was then she realised that the blood didn't

bother her that much. She could filter most of it out, the scent becoming so familiar that it was as if it wasn't there anymore.

Then the bullet was gone from him and she flung out somewhere over the side of the tray. Alex slipped into unconsciousness.

Liz bit her wrist open and forced it to her friend's mouth. *Please swallow, please swallow…* She grimaced as he instinctively gag, but finally swallowed. She'd never used her blood to heal another before and hoped it wasn't too late. *It couldn't be too late.*

They were twenty minutes from Alex's place before Liz knocked on the back window of the cab to let Gabby know it was okay to move Alex inside. The wound had healed over, but it would still take time for him to feel completely better, but he was going to make it.

Once she was inside the cab with Alex in the middle, she called Sam and explained what'd happened—every sordid little detail.

"I don't know what it means," she said, "but Arturius wasn't there."

"I'm so glad you're all okay," he said after acknowledging her warning. "Liz, I'm so proud. God, I love you."

"And I love you."

When she hung up, Gabby looked at her. "He's going to come and meet us in Mobile when he can," she said.

Gabby could only nod, but the moment she turned back to the road, she slammed on the breaks.

Liz grasped Alex, one hand landing on the dash, as she caught sight of an ominous figure standing in the middle of the road. The screeching of tires and burned rubber filled the air and Liz prayed they'd stop in time.

It was then she realised the man was Arturius.

At the last second, she caught the sly smile on his face as the truck collided with his body, sending him spinning onto the hood, shattering the windshield, throwing him clear over the tray and onto the road behind.

The truck skidded to a halt, turning ninety degrees from the forward momentum, rocking side to side before finally settling. The smoke churned up by the burning tires choked the air as the engine sputtered and died.

"Shit," Liz hissed.

"Are you guys okay?" Gabby's voice wavered, hands still clutching the steering wheel, her knuckles white.

"Yes. Yes, we're okay. Alex is still out." Liz peered out of the passenger side window where there was a dark lump lying in the middle of the road. *Arturius.*

"Call Sam back, now," she said to Gabby and jumped from the cab, laying Alex down along the seat.

Liz wasn't stupid enough to presume the Roman was dead, but from the crunching sound the truck made, she knew the engine was. She pulled open the hood and checked anyway, trying to remember the things her dad had shown her about cars when she was little. Cursing, she slammed it closed. They would have to make a run for it.

That was when she glanced down the road and gasped. *Arturius was gone.*

"Gabby?" she called out, the warning in her voice desperate.

"Yes, dear?"

Liz spun and came face to face with the Roman, who was smiling down at her, triumph plastered on his twisted face.

She stumbled back, but he already had her head in his hands... and twisted.

Turned out, Gabby should've slammed her foot on the gas instead.

Liz's eyes snapped open and she gasped for air as her heart started beating with a painful thud. Powerful hands were on her shoulders, calming her. It took a moment for her eyes to focus, but when they did, she was relieved to see Sam looking down at her.

"Gabby," she exclaimed, trying to sit up.

"Easy," Sam said, soothing her. "You've had a nasty shock."

"Arturius, he—"

"I know. He's got Gabby."

"Alex! He was shot, he…" If anything had happened to him, she wouldn't know what to do.

"Alex is okay," he said, stroking her forehead, trying to calm her. "He's awake and perfectly fine, thanks to you."

"His truck…" she grimaced. "It's totalled. He loved that stupid truck."

"We had it towed here for the time being," Sam told her. "I had to compel the poor tow driver so he didn't rat us out to the cops." She scowled and he chuckled. "Don't worry, Liz. We'll get him a new one. What's the point of being rich if you can't spend it?" She sat bolt upright and hugged him. "Careful."

"I'm fine," she said, burying her face into his neck. "It's horrible. I don't know how you can stand it."

"Having your neck snapped? No, it's not pleasant and I definitely don't ask for it."

"How did we get back here?"

"Gabby called and told us what had happened. Zac and I, we came as fast as we could, but it was already too late." He grimaced and held her face in his hands. "When I saw you laying on the road…"

Liz clutched Sam like her life depended on it. "What are we going to do?" she whispered.

Sam stroked her face. "Zac and Aya are on it. They'll get her back."

"What if Arturius finds out?" She remembered when Gabby told them what Arturius was looking for

—the secrets to power. What would happen if he got what he was looking for? What would they do then?

"Gabby said she didn't know, remember? She didn't understand what Aya did to banish Katrin."

Liz frowned and bit her bottom lip. Maybe Gabby didn't understand, but what if Arturius had someone who did?

Aya was hiding in the kitchen, as much to listen to what was going on as to get away from it. It always took her a few days to acclimatise to life after coming back. And this time was no different.

It seemed like her senses were still running overtime after she'd drunk Zac's blood to finish healing herself. It was the most in-tune she'd felt with her Celestine side since she'd been turned.

Turning her thoughts away, she listened for the others. Sam was upstairs with Liz, waiting for her to wake up. Apparently, it was the first time she'd had her neck snapped. Aya snorted. At least she'd done it in spectacular style. That little girl was finally catching on and growing a spine.

She jumped up onto the countertop and sat swinging her legs, listening to Alex argue with Zac in the other room. She was impressed by his ability to bounce back from his brush with death—physically and mentally. Shot in the stomach and healed by his best friend. He was one tough human.

He wanted to go after Gabby, which was understandable, but he wouldn't have to. Zac was telling him as much. Going after the witch was her job. After all, she was a witch hunter.

Feeling a shift in the air, Aya frowned and looked out the back door that she'd opened to let in the fresh air. Arturius' stink was still through the house and it made her gag.

The afternoon sunlight was streaming in, lighting up the little kitchen, bringing the scent of wisteria and bougainvillea with it. When she caught sight of the blonde-haired vampire—the one Zac had called Morgan—she scowled. *So, that's who he was talking to on his cell earlier. The vampire who knew too much.*

Morgan saw her through the window and hesitated. She was intimidated, the emotion rolling off her in sickly waves, making Aya oddly satisfied. She suspected Zac had told her things that she shouldn't know, but that was when he thought her permanently dead and the dreams hadn't played out. What she was worried about the most was that Morgan knew that she was alive. If the vampire was here for the reason she suspected, then it could be a problem.

Aya peered at her through narrowed eyes as she hovered by the door, unable to come in until Alex invited her, and she definitely wasn't in a hurry to let him know.

"You must be Aya," she said in a quiet voice, betraying her apprehension.

"Yes," she replied bluntly.

Morgan hesitated, not knowing what to say next, but came out with a spectacularly annoying question. "How did you come back? Zac told me your heart was torn out."

Aya rolled her eyes. "I don't think that's any of your business."

"Are you a founder?" She just kept going. Did this woman have a death wish?

Aya snorted, shaking her head. "I wouldn't push it, Morgan."

"I'm just trying to protect him."

Aya laughed at her blatant proclamation and slid to the floor, walking towards the vampire who was still stuck outside.

"From what?" she sneered, inches from her face. She wanted to make her say it—that she wanted her out of the picture so she could have Zac all for herself. It was written all over her face and all over the emotions that bled from her skin. What a stupid little girl.

"Aya."

She didn't break eye contact with Morgan when she heard Zac behind her, the sound of his blood radiating around him. She shook her head and turned towards him, annoyed at the sudden territorial feeling that'd threatened to overwhelm her.

Alex walked into the kitchen and glanced to Morgan hovering in the doorway.

"She's with us," Zac said, not taking his eyes of Aya. "You can invite her in."

"I'm Morgan," she called out towards Alex.

"Oh," he said, glancing towards Aya, then back to the blonde-haired vampire outside. "Come on in."

As she stepped into the kitchen, Aya sighed loudly, the silent conversation she'd been having with Zac over. How exactly had Morgan helped him? When she'd tracked him after his fight with Sam, he hadn't been *that* bad. None of the humans he'd stalked ended up dead, but from experience she knew that it could get much, much worse. And from the emotions she'd sensed from Zac last night, she knew he'd been right at the bottom. That's why he felt so trusting of her, it had to be.

When Zac turned his gaze onto Morgan, Aya stepped around him and walked into the lounge, needing to get away before she said something she'd regret.

It was dark here now that the windows had been boarded up with plywood, most of the glass gone from the floor and where it had embedded into the furniture. Sam had generously offered to replace it all.

Alex had followed her in from the kitchen and was looking at her curiously. "You don't like her?" he asked when she didn't acknowledge him.

Aya frowned, pulling him into the opposite hallway by the front door. "I don't trust anyone."

"I really hope that's not true," he replied wryly.

"Oh, Alex." She rubbed her temples. "Of course, I trust you and the others, but I don't entirely trust her. She's hiding something."

"Okay..."

"She has an air of desperation that I don't like." As soon as she said it, she understood. Morgan didn't just have feelings for Zac... she was in love with him.

God, it annoyed her. She knew he didn't feel the same way, but what would Morgan do about it? She shook her head. They had bigger Roman fish to catch.

Grabbing Alex's arm, she said, "I need to go see Gabby's grandmother."

"Sophia? Why?"

"For much the same reason Gabby went to find her," she replied.

"She can help us find her?"

"Yes, exactly. And we know she's sympathetic to our cause, and not just because Gabby is her granddaughter."

"But can't you do something to scry for her?"

"No. I can't do anything like that. Not anymore."

Alex seemed to think about it for a moment. "I'm coming with you. She knows me and it might be better if one of us is at least human."

Aya grimaced. "I have a feeling it doesn't

matter. After all, I'm the only star left shining in the universe, even if I've been dulled."

"And Zac?"

"He would be less than welcome in a witch's home. He's vampire through and through. It's a miracle Gabby likes him."

Alex glanced back towards the kitchen. "I saw the way Morgan looked at him, you know. Are you sure you want to leave him alone with her?"

Aya was surprised at Alex's observation and he was right. It did bother her, but she couldn't put herself before Gabby. "I trust him to do the right thing." Alex didn't look convinced by her statement and she said, "With me, after everything... I know he'll do the right thing by me."

Alex nodded. "Just let me know when you want to go."

"Just let me talk to Zac."

"Sure." He looked back through the lounge room to where Zac was leaning against the doorjamb, Morgan hovering in the kitchen. He was watching them, waiting.

Alex grasped her shoulder before he went through to the dining room, giving them some privacy. A moment later she heard him talking to Morgan.

When Zac stood in front of her, placing his hands on her waist, she said, "I have to go see Gabby's grandmother."

"Now?"

"The sooner, the better."

"Are you sure? I mean, it's only been a day..." he began.

"Don't coddle me, Zac."

He took a step back at her sharp tone, letting his hands fall away.

"I've done this before," she whispered, caressing his face. "Don't worry about me. This is what I've done for thousands of years. I know what I'm doing."

He nodded, placing his hand over hers.

"Keep an eye out for trouble," she told him. "If anything goes wrong or if you feel uneasy about anything, call me."

"You don't have a cell."

"Then call Alex."

"He's going with you?"

"Don't be jealous." She resisted the urge to roll her eyes.

"I'm not. It's just... He was shot this morning."

"And Liz healed him," she replied, leaning her cheek against his chest. "It'll be fine, Zac. Just... keep an eye on Morgan."

He took her shoulders and pushed her back, his green eyes searching hers. "Why?"

"There's something off. I don't know what... but I can feel it."

"Aya, she's a good person. I trust her."

"I'm not questioning her goodness, Zac. The

greatest mistakes come from the best intentions. Please, just—"

"*Okay.*" He cupped her face in his hands and kissed her, his lips lingering against hers. "Okay."

She smiled. "Okay."

It was time to go hunting again.

CHAPTER 16

Morgan walked along the main street of Ashburton, her thoughts troubled. She never thought someone like Zac could ever love her—plain old Morgan Knowles.

She might be an immortal, but it came with a heavy price tag. Everyone around her would wither and die and she would go on, frozen in time. Kind of put a sour note on dating.

Watching another woman in his arms hurt, especially when that woman had threatened her. How could he love *her*? What was it that Aya had that she lacked?

Morgan closed her eyes and sighed. The mysterious woman who'd resurrected from certain death, a fact they wanted to keep secret from Arturius.

There was more to Aya than met the eye, she was sure about it.

Pushing through the door to *Max's* bar, Morgan

took a seat at a table along the far wall. She knew Zac wouldn't be here tonight. After Aya had left with the human Alex, he'd gone back to the manor with his brother and girlfriend. She'd be alone here.

Looking around the bar, she tensed as a man walked through the door—a man she knew to be a vampire. From the look of him, it must be Arturius.

He had short-cropped brown hair and a hard face that'd been marred by a long scar that travelled down the right side of his face. Now she understood why everyone was so scared of him. Not because he was a founder, or he was two thousand years old, but because he had an overwhelming appearance of power.

She watched as he sat by himself at a table across the room, his back to her. It would be naïve to think he hadn't noticed her gaze. She was in it now, whether she liked it or not.

Morgan had two choices. She could align herself with Zac and the others or she could cut herself a deal that could change her life for the better. She could have everything she ever wanted.

It was an easy decision. Morgan stood and walked towards the Roman before she could talk herself out of it. Pulling up a chair, she sat across from him, ignoring his raised eyebrow.

"And who are you?" he asked, narrowing his eyes.

"Morgan Knowles."

"I see." He raked his eyes over her and gave an

appreciative nod. "And what do you want from me, Morgan Knowles?"

"I have some information you'll find very valuable," she replied, not letting him intimidate her. How he knew who she was unsettled her, but she expected as much. Zac told her it was pretty much too late already. They knew she was here five seconds after she arrived.

"Well," Arturius drawled, "out with it."

"On one condition."

"What?"

"I want Zac. You leave him unharmed."

"Oh, I see." He looked her up and down. "You're in love with him."

Morgan narrowed her eyes at the Roman and kept her mouth shut.

"Really, what do you women see in that vampire? I have no idea." He waved his hand, dismissing the notion.

"Do we have a deal?"

He rolled his eyes. "Yes. Now out with it, love. I'm not wasting my eternity on you."

"Aya is alive."

Arturius sat up sharply at her statement and grasped her wrist, squeezing hard enough to bruise her skin. "You better not be lying, vampire, or this will be your end."

Morgan shifted uncomfortably in her chair, trying to squash the terror that'd suddenly surfaced within her. Defiantly, she raised her gaze to meet the Roman's, who was staring at her with a look of complete and utter darkness.

"I have no reason to lie," she spat, trying to wrench her arm free. "We both have things to lose. I'm offering her in exchange for him."

Arturius let her wrist go and a wicked grin crept onto his hard features. "If what you're saying is true, dear, then Aeriaya is much more than we ever imagined her to be. So, the witch grew a heart," he mused. "Took her time with it."

"I can lead you to her," Morgan interrupted.

"Where is she now?"

"She's gone to Mobile with the human Alex. They'll be back."

"They're trying to locate Gabrielle."

"Yes."

Arturius leaned back in his chair and regarded her thoughtfully. "Give me your phone," he said sharply, and Morgan slid it across the tabletop. He punched his number into her contacts and gave it back. "The moment you know when they'll be back, let me know."

"Is that all?"

"Don't underestimate me, dear. I've hunted the witch for two thousand years. I know how to trap her."

"And Zac?"

He sighed dramatically, rolling his eyes. "He will be free to go on the condition that he does nothing stupid. If he or any of the others get in my way, then I won't hesitate. They will die and that little courtesy also extends to you."

Morgan tensed, but nodded her agreement. "Understood."

How could she complain? After all, she'd just made a deal with the devil.

Aya and Alex left as soon as they'd got themselves together.

Borrowing Zac's car had been easy since Alex's truck was totalled. He drove, as she had no idea how to. Besides, he knew the way to Sophia's, having taken Gabby there a few weeks ago.

As they passed through the outskirts of New Orleans, Aya peered out the window at the passing buildings. It was different from how she remembered, it'd been over a hundred and fifty years since she'd set foot here, but she wondered if it was as seedy and seeped with unruly magic as it had been in the 1800s. It probably was. Power like that had a tendency to stick around for hundreds, if not thousands of years.

"Mardi Gras," he said.

"What's that?" she asked, realising that he'd been speaking to her.

"It's a huge street party. Crazy costumes, parades... It's a carnival. Goes on for like two weeks."

"Oh," Aya said. "A party of excess." It sounded familiar now.

Alex laughed. "That's one way of putting it. I should take you next time. Or at least get Zac to take you. I'm sure you'd like it."

"What do they celebrate?"

"You know what? I don't really know anymore. Being alive? They hold the big parties on Shrove Tuesday."

"Oh, so it's a religious thing? Catholic?"

He smiled. "Not anymore."

Aya turned back to the window and watched the city limits turn into countryside, her thoughts turning to Zac. He'd asked her to trust him with her heart and she wanted to, she really did, but it was difficult to break two thousand years of conditioning. Truth was, she had a hard time trusting anyone, even herself.

"Do you really trust Zac?" Alex asked suddenly. "I mean, with Morgan and everything?"

"I don't know," she told him. "I've always known what to do in one way or another, but this? It's a new thing for me."

"You've never been in love?" he asked, surprised.

"No. Not until now. I was never meant to."

"What do you mean?"

"I was the last. If things went the way they should've, then it would've been me and my brother. We knew that was it. We both had a duty to see through."

"Wow," Alex murmured. "I'm sorry."

"Love hasn't been high on the priority list," she added. "Hunting and being hunted doesn't really give one much opportunity to settle down. Besides, I'm not the kind of person who is easy to know. I can't exactly be truthful."

"Not until now, at least." He glanced over to her and smiled, ever the gentleman.

"Alex, you're one of a kind, you know that?"

He shrugged.

Aya sighed, resting her head back on the seat. "I don't know if I'm right for him. Or anybody."

"I don't believe that," he scolded her. "There's someone out there for everybody. You and Zac belong together."

"Sometimes I think I was born whole to begin with. It's just me against the world."

"Don't even think it, Aya. We'll get Gabby back, kill that a-hole Arturius, and you and Zac will live happily ever after."

"It's a lovely dream," she whispered, her tone warning him to drop it.

Alex pulled alongside the curb, yanked the handbrake on, and turned off the engine.

They sat outside a ramshackle little cottage, the

garden so wild, it almost hid the house entirely from the street.

Aya snorted at the irony. It was a witch's house through and through.

Not wasting a moment more, she got out of the car and was on the doorstep in the blink of an eye, Alex running up the path behind her.

"Hell," he said. "Some of us don't have superhuman speed, you know."

"Sorry."

When the door opened behind them, Aya turned back around, coming face to face with a woman she knew was Sophia.

She was in her late seventies, *perhaps*, and the spitting image of a Cohen she once knew. All wild hair, olive complexion, and curious, chestnut eyes. Yes, she was a Cohen.

Sophia was looking at her with something akin to reverence. Aya needed to be careful around this one. The witch knew exactly who she was with a single glance.

"I never thought I would ever see a star standing on my front porch," she said, making Aya smile despite herself.

"Hello, Sophia," she said, not giving away her surprise. "I understand you know why we're here."

"Yes, yes, of course." She gestured for them to come inside, Alex smiling shyly at the old witch.

"As you can see," Aya said evenly, "I don't need to

be invited. I can walk wherever I want. You know what became of me and you know what I am capable of. But know that I am asking for your help, and you are free to give it if you wish. If you wish the opposite, then know that I will leave, no questions asked."

Sophia chuckled. "You said the same thing to my great-great-grandmama."

"Violet Cohen." Aya tilted her head to the side as the old witch sat in a well-worn armchair.

"That's the one."

Aya and Alex sat on the sofa beside her, the latter glancing around the home curiously.

Sophia watched them for a moment, then asked, "So what brings you to my home... Aya, is it?"

Aya nodded, but Alex was the one to explain. "Arturius has taken Gabby and we need to get her back."

"Arturius?"

"He's one of the founding vampires," Aya explained. "She's in a lot of trouble."

Sophia's expression turned grave. "There've been vampires lingering about. I expected as much after she came to visit me."

Aya felt a pang of remorse. They were here because of her. "Have they been bothering you?"

"Don't worry about me," the witch replied with a wave of her hand. "They'll never get close."

"Sophia..." Aya glanced at Alex, before she

continued, "We need your help in locating her since you are of the blood."

"Of course."

"Do you need anything?"

"No, no. I just need myself."

Aya sensed Alex's unease and grasped his hand. He radiated a fear of the unknown and she realised he hadn't seen a witch practice before, not even Gabby, but there wouldn't be anything for him to worry about. Sophia would close her eyes and meditate on her granddaughter. Everything would happen inside her mind.

They silently watched the witch as she seemed to drift away, searching. Aya had faith it would only take a minute. Those from Ismena's line were of the ether, the spirit. Magic was easy for them.

"She's still in Ashburton," Sophia said, opening her eyes. "An old house with a red mantle, falling into disrepair. Outside the town, but still within it. There are roses in the garden and the grass has grown high. There are no fences, but there's a broken white letterbox by the sidewalk."

Aya looked to Alex. "Do you know it?"

"Yeah." He nodded. "It belonged to Mr. Forester. He died last year, and it's been empty ever since. He never kept it in good shape when he was alive, and it's been for sale forever. No one wants to deal with it."

"Well, it's the perfect place for vampires to hide." Aya rolled her eyes. "No human occupants."

"I would say someone is there now," Sophia added.

Aya nodded. "A human security system."

Arturius would've found a sympathiser or compelled someone to sign the deed. With so much at stake with Gabby, they'd take no chances of the brothers finding and taking her back. What they didn't count on was Aya still being alive.

"We need to go then," Alex said. "Who knows what's happening to her."

"Gabby's strong," Sophia told them. "She won't give in so easily."

Aya shook her head. "I know Arturius. He'll have a plan and if it's what I suspect, then we are in serious trouble."

Sophia drew in a sharp breath and placed a shaking hand over her eyes. "It's the same, isn't it?" she asked quietly.

"Yes."

"I sensed it in her and I said nothing," the witch murmured. "I believed we had time..."

"It's not your fault, Sophia," Aya reassured her. "None of us expected the paths our lives took these past few weeks."

"The same as what?" Alex asked, looking between them, his features panicked. "What's wrong with her?"

Aya turned to him and took his hands in hers. "When I first came to Ashburton, I was looking for a witch who'd been practicing dark magic. Evil magic. That witch was one Violet Cohen, a servant in the service of the Degauds. It wasn't long before I understood that she could be saved, that the darkness was controlling her, not the other way around. She wasn't practicing of her own free will. Gabby's magic is like hers, of the ether."

"Ether?" he asked.

"Spirit," Aya explained. "It's powerful and dangerous magic and can leave a witch open to certain... darkness."

Alex looked between her and Sophia. "You saved her, right? You saved Violet?"

Aya nodded. "I did..."

"So, you can save Gabby?"

Her gaze flickered to Sophia's "I hope so... but we have to save her from Arturius first."

"Then let's go." Alex went to stand, but Sophia placed an arm on his, pulling him down again.

"Wait," she said. "I have a gift for you, Aya."

Her eyes narrowed. "A gift? Why?"

"In case you ever came back, I was asked to show you something that might help you. After all, you helped our family. If Violet died, then our line would've ended."

Aya shook her head, frowning. "You witches and your cryptic messages. I don't remember that being part of the gift."

Sophia ignored her. "There's something you need to remember."

"I've had two thousand years of remembering. I think I'll be okay."

Sophia chuckled. "This is a courtesy, dear. There is something weighing on your heart and this might help you decide."

Before Aya could complain, Sophia had placed her hands on her temples and her vision blurred.

Damn witches, she thought before she was taken away.

Ashburton, Louisiana
June 1863

Aya stood at the edges of the lavishly decorated parlour in the Degaud Manor and watched the annoyingly uptight socialites partake in the exasperating human event known as a ball.

Louis and Marie Degaud had invited her the previous day over tea in New Orleans. Well, they hadn't done it on their own—she'd compelled an invitation from them—but she needed to be here. She was looking for the Cohen witch, a maid in their employ. She needed a way into the house, and this was it. It may be the only time she could corner the young witch and save her from herself.

As decorum demanded, she wore the

appropriate attire and spoke the appropriate pleasantries, but she did nothing but watch and wait.

Aya's dress was over-the-top and got in the way every time she took a step. It was a simple emerald blue with a tight corseted bodice and what seemed like thousands of skirts. How she hated what women had to wear to be considered *respectable*. She'd rather dress in trousers and a shirt and be done with it, but she was a lady and had to conduct herself as such. *What rubbish*.

Letting her gaze wander around the room, she found a few familiar faces amongst the attendees. Businessmen from New Orleans and Baton Rouge and their wives, socialites from Ashburton and beyond.

Since New Orleans had been declared a free city the year before, it'd become difficult for the Degauds to ascend farther in social and business circles. The ball was a blatant attempt to gain another foothold on the mysterious ladder of success. Most, if not all the attendees, were Confederates, which was another story.

Aya's gaze slipped over them, uninterested. The young man dancing with a young chestnut-haired woman to her left was the Degauds' youngest son. Her gaze swept the room a second time, but she caught no sight of any servants and would have to excuse herself the first moment she could. But when her gaze met a pair of green eyes, she faltered. She vaguely recognised the man to whom they belonged, but what gave her pause was the uniform. He was blatantly with the Confederacy.

She turned her head and watched him approach with an air of apprehension. Wasn't he the eldest son of Louis Degaud? The one who had caused all that scandal? Running off to join the Confederacy to spite his parents, who wanted him to become the next tyrant of their family dynasty. It seemed this young man had some spine at least.

"Good evening," he said, bowing his head to her.

"Evening," she replied politely, dipping ever so slightly into a curtsy as society demanded of her. She offered her hand and he took it, his grasp on her fingertips light and hesitant, as if he was afraid of hurting her.

"Captain Zachary Degaud." He bowed his head, kissing her lightly on her outstretched hand.

She looked him up and down and he laughed quietly at her blatant perusal.

"Captain?" she asked. "You're a little young, are you not?"

"Age has nothing to do with skill," he replied, a grin playing at his lips.

"I suppose not."

"May I ask your name?"

She looked him up and down again, earning herself a wicked grin. "I am Lady Anastasia."

"Ah, so you're the English woman I've heard so

much about."

"It would seem so."

"And may I ask, Lady Anastasia, what a beautiful lady is doing standing here alone?"

Aya snorted. "I care little for these social gatherings. A lot of pomp, if you ask me."

The captain let out a laugh and shook his head. "I am inclined to agree with you," he said. "May I ask you for a dance?"

She looked at his outstretched hand and then towards the middle of the room where couples were turning demurely, hardly touching. It didn't take her fancy.

The captain frowned and glanced over his shoulder, following her scowl. "Perhaps not." He sounded disappointed but offered another solution. "Perhaps you would do me the honour of accompanying me on a tour of the house? There are some rather lovely paintings in the hallway and study."

"Unchaperoned?" She let her head fall to the side, a quizzical look on her face.

"We do things differently here in Louisiana," he said with a grin, offering her a challenge.

Sighing, she let the captain take her arm and lead her into the hallway and into the study, which was dark and empty. She suddenly felt awkward, being alone in the dark with a human man while she was very much a vampire.

"I apologise if I'm being presumptuous, Lady

Anastasia, but I would like to dance with you without jealous eyes watching." His voice was hushed as he leaned close to her ear, his arm dropping away as he turned to face her.

"Oh, so this was a ploy to lure me away?"

"I admit some deceptiveness on my part," he said with a wink. "Am I forgiven?"

"Not at all, captain." She inclined her head, amusement in her voice.

He let his gaze drop to her lips before meeting her curious gaze and she faltered. Stepping forwards, the captain slid his palm over her waist and took her hand lightly in his—much too close than society deemed appropriate. There was an annoying amount of space between them and Aya stepped forwards impulsively, pressing herself against him.

His lips brushed her hair as he moved her side to side in time with the music drifting down the hallway.

She was all too aware of the intoxicating sound of his racing heart. Letting her head drop to the crook of his neck, she listened to the blood rush through his veins and the hitch in his breath when she sighed. The entire world had dropped away as she stood there, his arms circling her waist, his lips against her hair. She forgot that she was a vampire, that his blood would sustain her life. She didn't feel the inclination to bite into his neck and she was surprised at her restraint. She caught herself thinking what it would be like to kiss him, his hands on her bare skin.

She was tired. Tired of running. Tired of hunting. Just... *tired*.

"Where did you come from?" the captain whispered, breaking the spell that had fallen over them. "Are you a dream?"

Reluctantly pulling herself away, she gazed up at his green eyes. She couldn't tell him anything. Where she came from, what she was doing. She would have to send him away.

Aya dropped her gaze and offered her arm. He took it with a frown, and they walked back to the parlour and into reality.

"I leave for Virginia in the morning," he said, releasing her from his grasp.

"Well..." She smiled to cover her reluctance. "Fair thee well, Captain Degaud."

He bowed, taking her hand and brushed his lips lightly across her knuckles as if it were a gesture between secret lovers. Green eyes sparkled up at her in the warm lighting of the parlour, and she caught herself flushing. He turned with a lopsided grin and walked away.

She watched him move across the room, frowning as he stopped to talk to many other ladies along the way, kissing a hand here and there.

Looking away, she sighed. She wasn't here to prey on innocent humans, no matter how alluring they were. Catching sight of Mr. Rochester through the window, she moved through the crowd, promptly putting the handsome captain out of her mind.

She had work to do.

***

They'd met before.

Aya didn't understand how she could've forgotten. Now Sophia had stirred up the memory, it was as clear in her mind as if it'd happened yesterday.

Zac didn't remember. If he did, he would've told her. He would've gone off to war and promptly forgotten about it, and she'd gone off and saved a young witch's life. There were bigger things to think about than a pretty lady.

Why this memory? To remind her of the things she wanted and the things she'd felt the night he'd held her in his father's study. To remind her she was capable of love, compassion... and she could live in both worlds if she chose.

But Gabby was still at the forefront of her mind.

Aya remembered Mr. Rochester was having a torrid affair with Violet and he'd ultimately led her to the witch. It'd taken most of her strength that day once she'd finally convinced Violet to let her help.

Aya knew if she didn't do anything, the same fate awaited Gabby. Arturius would awaken the dark powers inside of her, use it to his advantage, and it would destroy them all.

If Gabby succumbed she would be lost to the dark forever and Aya would do what she had to, but there was still time to stop it.

Glancing up at Sophia, Aya said, "I will get your granddaughter back. Even if it's the last thing I do."

CHAPTER 17

Gabby guessed it'd been maybe two or three days since Arturius had taken her, but they had all blurred together. It could even be four by now.

Since she'd been here, she'd been tied to a chair in a room that'd been converted into a study. One wall was lined with a bookshelf crammed with books and novels, a desk littered with papers sat against another wall, and a sofa and coffee table were in the centre. The windows were closed tight, heavy drapes blocking out the sunlight, so it was hard to tell what time of day it was.

For at least two of those days a witch by the name of Rhian had been coming to speak to her. She was perhaps in her late twenties or early thirties, with wild, curly auburn hair and feline eyes, her face dusted with a healthy dose of freckles. She said she was of Katrin's bloodline and Gabby could definitely see it. Rhian was so much like the founding witch, even her magic had the same coppery tang.

Now the witch sat across from her, her voice laced with power as she spoke.

"You're very powerful, Gabrielle," Rhian told her, "and you don't even know how to tap into it without hurting yourself or others."

"And that's the only reason you're here?" Gabby didn't really believe her.

"I'm here to help you control it."

"You mean control the darkness and use it for evil?" she asked, the sarcasm dripping from her words.

Rhian laughed. "Arturius said you were feisty."

"Feisty has nothing on me." It was meant as a warning, but the witch only smiled at her.

"You're one of the most powerful witches I have ever met. Your potential is endless."

"How would you know?"

"You're powerful because you come from the ether. Any time is a good time for you. The centre of all things."

"What do you mean?"

"Arturius said your education was lacking, but I'm surprised."

"Why?"

"This is basic witchcraft, Gabrielle. Every witch has an elemental affinity."

"And you said I'm of the ether? You mean, the spirit world?"

"Yes," she replied. "You're descended from Ismena. Her power comes from the other side, from the thing that lives in us all. Your power encompasses life and death."

"That's why—" she began, but clamped her mouth shut. That's why she could summon the void so easily. That's why she could walk in between life and death and come back to tell about it. Life and death was a never-ending circle and she could tap into it without even thinking. It was natural. Her power was never ending. This is why Arturius wanted her so much. He'd seen her enter the void and he knew.

"Now, I see you understand... at least a little," Rhian said, turning towards the bookshelf.

It was cluttered with old books, westerns, and detective novels. The previous owner of the house, Mr. Forester, had been a bit of shut-in and now Gabby knew what he'd spent most of his time doing.

Rhian ran her finger along the spines of the books before pulling out an old leather-bound tome. It was unusual and didn't fit with the other books, the house, or its previous owner. When the witch sat down before her, Gabby knew it was a grimoire, but it was different to hers. This one oozed something foul, like it'd been coated in a thick sludge of evil.

Gabby looked up into Rhian's smiling eyes and said, "What's that for?"

"What do you think?" she asked, shaking her head.

She knew that the grimoire was dark. That it used

the same darkness inside of her. Afraid of what Rhian was going to do, she tried to stall, "Why do you do it?"

Rhian smiled and placed a hand on hers. "Arturius made me an offer I couldn't refuse."

"He offered you the same thing he offered me."

"Yes, I assume it was the same."

"Control."

"Something like that."

"He's using you... can't you see it?"

"I owe him, Gabrielle. He saved my life. My power would've consumed me and everyone I ever loved."

"He turned you to darkness. *It's not the way.*" How could she not see that this was wrong? It went against everything that was trusted to them. *Everything.*

She looked up from the grimoire, her expression sharp. "There *are* other ways. They may not be conventional and they may not be pure, but it gets the job done."

"What job? What are you doing for him?"

Rhian laughed at her questions. "You're very curious. That's good. When you've learned to harness the dark inside you, you'll understand. Then you will help him just as I do." She reached out and touched her fingertips to Gabby's temples, closing her eyes.

Gabby tried to jerk away from the witch as Rhian murmured an incantation. Breaking contact would sever whatever she was trying to do to her, but it was useless. Her fingertips wouldn't budge, and Gabby panicked as she felt Rhian's power seep through her skin.

Gabby had no choice. She wouldn't let them turn her to the dark. *She couldn't.*

In a moment of desperation, she let go of the coil of power she'd kept locked deep inside of her and pushed it into Rhian with all her strength. The witch's eyes snapped open in surprise and her mouth dropped in a silent scream.

The power seemed to recoil backwards, and Gabby pulled away as the shock splintered into her, then Rhian's hands fell away.

For a moment it was as if time had stopped. They were face to face, both sets of eyes in different kinds of pain. Then the witch let out a choked cry and fell limply to the floor.

Gabby stared down at her in shock. It wasn't supposed to go that far... she was just meant to stun her.

Realising her hands were free, Gabby dropped to her knees, checking Rhian for a pulse, her hands shaking. Taking a deep breath, she pressed two fingers into her neck, hoping to God she hadn't killed her. She couldn't have. All she wanted was to get away. As she felt a faint flutter, she let out a relieved breath.

Aya could save her. She'd get out of here and Aya would come back, free them of Arturius, and bring Rhian back.

Standing, Gabby turned towards the door. It was

time to get out of here before someone came looking. When her nose tickled, she wiped her face with the back of her hand and gasped as it came back wet, blood smeared across her skin. The power was too much for her.

Gabby needed to get to Aya.

Pressing an ear against the door, she listened for any sounds in the hallway, but she was only greeted with silence. There was no way of telling who was in the house without her power. Cautiously, she turned the knob and eased the door open, peering through the crack into the hallway beyond. Abruptly, she was pushed back into the room as the door opened, banging against the wall. Arturius stood just inside the room, his hard gaze on her.

Gabby glanced to the floor where Rhian lay unconscious and back towards the Roman, who was now surveying her with amusement.

Before he could speak, she said, "What do you want from me? You better start talking."

Arturius just stood there staring at her, his expression indecipherable.

"You can see what I can do. Tell me or I'll—"

"Sweet, poor, Gabrielle," he murmured as he sat on the sofa, leaving the door wide open.

What an arrogant a-hole. He knew she couldn't run from him and just had to rub it in her face.

"I mightn't be able to run from you, but I'm not afraid to hurt you, either."

"You know," he glanced to Rhian, not perturbed in the slightest, "I think I might like that."

Gabby scoffed, making the Roman laugh at the disgusted look on her face.

"I do so love getting a reaction out of you," he said. "Take a seat, Gabrielle. We're not going anywhere."

She sat heavily on the sofa opposite. "Tell me what you want, and I might be more willing to co-operate," she tried to counter.

Arturius said nothing for a moment, content to sit and stare at her. She could see him trying to decide if he should tell her anything. Or at least, how much was too much. Leaning forwards, elbows on his knees, he said, "My brother is looking for something and I want to find it before he does. That's where you come in."

"Is that why you kidnapped me?" she asked offended. "You want one up on your brother?"

Arturius laughed. "One of many reasons."

"What's he looking for?"

"That I won't tell you until Rhian has finished her work," he said, looking down at her again. "That is, if she deigns to wake up. You're really a spectacular piece of work, love."

"You'll never make me do anything for you," she declared, holding her chin up in defiance.

The Roman smirked. "Oh, Gabrielle... do you think you were the first to say no?"

She narrowed her eyes. She wasn't sure how long she could hold out against him and Rhian. They wanted the darkness to take her. She'd fight them tooth and nail for as long as she could.

Aya would come help her. *She had to.*

Aya let out a sigh as Alex pulled up in front of the manor. He'd asked no questions about what she'd seen when Sophia touched her, but she was sure he could guess. She'd never felt so vulnerable in her life.

Casting her thoughts aside as they got out the car, she focused on Gabby. They had to work out a plan to get her back. Alex would show them the house from Sophia's vision and then they would plot. Aya was confident she could get her back before Arturius awoke the darkness inside her.

Walking inside and standing in the doorway to the parlour, Alex in tow, Aya smiled. After Sophia's vision, she had a fresh sense of purpose where Zac was concerned. She wouldn't let Morgan worm her way into his heart. It wasn't a case of who saw who first. She loved him even before she understood what it was. Ironically, she always liked to sit in the study. Mainly because it annoyed the hell out of him, but now she understood—it was where she had first felt it.

Seeing Zac standing there in the parlour brought back the memory Sophia had given her even sharper. She wanted to press herself against his body and kiss him like it was the last time, but Morgan was sitting on the sofa, her back to them and she felt it. It washed off her in waves, making her gag.

Aya stumbled to a stop, grabbing Alex's arm. "*Run*," she hissed and when he hesitated, she pushed him away. "Run!"

Zac snapped to attention, his expression falling into surprise. "Aya?"

She heard the front door slam and the engine of Zac's car start. She hoped Alex would get away before he was caught.

"Aya?" Zac was in front of her, shaking her by the shoulder.

"They're here."

"Who?"

She glared at Morgan, who was on her feet looking guilty as hell. "*Ask her*." She jabbed a finger at the blonde vampire.

Zac looked at her, the confusion clear on his face.

The guilt Morgan's eyes was unmistakable. "Zac—"

"What did you do?" he roared, making the blonde vampire shrink back.

Aya shook her head. It was too late to run now. A familiar presence was already hovering outside. They'd have to fight their way out of this one.

Turning her back to Zac and Morgan, she snarled as Arturius sauntered into the parlour, a sickly look of triumph plastered on his ugly face.

"Nice to see you again, Aeriaya. Sorry about last time, but you know how much I like surprises." The

Roman leaned against the doorjamb, crossing his arms over his chest.

Aya narrowed her eyes, feeling the familiar coil of power awaken deep within her. It would be so easy to end him now, but if she did, they mightn't find Gabby.

"Don't be like that, love," he said, grinning at her.

"You've no right to call her love, asshole," Zac spat from behind her.

Arturius laughed, pushing himself off the wall and walked into the parlour, unafraid of her. "I can do whatever I want, Zachary. Don't you ever forget that." His gaze shifted to Morgan and he winked. "And that goes for you too, blondie."

Aya didn't have to turn around to know Morgan was afraid.

"Where is she, Arturius?" Aya snapped, cutting to the chase. "Where's Gabby? Tell me now and I'll spare you this time."

"Well," the Roman pretended to think about it and rolled his eyes, "that's something I'm not at liberty to divulge, sweet one." He snapped his fingers and three vampires she'd never seen before walked into the parlour. She sensed Zac tense behind her and before he could move, two of the vampires were across the room, holding him down as he roared in fury. Aya turned as the third grasped Morgan around the neck as she struggled to free herself.

Aya felt her fury pour to the surface and her vision blurred as her vampire side took over. She'd only taken a step when Arturius grabbed her from behind, an arm around her neck and waist, pulling her back hard into his chest.

"*Shh*," he crooned into her ear. "Don't struggle. I only have to give the word and your little boyfriend is dead."

Aya seethed in his grasp, trying to keep herself under control. She drew sharp breaths as her fingernails dug into the skin of his arm, pushing her power back down. She couldn't take him now... *Zac*...

"Bastard," she spat as his arm dropped from her waist.

"Yes," he said, still holding her tightly around the neck. "Yes, I am."

She hissed and writhed in his arms as something sharp and metallic pierced the skin in her neck and a strange sensation crept through her veins.

Something warm and poisonous spread through her and within a few seconds, she felt herself slipping away. Arturius clutched onto her as her world went dark and there was nothing she could do.

"Zac..." She managed raise her hand towards his as she fell.

No, no, no!

As Aya crumbled to the ground, Zac's heart almost stopped. He couldn't lose her again, *he couldn't*.

Arturius seemed extremely pleased with himself as he scooped her up in his arms. Zac desperately tried to struggle against the two male vampires who held him, a strangled roar of pain tearing from his throat, but even he wasn't strong enough to break free.

"I must thank you," the Roman said to Morgan, who hadn't made a sound.

"Morgan?" Zac asked, disbelief in his voice.

"I'm sorry, Zac," she sobbed.

"Oh, it's so heartbreaking," Arturius said, the sarcasm dripping from his words. "*Boo hoo.*" He gestured to the vampires holding them and walked backwards out of the room, Aya limp in his arms.

"But," Morgan cried, but was cut off sharply as the vampire snapped her neck. She fell heavily to the floor, her head at an odd angle.

Zac hissed and tried to lunge forwards, but firm hands held him back. "You'll pay for this, Artie," he sneered, feeling his eyes change. He didn't care what happened to him, as long as he could kill every single one of them. He couldn't let Arturius take Aya.

"Well, look at you." The Roman laughed and gestured to his thugs.

As they slackened their grips, Zac twisted to the side, trying to break free. Before he could do anything else, he felt hands on his head, and he was dead before he hit the ground.

Alex ran from the manor, jumping into Zac's car, shoving the key into the ignition with shaking hands.

Aya said they were coming. He'd heard it as he ran down the hall. It could only mean Arturius was here. There was nothing he could do. He had to get out and warn Sam.

The engine roared to life and he slammed his foot on the gas, the wheels spinning in the gravel.

He was hurtling down the long drive when he saw a figure in front of him. A man was standing in the middle of the unsealed road playing some kind of twisted game of chicken.

He didn't dare stop. If he did, he was as good as dead, so it only took him a split second to decide—he'd run the guy down.

Alex had driven around on country back roads all his life. He knew that when an animal was on the road, the safest thing to do was to hit it. It seemed cruel, but if he swerved, he'd flip the car and wrap himself around a tree. With a grimace, he flattened his foot on the gas, pushing it right to the floor. The car shot forwards, the vampire illuminated in the headlights. He had to give it to Zac. He sure knew his cars.

There was a sickening thud as the vampire collided with the car, but Alex didn't stop. The body hit the hood, then the windshield, before sailing over the top and into the air. He didn't even look up into the rearview mirror to see where he'd landed.

The windshield was cracked and blood trailed

across the glass in the wind. Alex flicked on the washers as he drove out onto the main road and let out a shaky breath.

He had to get to Liz's. That's where Sam was.

His panicked flight across town didn't register until he screeched to a halt outside the old hardware store where Liz's apartment sat above.

Jumping from the car, he pushed through the glass door without taking a breath. Running up the two flights of stairs, he banged on her front door with a trembling fist, his heart hammering.

"Sam? Liz?" he yelled, thumping the door again. He almost fell inside as Sam appeared in front of him, a worried look on his face.

"Alex?"

"*Sam*," he gasped. "He's got them."

"What? Slow down..."

Alex leaned against the door, catching Liz's eye as she came up behind Sam. Clutching the stitch in his side, he said, "Arturius has Zac and Aya."

"What?" Her eyes were wide as she clutched Sam's arm. "How?"

"Morgan betrayed us."

CHAPTER 18

When Aya finally came to, she found herself face down on a cold concrete floor.

Rolling over with a groan, she was greeted with murky light filtering in through a blacked-out window that was barely three inches wide and a handspan long. Turning her head, she saw Zac lying next to her, unconscious. Sighing in relief, she reached out for him, taking his limp hand in hers.

She sent out her mind but could feel nothing. It was just her and the soft hum of Zac's blood. Wherever Arturius had taken them, it was shielded. Another witch in league with the devil.

Why did they keep doing this—forsaking their true calling and falling into evil? Humans were too easily corruptible, that's why.

Sitting, she looked around the room and decided that it must be a basement. Where it was, could be anywhere. If they were lucky, it was the same house

Sophia saw in her vision—the one where Gabby was being held. But there was no way of knowing for sure.

Zac gasped for air next to her as he came round, and he sat up, rubbing his temples. She placed a reassuring hand on his arm and waited for him to get his bearings. They'd work out what to do. Once he'd fully woken, they'd formulate a plan to get out of this place. Suddenly, his breathing became sharp and he tore at his skin.

Her heart skipped a beat as she realised what Arturius had done.

It was payback time for Caius.

Zac gasped for breath and sat up sharply, holding his head. He felt Aya's hand on his arm, but strangely, her touch didn't seem to calm him. He felt it then, his blood boiling inside of him.

He let out a strangled cry and writhed, clawing at his skin.

"*Aya*," he gasped, eyes wide.

It was then that he realised he hadn't been invited in. Arturius had a human in the house and he *hadn't been invited in*.

Before Aya could do anything, he was on his feet, hurling himself at the door. He collided with it with a bang, jarring his shoulder, but it didn't budge. He let out a strangled cry of pain as he flung himself against the opposite wall, almost cracking the brickwork.

Falling backwards, he landed heavily on his back, clawing at his skin, drawing blood. His eyes became dark and he got up, every inch of his body burning.

Aya was on top of him in an instant, holding him down with all her strength. "It's going to be okay," she said, her hands on his face.

He wanted to believe her, but if he didn't get out of here now, he'd tear himself apart in the attempt. For him, it was a death sentence.

Grimacing, Zac fought against her, drawing sharp breaths between his teeth, desperation taking over.

"I can't," he gasped. "I have to get out. I can't be here. I..."

Aya cradled his head in her hands. They'd been through so much. Why couldn't they have some peace? She was looking down at him with such sorrow, it reminded him of that night in the clearing. The night she'd died.

"Do it," he told her.

"Zac," she whispered. "It's going to be all right. I'll get you out of this."

"*I trust you.*"

She smiled down at him, her hands caressing his face, tracing his jaw.

"I love you," she said, then twisted.

Aya knew he was at the door before it opened. Cradling Zac's head in her lap, she glared up at Arturius as he sauntered into the room, closing the door behind him with a dull thud.

It'd been hundreds of years since she'd seen the Roman and the years had changed little. He was still the hard, vicious, calculating man she had known back then, but when she'd first met him, he hadn't been like that, had he? He had a kindness about him, but Katrin had firmly erased it and shaped him into something else.

"How many times do you think you can snap Zachary's neck before his head comes off entirely?" he asked with a sneer.

Pursing her lips, Aya stood, placing Zac's head gently on the hard floor. Breaking his neck was the only way to take him down without killing him. "I know it's payback, Arturius. For Caius."

"Oh yes, you did the same thing to him once if I remember correctly. Except he actually tore himself apart." He scowled at her and shook his head, remembering. "Who do you think was the one who stuck all the pieces back together?"

"There was no way he would've died."

"Of course not, but you're as sadistic as we are, love. You enjoyed that little show. Let me enjoy mine."

"*Invite him in.*"

"Oh, come on. We've plenty of time to do that."

"Go and die, Arturius."

"Oh, my dear," the Roman retorted, "what happened to your sense of humour?"

"Get it over with. Whatever you have us here for, just *get it over with.*"

The Roman regarded her for a moment then said, "How long has it been? Four hundred, maybe five hundred years since we've seen each other?"

"I don't really care."

"Ahh," he held a finger up, "Tudor England. 1500s. Spanish Armada and what-not."

She rolled her eyes. "I'm not in the mood for a catch up."

"Always so impatient, Aeriaya."

"Only when it comes to you lot."

He let out a slight laugh, his eyes sparkling in the gloomy light.

Aya didn't have the stomach for his games, so she cut to the chase. "Did you go to Morgan or did she go to you?"

Arturius smirked. "She came to me."

She knew it. Morgan was in love with Zac and wanted her out of the picture. Her greatest mistake was dealing with the Romans. She wouldn't have to seek retribution for this—they did the job for her. *Stupid woman.*

Arturius glanced down at Zac with a confused look. When his gaze met hers again, they were nothing but cold.

"What have you done with Gabby?" she asked.

"I'm helping her," he replied.

"You and I both know that your idea of help will destroy her."

"That's a matter of opinion." He turned his back and pulled a chair into the middle of the room and sat to face her. He wasn't going anywhere anytime soon.

Aya regarded the Roman. She knew he had no idea what to do with her. She couldn't be killed by any means they knew; even she didn't know how she could die.

Her gaze flew up to his as he sighed and leaned forwards, resting his elbows on his knees.

He traced the point where his scar reached his jaw with a finger. "The world I knew, Rome, it was all a lie." His voice was unusually quiet, making her regard him with suspicion. "The gods didn't exist. Everything I had sacrificed myself for was meaningless. Katrin offered us a new life. One where we had the control. One where we had the truth."

"But she lied to you, too," Aya murmured.

"She lied to us all, Aeriaya."

She flinched at the sound of her true name on his lips. "There's more?"

"More than you or I will ever know," he replied, leaning back and crossing his arms over his chest.

"Why did she do it?" She didn't have to explain what she meant, Arturius knew better than anyone.

"She never told us her reasons for betraying the

Celestines and the other witches. I would suggest you speak to her, but she's dead."

"What about you?"

His eyes narrowed. "We were tricked, Aeriaya. All of us... except maybe Regulus."

"He wanted this?"

"He was the one who convinced us all. I didn't want to be this... this monster, but he convinced me and there was no going back. I had no reason to desert the Legion. None at all. I was content."

Her eyes narrowed. "Content to conquer and kill."

"It was a different time. A different world. It was what I believed in."

"So, that's why you hate him so much," she murmured, but Arturius didn't seem to hear her.

"Katrin doted on Regulus. He'd been disgraced and she took him in when he was little more than filth to the people he'd dedicated his life to. He went along with it in the beginning, but he soon came around. We were at each other's throats from day one."

Aya didn't know what to say. Why was Arturius telling her all of this? Perhaps he needed to repent since this had been the first time they'd sat in the same room in two thousand years without trying to kill one another.

"Katrin ordered me to seduce you," he said absently. "Of course, I had to do it, but it wasn't all a lie."

"What do you mean?" she asked, frowning. He couldn't mean...

"The day Regulus dumped you at my feet, a terrified slip of a thing, I was transfixed."

"*Please...*" She rolled her eyes.

"That's the truth. And it's more truth than I have ever given anyone."

Aya didn't want to believe he'd had feelings for her in the beginning. Not after what he'd done to her. "Do you even feel any remorse for the things you've done?"

Arturius smirked, leaning back in his chair. "Remorse? Me?" He said it like the answer was glaringly obvious. He didn't have any. "How about you?"

"You can't admit to it, so how could I?"

He narrowed his eyes. "Try to separate the truth from the lies, Aeriaya. *I dare you.*"

"I don't want to play your games, Arturius."

"I didn't want to do it," he said, his voice strangely quiet. "I was the one who tore your brother apart."

She shot to her feet, a snarl erupting from her throat, eyes threatening to change.

"I knew how much you loved him, but I had to."

She took a step forwards, hands trembling in tight fists at her sides.

"It was my punishment for turning you, for having feelings. She made me take away the thing you cared about the most."

"*No,*" she hissed. "How could you?" Even as she

said it, she knew he'd had no choice. Katrin had ordered it and her power had bound him to follow through.

"If you hadn't been so hell-bent on killing me for the past two thousand years, I might've explained myself."

"Why do you care about explaining yourself? I could never forgive you for any of it."

"Sometimes I think I'm still a man underneath all of this," he gestured to himself, "under the beast."

Aya shook her head, trying to clear her rage. "There is no man left."

Arturius stood abruptly, the chair falling over behind him. The Roman was an inch away from her face, their eyes boring into each other's. All Aya had to do was reach out and touch him, then he would be hers... but she had to know. "Why did you do it? Why did you turn me?"

"I wanted to destroy you," he spat, "like you destroyed me."

"Katrin destroyed us all, Arturius. Not me."

"If it wasn't for you, I would still be human." He pushed her up against the wall, her head cracking on the brickwork. He wrapped his hand around her neck and began to squeeze. Pushing himself into her, she felt his lips against the skin of her neck.

"I wouldn't do that if I were you," she rasped, the warning clear in her voice.

He brought his head up, his eyes glaring into hers.

"Where is Gabby?" She didn't falter. She could kill him now if she chose.

Arturius let his grip slacken and he dropped her, her feet touching the ground. "You've become a monster, Aeriaya. What would your precious Celestines say if they were still alive to see you?"

"I'm no longer a Celestine," she said, the emotion dropping from her voice. "You saw to that the day you snapped my neck."

Arturius took a few steps back and snorted. He ran his hands over his face and took a few sharp breaths. She'd gotten under his skin and she didn't care in the slightest.

"We can feel when one of us dies. That was the only reason you escaped that night. When you killed Titus, none of us understood what was happening until we found what was left of him. It was that moment that caused Katrin to order us to kill your family." He seemed to be trying to make it better.

"You're talking to me like an old friend, Arturius. What do you want? Sympathy?"

"You think everything we do is about you," he said with a sneer, his eyes darkening. "There are bigger things at stake than a rogue hybrid."

"Like what?"

He remained silent, eyeing her with distaste. *What were they up to?*

"I know I won't survive you," he told her. "Whether it be tomorrow or in a thousand years... but damn if I let you kill me before I'm ready." He turned his back to her, dropping his head.

She found it insulting that he thought he had all the power.

"I haven't decided what to do with you yet," he murmured. "That depends on my friends upstairs."

"Lucky me," she drawled.

He looked back at her, a frown creasing his brow. "How did you do it?"

"Do what?' she asked, knowing he meant how she had killed the other founders.

"Titus, Marcus, Octavia... Caius."

"When you made me, not all parts of my old self withered and died."

"Though, time has," he said absently. It was this comment that made Aya understand. He knew her power had faltered when she'd killed Caius, and he thought it was all gone.

She said nothing, instead waiting to hear what he would say next. It would all be over if he found out. Arturius would kill everyone she cared about in a heartbeat if he knew even a drop of the truth.

And Zac would be the first. He would be dead, and she would be imprisoned for eternity.

Arturius sighed, looking back down at Zac before walking towards the door. He paused, his hand on the knob, and looked back over his shoulder at her. "For what it's worth, I'm sorry about your brother." Aya tensed. She went to speak, but he continued, "I died a hero, but I lived long enough to become a villain. Don't make the same mistake I did."

"Poor you." She rolled her eyes, not believing him for a second.

"No," he said, "poor *you*."

The Roman strode back across the room and hauled up Zac's unconscious body, hooking his arms under his shoulders. Aya took a step forwards, ready to do whatever it took to stop the Roman from taking him, but he shot her a warning glare that stopped her in her tracks.

"Don't think about it, Aeriaya. If you want him to live, you will not lift a finger to harm me."

Aya backed up against the wall, her gaze cutting straight into him as he dragged Zac out of the room. The door closed heavily behind them, leaving her to her imprisonment alone.

If he did anything to harm Zac, she would stop at nothing to tear Arturius to pieces.

And she would enjoy every moment of his torment.

CHAPTER 19

D*orset, United Kingdom*
43 A.D.

Lucius Arturius Quintillus was a man to be reckoned with.

He was typical for a centurion of the Roman Legion. Broad-shouldered, heavily muscled, and imposing. His men would follow him to the bowels of the underworld or suffer at the end of his blade. They feared and respected him and never questioned his logic. His men came back alive. That's what made him the best.

It was this new crusade that had the entire Legion rattled. Cesar had ordered the expansion of the empire into Britannia—wild lands that lay across the channel.

Stories about the Britons, ferocious tribes of men stained with blue war paint, had the younger, more unseasoned soldiers nervous. Julius Caesar had tried to conquer them some eighty years before without success, but it would be different this time. This time they understood their enemy.

Arturius' legion, II Augusta, was led by General Vespasian. While the other legions travelled northwards into the wilds, they were tasked with the capture of the southwest—old country that the tribes held sacred and fought fiercely to protect. They were battle hardy men, and the only ones who were fit enough to conquer this stretch of land.

On the morn of the eleventh day, they marched upon a small castle that nestled upon a green hillock. It was hard for the people there not to be aware of the Legion's approach, so when the Romans crested the rise and saw the castle for the first time, they were greeted with the sight of a group of Briton's amassed on the hillside. They stood to defend their homes, but Arturius knew they only stood to face their deaths.

Vespasian ordered Arturius to take his men and deal with the savages. The Britons had amassed a mere one hundred men and boys to defend the fort and eighty of the best and brightest Roman legionaries would slaughter them in minutes. Here, skill would prevail over numbers.

"Don't disappoint me, Arturius," Vespasian said, gesturing down the hill. "You are one of my best *primius pilus*, are you not?"

He *was* one of the best and that meant knowing

that the general just wanted to sit back and be entertained by the bloodshed.

Still, Arturius hesitated a moment. This seemed wrong. They were just a group of old men and children, not seasoned warriors. They would hardly have a chance to defend themselves or even surrender before the Legion squashed them. "But, general, it will be a massacre."

Vespasian turned and glared at him, his gaze cutting straight through to his bones. "Are you questioning your orders, Arturius? If you are, know that you are replaceable." He gave him a look that suggested his replacement would put him in the ground.

"No, general," he said, quickly covering his doubt.

"You have your orders, now go and execute them. For the glory of Rome." The general clapped a fist over his heart.

It was the first time he'd questioned his superior and Arturius felt sick. He'd always followed orders unquestioned, trusting he was doing the right thing for Rome and the gods. He had always known he was replaceable, but it was now glaringly apparent just how replaceable he was. To speak out to his general was treason and his sentence would be waiting for him at the end of a sword. He hoped he could make up for his slip. He had to.

"Yes, general," he said sharply, clapping a fist over his own heart. If it was a spectacle Vespasian wanted, then he would get one grander than the gladiators of Rome could ever hope to put on and he would be the star.

As Arturius marched forwards with his men, he couldn't help scoffing at the sight before him. The Britons were all over the place, their line haphazard and weak, their vanguard full of old men and children. They had no idea what they were doing. It was a stark contrast to the Roman formation, which suggested order, precision, and training. It would be a senseless slaughter, but by then, Arturius was more interested in saving himself.

His attention was pulled back to his own front line as he saw the man to the left veer too far from his shield-mate.

"Titus, keep in formation," he barked at the soldier. He didn't care to know all their names, but this one was a particularly bloodthirsty fighter, along with Marcus, Paius, and Augustus. These men he'd made his elite.

As the two forces met in a clash of weapons, Arturius surged forwards with a roar, bringing his sword down on a stout man, whose face and chest was smeared with blue paint, while willing himself not to think about what he was doing.

The man had no hope of escaping the Roman's blade as it sunk deep. Wrenching it away in a shower of hot blood, Arturius crashed into the next man, slashing upwards. His victim stumbled forwards in surprise at the sudden pain, exposing his back. Arturius didn't hesitate. He plunged his blade clean through his heart.

For the glory of Rome.

There was a savage roar behind him as the dead weight of the man slumping to the ground freed his blade. Pivoting on his heel, Arturius was a fraction too late lifting his sword to parry the axe that was arcing towards his face. Everything seemed to slow down as he stumbled backwards, trying to arc his head out of the way, but it wasn't quite enough. The sun glinted off the crudely forged iron weapon as it sliced into his face, narrowly missing his right eye.

Arturius was stunned for a second as the Briton heaved the axe back to swing again. He blinked hard as blood began to drip into his eye. Eyesight intact, he grimaced, cutting his blade upwards and cleanly sliced into the man's weapon arm. He dropped the axe with a wail as blood soaked his crude shirt and Arturius kicked him viscously in the stomach. The Briton doubled over, the air pushed from his lungs, and tripped backwards, falling hard on his back.

Then, it was as if Arturius was overcome by some demon. Straddling the man who had tried to hack his skull open, he brought his sword down hard into his chest, narrowly missing his heart. Pulling it out, blood poured from the wound at an alarming rate, but he wasn't done at all. As his own blood ran from his face, blinding his right eye, he sunk his hands into the Briton's chest and tore, digging straight into his chest cavity. As his hand came into contact with his still beating heart, Arturius paused. It was insane what he was doing, but he felt powerful... like a god himself.

With a guttural roar, he ripped out the man's heart and tossed it aside, his chest heaving.

His head snapped up as he caught sight of two Briton's staring down at him in horror. Before they could turn and run, he grasped his sword and cut them down with swift, efficient blows to the heart and neck.

He cut down three more men before he realised there were no more. His men had made short work of the skirmish. All they had left to do was to enter the castle and establish order. There would be women and younger children inside who would be put to work. The castle would be fortified and improved.

Arturius stood in the battle's aftermath, hardly aware the general had approached him, stepping over the carnage to come congratulate him.

Vespasian clapped him on the shoulder. "That was quite something, Arturius."

"Thank you, general," he muttered, wiping the back of his hand across his face. He hissed when he remembered he had a gash running the length of it.

Vespasian turned towards his entourage and barked an order to them. "Take the castle and secure its people. I want this place ready to be built upon as soon as possible." The general regarded Arturius a moment and said, "Get your face seen to, Arturius, and rest. You deserve it."

Arturius nodded, knowing he'd been dismissed. It seemed he'd won back Vespasian's favour... for now.

Instead of following his orders, he collected his men from around the field, offering words of encouragement. Other soldiers had advanced from the opposite rise and had already begun dragging the corpses away to a ditch that ran along the side of the hillock.

Marcus clapped him on the shoulder and pointed up to the castle. "We will see to them. Return to your tent, Titus will go fetch Magnus."

Arturius only grunted and turned to make his way back to their camp. Magnus was their *medici*, he would see to his wounds before they could fester.

He left the carnage he and his men had wrought behind him without a second thought. Dwelling on these things—duty and honour—would destroy him if he let it. He liked his life too much for that to ever happen.

Maiden Castle was the name the Britons had given their construction and it was by no means a palace. To the Romans, it was little more than an outhouse, only suitable for an outpost.

They began work immediately, building stronger

walls, erecting a temple at one end, and improving defensive positions. This would make a fine mid-point for their journey into the southwest. The Britons were living in the past and would herald their conquerors and the knowledge they brought. All their lives would improve drastically.

Arturius was ordered bedrest for several days. His face throbbed, but he refused to let them sew up the gash. It would serve as an impressive scar and instill fear in his men—fear that would keep them under his thumb. Especially after he'd only cut down two men before he was wounded. It hadn't stopped him from continuing, but he felt ashamed of his weakness.

To keep himself occupied, he worked hard to keep the wound clean, despite the pain that shot through him when the tinctures and salves Magnus had concocted to prevent infection were slathered on his face.

He had little else to do but contemplate their next journey. There were many miles to cover until they'd secured their portion of this wild place. What he tried *not* to dwell on, was the moment he'd torn a man's heart from his chest while it was still beating. He'd gone too far and wondered if the gods would punish him.

The evening a few days after they'd captured the castle, Arturius lay in his makeshift cot, staring at the ceiling of his tent and thought about home.

He was rich enough to own land and a villa if he so

chose, and the Legion would certainly not oppose it. He was devout in his religion and loyal to Rome—a model citizen in every way. After he'd served his time in Britannia, he would make a home for himself and take a wife. It was all he wanted.

He dreamed of a white-washed villa on a sun-soaked hillside, the field below dotted with olive trees, horses grazing in the warmth of the afternoon light. A son to raise into a strong and honourable warrior, taught by his own hand. A beautiful wife to make love to. Drinking wine together under the stars...

Yes, that was the life he wanted for himself. A good life. A quiet life.

When the flap to his tent was pulled aside, he sat up sharply as he caught the sight of a woman entering. The coarse material swung back into place as she stood there staring at him. She was beautiful in an otherworldly kind of way—tall and slender, skin as pale as milk, and hair that was as rich and wild as honey. She did not look to be at all Roman or from any one of the lands they'd conquered, but she was dressed in the way of one.

"How did you get in here?" he barked at her. If she was here for his entertainment, she could go away. He wasn't in the mood for it.

The woman ignored his question. "I've come to offer you a gift, centurion."

"A gift? Why?"

"You've proved yourself to be one of worth."

He glared at her, raking his eyes over her body, not caring if she took offence. "What are you offering, woman?"

"I'm offering immortality, power, and strength beyond reckoning."

"What do you mean... immortality? I am no god." He said it like she was offering blasphemy. The gods would punish him for being tempted by this *witch*. This had to be a test of his faith, for what he'd done on the battlefield. There was no other explanation for this intrusion.

She laughed, her voice filtering through the tent like music. "Not a god," she told him. "But you will feel like one. All will cower before you, and you will rain death and destruction as easily as you will light and love."

"You want to turn me into a demon?"

The woman narrowed her eyes, a sly smile playing at her soft lips. "But you already like killing, don't you, Arturius?"

"How do you know my name?"

"I've been watching you."

He stood sharply, his lip curling into a sneer. "Be careful what you say to me, woman."

She only smiled at his reaction and reached out, taking his rough, calloused hand. "Come."

Hardly aware of what he was doing, Arturius followed her from the tent. *What kind of trickery was this?* He seemed to have lost control of himself as she led him away from the camp like a lamb to the slaughter.

They'd gone some way into the darkness, over the rise and hidden from the sight of their camp and the captured castle, and it was not long after that that he saw the warm light of a campfire through the trees. As the woman led him closer, he saw it was a large circle of flame, too large to be a simple campfire. There was something unnatural about it.

He began to hesitate, suspecting some kind of ambush, but she wouldn't let his hand go. He didn't think he could release from her grasp even if he wanted to.

Emerging from the tree line, he wasn't sure what he was looking at. Within the circle of flame stood faces he recognised, and they were all as bewildered as he was.

To one edge stood his men, Marcus and Titus. There was a *primius pilus* he knew to be Caius, new to his post, but well deserving. And behind the young Roman was the woman he knew was named Octavia.

Arturius was shocked to see her here. She was Vespasian's plaything, his whore.

When he'd first seen her at camp, he was surprised. He thought their general had preferred little boys, but perhaps the reason she was here in Britannia was to stop such rumours. From the look of her, he knew that was Vespasian's reason, not hers. A woman in a man's world only meant one thing. She was cutthroat and prepared to do whatever it took to secure her ambitions. Octavia wanted power.

A fifth figure stepped from the shadows as the woman led him into the circle of flame. Arturius recognised him instantly.

Regulus.

If he was here then it meant he'd escaped. Everyone knew what he'd done. He was third to Claudius himself in the Legion and he'd been caught plotting to assassinate the emperor. Last he'd heard, Regulus had been locked up, awaiting passage back to Rome for trial and execution. He should've been killed on the spot. Trial was merciful.

"Regulus," Arturius sneered as he came face to face with the tall Roman. "What are you doing here? Shouldn't you be clapped in irons and left to rot?"

Regulus stared coldly into his eyes as if he was daring him to look away.

"Did you really plot against the emperor?" Caius asked, looking him up and down.

"Whatever they said I did, it hardly matters now," Regulus replied.

"Welcome," the woman said, opening her arms. The firelight danced over her skin, giving her an air of otherworldliness. "My name is Katrin, and I have brought you all here this fine evening to offer you all a gift. I have seen glorious things in all of you and they deserve to be rewarded."

"Rewarded with what?" Marcus asked with a note of doubt in his voice.

Katrin smiled. "You will all have new lives. Your futures will be in your hands."

"What do you want in return?" Caius seemed as skeptical as Arturius felt.

"I want your allegiance," she told them. "And your help with a little matter."

"What matter?" Arturius was the highest rank in attendance and felt it his right to speak for them. Regulus didn't count anymore; his rank had been stripped.

"I want information and you will be in the position to gain it once you have been transformed."

"And that's all you want?"

"Yes."

"In exchange for immortality?" Octavia scoffed. "There has to be something else you want."

"Don't underestimate the value of what I want you to do, Octavia. There are certain side effects to your transformation."

"What kind of side effects?"

"You won't be able to go out into the sunlight for a time. And you will have to drink blood to survive."

"Blood?" Octavia was disgusted at the notion. "Only the denizens of the underworld drink blood."

Katrin sneered at the Romans, "I'm sorry to be the one who divulges this to you, but your gods don't exist."

"*No*," Arturius hissed, turning to the others. "This is a test. The gods will punish us if we agree to this. Can't you see?"

Regulus rolled his eyes at the five other humans. "Are you all stupid? She's a witch *and* a human being. In what world does that exist? A god didn't give her this curse. A *creature* did. A living, breathing creature who can die just like the rest of us."

"I wouldn't call it a curse..." Katrin crooned. "I would call it a gift."

"Whatever you call it, I agree with your terms," Regulus said before turning to the others, staring each of them down. "Are you with me?"

"Regulus, you can't," Arturius tried to reason with him. "Your soul—"

"My soul was destroyed a long time ago, brother. Can't you see that this is something great? We'll have the power to make a better world. Create something *worth* fighting for."

"Rome is worth—"

"Rome is worth *nothing*," he spat. "The moment you try to do something good and right, they will stop at nothing to tear you down. They will kill everyone you ever loved in front of your eyes, then plunge a sword into your heart. Rome is *corrupt*."

"No..." Arturius looked around at the other Romans, but they were staring at him with closed expressions. They wanted this. They knew the truth of Regulus' words and he was the only one resisting.

"Why do you think I tried to murder the emperor?" Regulus grasped the front of his shirt. "Because he killed everyone I ever loved. He sold me a lie, then he took it all away. And he will do the same to you."

Arturius wrenched himself away, hardly comprehending what Regulus was telling him. *Rome was corrupt? The gods didn't exist?* If what Regulus was saying was true, then the life he wanted to go back to didn't exist. And if he found it, it would be taken from him with the flick of a wrist.

He'd seen a taste of it when he tried to question Vespasian's order the previous day, had he not? Death would follow the moment he disagreed with another order and it didn't matter if he was right or wrong. He was *replaceable.*

Rome was not a democracy. Deep down, he knew it, but he'd rather the denial. All this time he'd preferred the denial over the truth. *The coward's way.*

"Then what is right?" he whispered, looking up at the traitor who now didn't seem so traitorous.

Regulus inclined his head towards Katrin. "This is right."

Arturius glanced over to the witch and she nodded, a smile playing at her lips. Looking back to Regulus he said, "Then I agree."

CHAPTER 20

Zac sat bolt upright with a sharp hiss and clawed at himself. He was still inside the house and still not invited in. He felt like he was turning inside out.

When he looked up, desperate for an escape, he saw Arturius staring down at him with a look of amusement plastered on his ugly face. He was on his feet in an instant, launching himself at the Roman, who pushed him back with the slightest of touches.

"Invite him in," Arturius ordered a man who was lingering in the shadows, "before he hurts himself, if you don't mind."

"You're free to come inside," the man said and almost instantaneously, Zac felt the pain subside.

He slumped against the wall, fighting the overwhelming desire to rip the Roman's face off, but that's when he saw her lingering in the shadows, shoulders hunched forwards, head hanging low. It couldn't be anyone else.

"Morgan?" he asked, ignoring Arturius who stood by watching them with a curious expression.

She lifted her head and he caught the glitter of tears staining her face. "I'm sorry," she whispered.

"Has he hurt you?" he asked, trying to ignore the anger welling up inside him.

"*Has he hurt you*?" Arturius mocked, throwing his hands in the air dramatically. "She betrayed you."

"I would never..." Morgan cried.

"You betrayed him, not her," Arturius drawled. "Do you really think he would ever forgive you?"

"No..."

"You've been played, love." He said it with a note of triumph that made Zac sick. "If you truly thought I would honour a bargain with you, you are one stupid little girl."

"You have no shame, Arturius," Zac whispered, clenching his fists at his sides.

"That's the first intelligent thing you've said, Zachary. *Bravo*."

Morgan was sobbing. "I'm so sorry, Zac. I never meant for this to happen. I was blind. *I'm sorry*."

Zac knew he should be angry with her. She'd betrayed them all to the one man who wanted them dead. And what for? An empty dream? He couldn't love her the way she wanted. He would never be able to. Love didn't work that way.

Arturius sighed loudly, apparently bored with the lack of reaction. The Roman obviously wanted a show, but Zac would never stoop that low. He glanced back to Morgan, who was cowering back against the wall, a look of absolute anguish on her face. He'd never seen such emotion before. Even in the face of death, he'd never seen someone so desperate for forgiveness.

Zac knew she needed this from him, and he would give it to her. He'd led her on all that time ago. He'd slept with her in a moment of weakness, used her for comfort. He was the reason she was here in the first place. He was the reason she had these feelings. It was all his fault, wasn't it?

"I forgive you," he whispered and felt a pang of sadness as her fearful expression faded with relief.

Arturius scoffed, "Forgiveness is for the weak. If you're going to do something, do it without the regrets."

"Let her go, Arturius." Zac scowled at the Roman. "She isn't part of this. You've got what you want."

"You're right, Zachary," he sneered, reaching behind his back and pulling out a stake he'd hidden in his pocket. He flipped it in his hand a few times before looking back up at him. "She's outlived her usefulness. I don't need her anymore now that I have Aeriaya locked up safe and sound. But then again..."

Before Zac could move, Arturius plunged the stake directly into Morgan's heart. Her eyes widened with shock as she gulped for air.

"*No!*" Zac ran forwards and grasped her face as she turned grey, her body withering under his hands.

A tear slid from his eye and down his cheek as her eyes glazed over. Gently lowering her limp form to the ground, Zac closed his eyes, anger beginning to simmer underneath the surface.

"No," he hissed through his clenched teeth as he felt her life slip away, her heart thudding into silence. "*No.*"

He turned to face Arturius, who was surveying them with an amused grin.

"What are you smiling at?" he demanded. "Was all this just for your own entertainment?"

"Of course," the Roman declared.

Zac was too far gone to stop himself. He launched himself onto the Roman with such force, his fist almost punctured the flesh around the Roman's heart. Arturius' fist came back just as fast, clipping his jaw, splitting his lip against his teeth and sending him sprawling backwards.

"I won't be your pawn, Arturius," he growled, spitting blood on the floor.

Arturius laughed, his head shaking from side to side. "Unfortunately, you don't have a say in the matter, Zachary. I'll do what I want with you, when I want. And next time you think about trying to tear my heart out, remember how easy it was for me to stop you."

Aya scrambled to her feet when the door to her basement prison was opened and Zac's form came hurtling in.

He landed on his knees with a grunt and she rushed forwards as the door closed with a bang. When he didn't move, she knelt beside him, concern in her pale features.

"Zac?" she asked tentatively.

He stood without looking at her and crossed the room, resting his head against the brickwork of the far wall, his shoulders heaving as he drew in deep breaths.

Aya knew he was trying to calm himself down and she remained where she was, letting him be. A minute passed before he turned around, leaning back against the wall and sliding down until he was sitting. She was beside him in an instant, her blue eyes shining curiously in the murky light.

"Zac?" she asked again, knowing the news wasn't good. How could it be?

"She's gone." His voice was quiet, almost strained to a breaking point.

"Arturius—" she said, but Zac grunted, cutting her off before she could say it. Arturius had killed Morgan.

He let his head fall to her shoulder, closing his eyes.

"I'm sorry." Her voice was a whisper in the darkness as she stroked his hair.

He lifted his head and cupped her face with

shaking hands, pressing his lips against hers, kissing her with a desperation that was unsettling.

He'd just lost Morgan, a woman she never trusted, but he had had a connection with her that was deeper than just friendship. To a vampire on the brink of insanity, the offer of help and salvation was just as great a sensation as the one of love offered. Aya was jealous of her; she couldn't deny it.

Despite Aya's uneasiness, his presence was overwhelming and she kissed him back, sliding a hand up his chest, coming to rest over the pulsing vein in his neck. Even as he was coming to terms with what he'd obviously witnessed, she wanted him. It was selfish, but she wanted him.

"Please," he whispered, pulling away, his eyes searching hers in the murky light. "Please." He leaned back against the wall, exposing his neck to her.

Aya understood. She would give him this, regardless of the benefits his blood would give her.

Kneeling in front of him, she buried her face into his neck, inhaling his scent as deeply as she could, her fingers curling into his unruly hair. When he groaned, his hands grasping her waist, she let her fangs grow in and sunk them deep into his flesh.

Zac hissed at the sudden pain but let his head loll to the side as she pulled the blood from him in gentle mouthfuls. She would never get over how addictive it was to her, the rich coppery tang sliding down her throat like a fine wine, her power awakening deep inside of her.

Zac's blood was more than a lifeline; it was more than power. It was... There were no words.

He pulled her closer and she straddled him, pushing herself hard into him as she drank her fill. When his heartbeat slowed and his hands fell away, she drew back, running her thumb across the wound in his neck, encouraging it to heal. She didn't want to be anywhere else but in his arms. When he touched her, she forgot everything but him.

"Thank you," he murmured, his eyes still closed.

Running a hand lightly down his face, she said, "You're welcome." She tore herself away, sitting next to him, leaning back against the wall.

"I love you," he whispered, his head coming to rest on her shoulder.

Aya had no idea what to say to comfort him. She couldn't be selfish with him, but she didn't know anything else. Instead, she asked, "Do you remember the ball your parents had at the manor? The one they had the night before you left for Virginia?"

"When?" His head rose, but she didn't lift her gaze to meet his.

"It was 1863, if I remember correctly. During the Civil War."

"How do you know about that?" She felt his hand tighten around hers as he recalled the night she spoke of.

"Because I was there."

"What...?"

"Sophia helped me remember a few things." She turned to look at Zac in the murky light, taking in his features that were so familiar to her, remembering the vision. "The uniform suited you, though perhaps it was the wrong colour."

He snorted, shaking his head slightly. "Why don't I remember you? Did you..."

"No, I never compelled you. It was a strange time. Perhaps you had a lot on your mind?"

"How could I forget you," he whispered, his hand caressing her thigh.

Aya tried to force a smile, shivering at his touch. "How could I forget *you*."

"Do you think you could compel me to remember?"

She shook her head. "It wouldn't be real."

"None of this seems real."

"I assure you, it's all very real," she scoffed. Suddenly wishing she hadn't brought it up, she let silence descend.

"I want—" he began to say but stopped.

She felt the tension begin to build in his body as she pressed her leg against his. When she slid her hand along his thigh, he let out a sharp hiss, his unusual green eyes burning into hers.

"What?" she asked, but he remained silent, staring at her.

"I think all parts of you are beautiful. I love all of you."

"Zac..." Aya frowned at him. Did he think this was his goodbye? "You haven't seen the half of it."

"It doesn't matter."

"That was nothing when I tore those werewolves apart..."

"And you don't even know a quarter of the shit things I've done."

"It's not the same."

"It's exactly the same."

"*Zac.*"

"The circumstances might be different, but it's the same."

She let it drop, knowing he was right. They both had an unstable element. Hers was because of her genetic makeup. His was because of lack of instruction. The result was the same.

Zac turned away, leaning his head against the wall. "What are we going to do?"

"I don't know yet."

"You need to kill him, you know that, right?"

She glared at him. "Of course, I do. Just... not yet. I can't."

"Why not? After all the things he's done to you." He ran his hands over his face, trying to mask his anger. "Morgan didn't deserve that end. Even though she betrayed us, she didn't deserve it."

She sensed his impatience and it irritated her. "He won't come close to me. There's no chance."

"You only need to touch him."

"Yes, but we have no idea what's happened to Gabby. It's entirely possible that we're in the same house Sophia saw in her vision, but that's only speculation. If I kill him, then we wouldn't know for sure. We could lose her, Zac." She let her head fall back against the wall. "Arturius is trying to wake up something dark inside her. It was the same thing that happened to her ancestor and why I was in Ashburton to begin with. If we act irrationally, it could mean our freedom, but it would be a death sentence for Gabby and who knows how many other people."

"But the more time passes..."

"We have to be smart about this, Zac. It won't be as straightforward as Caius. Arturius is far more cunning than he ever was."

Zac sighed, covering his face with his hands. She knew he wanted to get it over with. As with the werewolves and Katrin, he wanted to dive headfirst into trouble and fight his way out.

Aya watched him struggle with his nature and resisted the urge to embrace him. He wouldn't want to be coddled any more than she did.

"Trust me," she told him. "We need to bide our time."

"What if something happens to you?"

"I won't let it," she said firmly.

"I can't lose you again."

She sighed and leaned towards him, her lips on the edge of his jaw. "I know." She kissed him lightly, the stubble on his face rasping against her lips. "I know."

Rhian was angry when she finally woke.

When Arturius had left them the previous night, or was it day, Gabby had been locked in the study with the unconscious witch until she came to. There had been sounds throughout the house that signalled something was happening, but no one had come upstairs. At first, she hoped it was Aya come to rescue her, but she soon let that hope slide.

Gabby regarded Rhian without remorse as the witch picked herself up from the ground, clutching her head.

"That was incredibly stupid, Gabrielle," the witch scolded her. "You could've killed me. You know I'm only trying to help you, right?"

"I don't want your help," she replied sullenly.

"The darkness *will* claim you. It will be much less painful if you accept it and stop fighting."

"I'll never stop fighting, Rhian. I never want to be like you."

Rhian sighed and bit her bottom lip, surveying Gabby with her strange feline eyes. She looked so much like Katrin it made her sick to the stomach. After all she'd learned about the founding witch and now Rhian, she never wanted to meet another of her descendants—and they'd be fortunate not to meet *her*.

Rhian sighed, then sat forwards in her chair. "You've left me no choice, Gabrielle."

Before Gabby could turn away, the witch placed her palm against her forehead and her eyes widened as she felt a burning sensation spread across her skin. Alarmed, she tried to shake her off, but she was caught in her power. Rhian's hand was stuck to her forehead and wouldn't move.

"Don't struggle," the witch told her with a scowl. "It's for your own good."

The burning sensation prickled in Gabby's skull, worming its way inside her mind. Rhian was trying to take her by force.

Her power was burning its way through the walls Gabby had placed in her mind weeks before, the barriers she'd put there to protect herself.

She struggled to remain focused, fighting with everything she had to keep Rhian out. But the truth was she didn't understand enough to keep it up forever. Even with the amount of power she possessed, it would still end the same way. It was only a matter of time before everything would crumble around her.

Gabby was terrified to think about what she would become when Rhian succeeded. She wouldn't be the same person anymore. The Gabby she was would disappear and she wondered if she would beg Aya to take her power or try to destroy her with it.

Grimacing, Gabby tried to hold on, but the burning was becoming unbearable. She had to do something... but what?

Suddenly, she understood. There was only one thing she could do to get away. It was her only option.

Praying she was strong enough to hold on until she got to Aya, Gabby let the walls she'd placed in her mind crumble. Instantly, she felt the darkness swirl alive, obliterating almost everything inside of her. It was a like a feral monster, salivating for blood and destruction. Gabby gasped with the force of it, her heart beating so erratically in her chest, it felt like she was having a heart attack.

The satisfied smirk that crossed Rhian's face made her angrier than she'd ever felt in her entire life.

The witch's hand fell away and she grinned. "Welcome, sister."

Gabby tilted her head to the side, her jaw set as she felt the thing inside of her that she was terrified of take over. Standing abruptly, she slammed her hand down onto Rhian's forehead, the heel of her palm resting against the bridge of her nose, her fingers splayed across the top of her skull.

The witch's eyes widened in fear as she beheld her fate. She would not escape her.

The darkness swirled out of Gabby and poured into Rhian, the witch's spine arching as she let out a blood-curdling scream in agony. Blood ran from her nose, leaving a crimson trail over her lips and down her chin before dripping onto her shirt.

Gabby looked down at her with a chilling expression as she watched the life bleed from the witch who had tried to ruin her. Perhaps she had already succeeded, but perhaps they hadn't realised just how dark she was inside. How dark the Cohen witches could really be.

When she was sure she was done, Gabby let her hand drop and Rhian slumped to the floor, her eyes wide and unseeing.

She wouldn't be coming back this time. This time, Gabby had taken her life. This time it had been easier than the last.

Is this what they wanted her for? Death, destruction... *Malice*...

She had to laugh, remembering when she had obliterated Caius' witches all those weeks ago.

Even though she hated him with the fire of a thousand suns, Arturius was right...

She did like it.

CHAPTER 21

Gabby's head snapped up as the door to the study opened and a male vampire strode in.

Once his eyes locked onto Rhian's lifeless and broken body, he looked up at her, lips curling back into a snarl. The fleeting look of fear that passed through his eyes didn't escape her notice as she turned to face him. The vampire took a few steps forwards, unaware that whatever spell Rhian had placed over him for protection had vanished. Even if she was still alive, her pathetic charm would be useless.

Glaring up at him through her eyelashes, Gabby let out a terrifying snarl, her gaze piercing into his. The vampire stopped dead in his tracks, transfixed.

She felt the darkness swell again, but this time she didn't have to raise a finger. A satisfied smirk pulled at her lips as he fell to his knees, eyes bulging and bloodshot. His mouth fell open in a silent scream as he clawed at his hair, trying to get her out of his head.

Blood fell from his eyes like tears, staining his cheeks and dripping onto the carpet, all while Gabby looked on with a sick sense of fascination.

How easy it was to bring this monster to his knees before her. How easy it was to choke the life from him.

Absently, she flicked her wrist and he fell onto the floor, eyes wide and vacant. His undead heart was abruptly silent as blood pooled beneath him, the cream carpet now resembling something from a horror movie.

As she looked down on the chaos she'd wrought, Gabby suddenly drew in a sharp breath. *What the…?*

The darkness lulled and she felt herself come back as the hunger from the beast within was sated.

Falling to her knees, she rocked back and forth, trying to clear her mind. She needed help. She had to call someone. She needed Aya, but she knew she couldn't link her mind with another vampire. It was impossible. Even if Aya was half Celestine, she still couldn't.

Alex.

He was the only human who knew. She didn't know if it'd work over distance—she'd only ever linked with her grams this way and she'd been right next to her. There was no other choice. She had to try.

Taking a few deep breaths, she covered her face with her hands and tried to focus. '*Alex…*'

It felt like her head was filled with static, like she was trying to tune in a radio but couldn't quite find the station. Voices faded in and out, blending into the white noise. Trying to focus on an image of Alex, she remembered one of the most vivid memories she had of him.

The first week at a new school, all alone, she'd walked the halls and Stacey Howard, captain of the cheerleading squad, tripped her on purpose and she'd fallen flat on her face in front of everyone. Mortifying for a girl of thirteen in a place where she knew no one. It was then her rivalry had begun with the vapid cheerleader, but it was also when she'd met Alex. He was the one who helped her up when everyone stood and laughed. He'd offered her his hand and she remembered his awkward smile and chestnut hair that was tinted red, his trademark hoodie pulled over his head. She'd met Liz later that day and the three of them had become inseparable, but Alex was the first friend she'd made in Ashburton.

Fixing the image of him in her mind's eye, Gabby tried again, willing her message to get through. '*Alex...*'

There was silence for a moment, the static dissipating, and she knew he'd heard.

His hesitant voice echoed in her mind. 'Gabby?'

'Oh, *God*, Alex. It's me.'

'Gabby, is it really you? Where are you?'

'It's me,' she almost sobbed. 'I'm in a lot of trouble. I need Aya... Arturius has me at Mr. Forester's old house.'

'We know,' he told her. 'We're working on it, but Arturius captured Aya and Zac. Morgan betrayed us.'

'What? No!' Her desperation was overwhelming. *If anything happened to Aya...*

'Are they there with you?' Alex asked.

'No... I don't know. Wait a minute...' Tentatively, she let her earth sense prickle through and allowed it wander the house, brushing past a few others, obviously other vampires and a human, before settling on two minds far below. One curious mind that she couldn't comprehend and one she recognised as vampire. That had to be Aya and someone else... She hoped to God it was Zac. 'I think so, but I can't be sure.'

There was silence for a moment and she almost panicked, thinking she had lost her link with Alex, but his voice came back through. 'Hold on, Gabby. We're coming.'

'I'm going to find them,' she said before he was gone. 'I will contact you again. Don't do anything until you hear from me, okay?'

'Okay,' he said. 'Be careful.'

As the link faded, she let out a shaky breath. Her head was feeling fuzzy, like someone had stuffed it full of cotton wool and her nose was itchy. Wiping the back of her hand across her nose, her heart skipped a beat when it came back wet with blood. Was this how it was going to happen? The more she fought the darkness, the more her body would breakdown?

She needed to find Aya before it was too late.

Edging her way around the doorframe, she was relieved when she found the hallway empty. No one investigated further, probably jumping to the conclusion that their friend would've taken care of it. Except now he was dead.

Moving down the hall to the top of the stairs, she set her feet down as quietly as she could. She could sense a human in the kitchen and three vampires in what she supposed was the living room. The sounds of some television program echoed through the otherwise still house.

Gabby couldn't sense Arturius and was thankful. If he was here, then she wouldn't have even come this far. He would've stopped her the moment he heard Rhian's screaming.

Setting her foot lightly on the top step, she descended the staircase, her hand clutching the bannister so hard, her knuckles were becoming pale against her olive skin. When she was almost at the bottom, one step let out a groan as the old wood buckled under her weight. Freezing, her heart thudded momentarily before she tried to calm herself. There was no way of telling what the vampires could hear, even if the television distracted them.

Gabby let out a shaky breath when nothing happened and took the last few steps to the bottom. Once in the entry hall, she peered around the corner into the living room, where three male vampires were sitting around drinking beer and watching what looked like to be an episode of the vampire TV show, *True Blood*. Gabby had no time to ponder the irony.

Crossing the hall, she came to a small dining room that adjoined an old-fashioned kitchen. Hardwood floors and 1970s-era mustard-coloured wallpaper. She stifled a gasp when she saw a familiar person sitting at the table. It was Hunter Cross. She'd gone to high school with him, he'd been a linebacker on the football team. Now he worked at the auto shop on Grant Street. He was a good guy and had obviously been in the wrong place at the wrong time.

Gabby had to get him out.

Hunter looked up at her when she stepped into the room, his face plastered with a look of absolute terror as he released who she was. "Gabby?"

"Yes," she whispered. "I'm gonna get you out, okay?"

"I can't leave," he said, his voice bland and unfeeling.

"I know. They made you, but I can make it go away." How she knew was beyond her.

Gabby looked back over her shoulder towards the living room, but thankfully, the vampires were still distracted. She crossed the kitchen and stood in front of Hunter, his expression lax as he watched her progress. Before he could protest, she grabbed his hand and led him across the kitchen, all the while looking back over her shoulder.

Pulling him out onto the back porch, she pushed

the door closed, turning the knob as gently as she could manage. She placed her palms on his temples, all while Hunter looked at her like she was a crazy person.

Gabby fought to separate the dark from the light. If she used the darkness, then she might kill him without meaning to. It was too much to use on a human being.

Finally, it separated like oil and water and she tapped into the light, using it to clear the compulsion over him.

Hunter hissed as something inside him snapped and he pulled away from her. He reached up and grabbed her wrist, his eyes wide with fear. "We've got to get out of here." He sounded more like himself, more like a human in control. If he was back to himself, it was entirely possible his hold over the house was gone. If that was true, then any vampire could walk inside. That meant Sam and Liz...

"I've got to stay," she whispered.

"Gabby, no. These guys are sick, sadistic bastards. I don't know why you're here, but we've gotta go. Like now."

"They have my friends locked in the basement," she replied. "I've got to get them out."

"Then let me help you."

"No, I'm the only one who can do this, Hunter."

He looked at her, panic-stricken. "No, I can't let you do it on your own."

"Please..." She almost begged. He had to save himself. He already knew too much.

"I've gotta call the cops," he hissed at her.

"No. The police won't be able to stop them." Gabby knew what she had to do. He would unknowingly endanger others by trying to do the right thing. Human law couldn't help with the supernatural.

Hunter jumped when she placed a hand on his face. *"Run,"* she whispered. "Run and don't look back."

She watched as he bolted across the yard and disappeared into the night. Hunter would run until he was at a safe distance, then he would forget. He would go home and be perfectly fine. He wouldn't remember seeing her here tonight, or whatever had happened when he'd run into Arturius. Hunter would be okay.

Gabby was too terrified to go back into the house with the vampires in the other room. It would be so easy to let the darkness take them, but it would drown her along with them. Until she found Aya and Zac, she couldn't risk it.

Venturing out into the yard, she surveyed the house, looking for another way into the basement, a window or a door. Old houses like this one had to have another entry.

Out here, the house looked massive. From the street it looked small, mostly because of the unkempt garden and enormous trees that filled the yard, but from out the back it was unreal... and falling down.

Gabby looked to her left and then to her right. The

back porch was so large it took up almost the entire stretch of the house. There was no way in here.

Around the side of the house she found old-fashioned doors that led down into the basement, covered in weeds and leaf litter. Scraping it aside, she cursed as she saw an old, rusted lock. Unsure of what to do, she focused on the annoying piece of metal and willed it open. The lock shattered with a crack and her head snapped up, listening to see if she'd given herself away. When silence greeted her, she hauled one side of the hatch open, dirt and leaves showering into the space below.

Descending warily into the darkness, Gabby came into a hallway that was lit from the murky moonlight outside. At some point the large basement had been divided into separate rooms. The walls looked new, so the renovations had to have been done in the last few years. One room, she supposed, for the boiler, others for storage. Mr. Forester had been a bit of a shut-in, so who knew what was hidden down here. For all she knew, he could have a secret laboratory.

Trying the first door, it opened without resistance. As the minimal light from the hallway spilled into the room, she came to an abrupt halt, her heart clenching. There was a dead body in the middle of the room. Looking closer, she felt an overwhelming sadness.

It was Morgan.

She was lying on her back, eyes wide and empty, blonde hair splayed out across the concrete floor. The greyness of her skin was odd, veins bulging from her skin like tiny road maps to nowhere.

Gabby looked down at the vampire's body and sighed. She may have made the wrong decisions, but all Morgan was guilty of was being in love. The most human emotion had led to her death. For a vampire to feel anything to begin with was nothing short of a miracle, but to love…? That was something else.

She knew what it'd taken for Zac to get to the point where he loved Aya. Well over a hundred years, if her suspicions were correct. She couldn't imagine what Morgan felt when she realised her mistake. That her feelings were unrequited, and she'd betrayed the one person she cared about most.

Was it love or desperation that had driven her? Or was it the promise of an eternity alone?

Gabby hung her head and frowned. Kneeling beside Morgan's body, she ran her hand over the vampire's eyes, closing them to the world. All she could hope for now was that she could rest and find what she was looking for in the next life. Gabby was sure Morgan would find her soul again—the nurse's afterlife had been dedicated to helping others. She would be forgiven.

Gabby went back out into the hallway, closing the door behind her. There was no sound coming from above and none around her. Stopping at the next door on the opposite side of the hall, she paused and listened. This was the one.

Placing a hand lightly against the door, Gabby closed her eyes. Trailing her fingers across the door, she felt the spell webbed over it. Rhian hadn't cast this. There was another witch somewhere.

Disregarding that realisation, she pressed her palm flat against the door. Instinct took over and her power trickled forth like an inky black smoke and the web that lay over the opening dissolved and crumbled. The mechanism clicked as the lock was forced open and she grasped the knob, pushing her way into the room.

A gust of wind was all the warning Gabby had as Aya appeared in front of her, the blue of her irises so pale her eyes were almost white.

"Gabby?" The shock jolted the vampire's eyes back to their usual iridescent blue and her hands came down on her shoulders. As soon as Aya's skin came into contact with hers, she pulled back as if she had been burned.

"Aya," she whispered, hardly believing she'd found her and barely aware that Zac was standing in the shadows with a curious look on his face.

"Aya," she said again. "I'm... I... I couldn't fight it anymore."

CHAPTER 22

When Aya touched Gabby, she recoiled as the shock of the witch's power seared through her. The darkness had surfaced and from the panicked look on Gabby's face, it'd already taken its toll.

"Have you..." she began.

"I had to get away."

Aya nodded in understanding. Surrendering must have been the only way Gabby could have freed herself.

"I'm afraid, Aya."

"I know," she replied.

"We need to get out of here." Zac's voice was quiet in the dark.

"There are others upstairs," Gabby said. "The human is gone. Anyone can come in now."

"What do you mean? Did they kill him?"

She shook her head numbly. "I broke the

compulsion. When he left, so did his hold on the house."

Aya was impressed. Gabby's power ran deeper than she'd thought. It'd been a long time since she'd heard of a witch breaking a vampire's compulsion, let alone a human's hold over a dwelling.

The young witch seemed to drift away for a moment before she said, "Sam and Liz are outside."

"How did they know?" Zac was confused.

"I linked with Alex. I had to warn them."

Aya frowned at Gabby's lack of emotion. It was unlike her, but she knew from experience she was trying to hold on to herself lest the darkness overwhelm her. She had to get her out before Arturius caught on that she'd escaped. She could bring her back once they got away from here.

"Let's get out of here," Aya said, looking towards the door.

Zac held Gabby's arm. "Stay with me."

The witch nodded and hung back behind him as he followed Aya out into the hallway.

Moonlight flooded into the hatch Gabby had left open, but at the other end, a staircase ascended into the house.

Aya placed an index finger over her lips to silence them. "Take Gabby outside to the others." She gestured towards the opening, then pointed upstairs with a sly grin. "I'll make short work of them."

Thankfully, Zac didn't try to argue with her and led

Gabby down the hall and up into the night. Once they had disappeared from view, she turned and took the stairs, opening the door on the landing as silently as she could. Stepping out into the hallway, she listened for a moment and snorted when she heard the television in the room to her left. The stupidity of Arturius and his choice in thugs was something she couldn't fathom. For someone as old as the founder was, it was laughable. He had been a *primus pilus*, a centurion. Commander and soldier. What'd happened to him over the years?

Eager to get back to Gabby, Aya sauntered into the den and folded her arms across her chest. When the vampires didn't stir, she coughed loudly.

When they realised who was standing behind them, all three vampires stood with a hiss and were across the room in a flash, but Aya was faster.

She pushed the first man with her palms and he went flying backwards into the second. Twisting, her hand plunged into the chest of the third. He fell to the ground with hardly a sound and she tossed the useless organ to the side, her hand and forearm coated with sticky blood.

Vaulting over the sofa, she pounced on the vampire who'd fallen to the floor, snapping his neck in one fluid motion. Ripping the leg from the coffee table, she plunged it upwards, directly into the heart of the last vampire, who'd barely had time to turn around, let alone try to attack. Pushing him away, the stake came free with a sucking sound and she slammed it directly into the vampire below, obliterating his heart.

Standing with a sigh, Aya pulled a throw off the sofa and wiped the blood from her hand and arm, tossing it onto the pile of desiccated vampires.

That was that, then.

When she emerged from the house into the backyard, Sam was in front of her, placing a hand on her shoulder.

"Aya," he said. "Thank God you're okay."

"Thanks go to Gabby," Aya said, glancing at the young witch, "not God."

Gabby was standing with Liz, her face ashen. If Aya was going to save her, now was the time.

"Arturius isn't here," Aya said. "But it won't be long before he comes back and when he does, he will be one angry vampire. We need to do this now."

"It's almost..." Gabby began. It was almost too late.

"Not if I have anything to do with it," Aya hissed. "Hold her." She gestured to the brothers, who came forwards and grasped Gabby around the upper arms.

Sam frowned. "Are you sure we need—"

"Yes," Aya told them.

Gabby's eyes widened in fear as she looked up at Aya. "What are you going to do?"

"I won't lie to you," she told her. "This will hurt, but it'll be so much better afterwards. You'll understand and it won't be so hard anymore."

"Do you promise?"

"I promise."

Placing her palm over Gabby's heart, Aya drew a sharp breath. Closing her eyes, she felt it—the same thing she'd felt in Violet and countless other witches before her. The thick darkness of corruption that came from the one thing the Celestines hadn't counted on—human emotion.

If she'd lived to fulfil her destiny, then it would never have gotten to this point. She would have been there to guide the witches in their true purpose, but it hadn't worked out that way. Now their emotions ruled much of their magic.

Gabby's heart was thumping in her chest, the beat so strong against Aya's palm, it echoed around her mind and reverberate in her bones. Reaching deep inside herself, she sought out her power and readied herself. She would only need a small amount. A trickle, a drop.

She drew a deep breath through her nose and looked into Gabby's eyes, dipping her head into a slight nod.

Aya let her power come forth and it pooled into her palm like a shock of electricity. Then she forced it into the witch—there was no way to be gentle about this.

As the shock splintered into her, Gabby's back arched as the darkness sputtered and died inside of her. She flung her head backwards, letting out a strangled cry as blue light poured from her eyes and mouth.

As soon as it had hit her, it was over.

The witch fell forwards, her knees crumbling and hair concealing her face. The only thing that kept her from hitting the ground was Zac and Sam's hold on her upper arms.

"Gabby?" Aya pulled the hair from her face, revealing her tear-streaked skin.

"You were right," she whispered hoarsely. "That hurt like hell."

"It'll pass soon enough."

The witch shook her head as if she was trying to clear it and stood up straight, both Zac and Sam loosening their grips on her arms.

Pulling away, she said, "I'm okay. It's gone."

Aya desperately wanted to ask her what Arturius had divulged to her, but she'd basically just restarted her heart. Perhaps that could wait a moment.

"Aya," Gabby said, "Arturius is up to something. There was another witch there who told me things."

"What witch? What things?" She daren't not contemplate what he was trying to do. It was never anything good.

"Rhian. She was one of Katrin's witches. She was the one trying to turn me."

"Rhian..." she said, trying to see if that name was familiar. She'd been asleep for a hundred and fifty years, but some witches had an annoying way of extending their lives, especially where Katrin had been concerned. "Did she or Arturius say what they wanted with you?"

"Rhian kept going on about how they wanted me to turn to darkness. How I was from the ether. I think they wanted me because I can draw power from life and death."

Aya's head cocked to the side. She already knew this. All Ismena's witches had the ability, but not all discovered it.

"Arturius said his brother was looking for something or someone. They must have needed my ability to find it or use it... I don't know."

"Regulus?"

"Yes. Whatever it is, Arturius wants to find it first."

"Damn it," Aya cursed.

"Do you know what they were talking about?"

"No idea," she replied. "But knowing them, it can't be good."

"Then Regulus is next on the hit list," Zac said. "After Arturius bites the dust."

Aya gave him a look. "We can discuss that once this is done."

He stared at her for a moment, his expression unreadable, before he looked at his feet.

"What?" she asked as Gabby went off with Liz and Sam, their voices low in the silent yard.

Zac looked back towards the house with a frown. He was struggling with something, but she didn't ask. She knew that he was thinking about Morgan. She supposed her body was still in the house. It'd only been a few hours since…

"I can't leave her," he said after a moment.

Aya looked up at him, concern in her pale features.

"This place wasn't her home," he said. "I can't take her to Britain, but I can give her this."

"Where?" Aya asked, slipping her arm through his, understanding exactly what he meant.

"When she came here, she told me that she thought the forest was magical," he murmured, looking across the yard to where a stream passed by the limit of the property, a willow tree growing by the bank.

"By the stream," she said, her eyes closed.

"Yes."

"Go," Aya whispered. "I'll keep watch for Arturius." She watched him disappear into the house and sighed. He'd been through so much over the past few weeks. It seemed ever since she'd come into his life there had been nothing but trouble. All she wanted was time with him. Time where they weren't watching people they cared about die. Time where they didn't have to look over their shoulders. Maybe one day.

"This is what he was like before," Sam said, coming up behind her. "When he was human."

Aya looked back over her shoulder at him and frowned.

He placed a reassuring hand on her shoulder. "His humanity is coming back."

"We seem to keep having these conversations."

"I don't know what you were like before, but you're different, too."

"How?"

"Compassionate."

"Don't get smart with me, Sam." She turned and picked up a shovel that'd been discarded in the overgrown garden. She felt uncomfortable talking about these things.

"What are you doing?" Liz asked like it wasn't obvious.

"I don't want him to dig this grave," she said curtly and walked over to the stream, surveying the shoreline. A short way from the edge of the water was an ancient willow, its roots spread out under the ground like skeletal fingers searching for life to consume. Closing her eyes, she felt out its pattern and settled on a space under its branches, the shower of leaves thankfully hiding her from the others. Aya didn't want to have an audience for this. Digging a grave for the woman who had betrayed them all for a dream. Once upon a time, she would've left her to rot.

Sinking the shovel into the dirt, she dug up the hard earth with little effort. It was important to Zac, so she would do it.

Sam was right about her. She'd changed.

It wasn't long before she was standing waist deep in the ground, a pile of dark and damp earth to one side. Without looking up, she knew Zac was looking down at her. Even if she couldn't hear his blood, she would have known it was him. He had that kind of presence.

"Thank you," she heard him say and she grunted, vaulting herself out of the grave.

He stood with Morgan's body in his arms. He'd wrapped her in a dark-coloured rug—not an inch of her was showing. Aya smiled sadly and caressed his arm. Without a word, he jumped down into the grave she'd dug and placed her body into its final resting place, arranging her just so.

Sam, Liz, and Gabby pushed their way through the willow fronds and congregated around the open grave, waiting for Zac to take the lead, but he just stood there looking down into the hole.

"Do you want to say something?" Aya asked, conscious of the mixed feelings in the air.

She could sense the tangled emotions from the others and guessed they hadn't entirely trusted Morgan, either. Rightly so, but that didn't make her a bad person. Aya knew enough about lies, deceit, and evil to know it was the case. Morgan had just been blinded by her heart. She'd seen it many times.

Zac sighed and said, "Morgan gave me hope at a time when I had none. I'm sorry this had to happen to her."

Aya looked up at the others and Sam shook his head. They didn't want to contribute. They hadn't known her, after all, so what could they say? Zac was the only one who did. She didn't exactly like her, but she was sorry that her life had to end this way. That's all she had to say, but she didn't dare utter the words.

When nobody moved, Aya picked up the shovel. She snatched it away when Zac tried to take it from her.

"No," she said. "This is one thing I won't let you do."

And she was relieved when he didn't argue; instead, he stood back and watched as she shovelled dirt back into the grave, covering the woman who'd saved his life. Giving her back to the earth.

When Aya was done, she tossed the shovel aside and backed away. He would want some time alone before things got out of hand. Arturius wouldn't be gone for much longer. It had already been the best part of an hour since Gabby opened the door to their basement prison.

Zac reached out and grasped her arm, pulling her hard against his body. His arms snaked around her waist and he buried his face into her shoulder, breathing in her scent as deeply as he could. Her eyes flickered to the others and met Sam's. He nodded and drew the others back out into the yard, leaving them in their own little cocoon.

"Did you bury your family?" he asked, his voice muffled.

Aya felt her body become rigid as his words cut into her. No, she hadn't. She'd just left them there to decay into bones. Nothing could enter the clearing where their house lay. She was the only remaining person alive who could. If she went back, what would she find? A ruin. A tomb. Broken bones and a broken future.

When she didn't answer him, Zac slipped an arm around her waist and gently pulled her to him. They stood this way for a moment, staring down at the disturbed earth that was now Morgan's final resting place.

"No," she said, "I didn't."

"Neither did I."

Then she understood why this was so important to him. He'd lost everyone he'd loved and had never had the chance to say goodbye.

Aya lifted her hand and lovingly stroked his hair. What she said next, she said for him. She said it for all those times he couldn't. "Rest in peace."

CHAPTER 23

"Arturius is coming," Aya said suddenly, turning towards the street.

"Have you had enough blood?" Zac asked, grabbing her shoulder, his sadness beginning to evaporate. They would have time to mourn later.

"Yes," she said. "I've had more than when I took Caius. I'll manage it. The stars have been speaking to me again."

Zac frowned at the cryptic message and pulled her close. "Whatever happens, Aya, know I love you."

"And I, you." She reached up and pulled him to her, kissing him deeply.

Aya stepped back abruptly, a queer look on her face.

"What is it?" he asked.

"He's not alone." She looked off into space, listening.

"How many?" Sam's steady voice came as Zac pulled her back out into the yard.

"I'm not sure. There's a witch."

"The witch that spelled the basement," Gabby said.

"Are you able to counter her?" Aya asked, hyperaware that she wasn't quite herself yet. She'd literally had a nasty shock.

Gabby nodded, wrapping her arms around herself. "I'll manage it."

Aya turned to the others. "I can't ask you all to stay," she said. "I know this is my fight and I can't protect you all—"

"Aya." To her surprise, it was Liz who had interrupted her. "We know. You're one of us. We'll do whatever it takes."

"And now it's personal," Zac murmured into her ear. "The moment he tore your heart out. The moment he staked Morgan. The moment he set foot in this town. It's personal."

She looked up into his green eyes and understood. She would do the same for him, no questions asked.

She tilted her head to the side, letting them know the Roman's arrival was imminent and a moment later, Arturius appeared around the side of the house, his expression complete darkness.

Aya turned to face her maker with an almost feral snarl as she felt her fangs grow in. Now it was time to deliver him the death he deserved.

Gabby came forwards and stood to Aya's left, her

expression strained as she fought against whatever countermeasures the other witch had placed around the Roman and his followers. Abruptly, she brought her palms together, and the six vampires in front of them shimmered into twelve.

Aya placed a hand on her shoulder and felt her power join with hers. They couldn't will all of their brains to explode at the same time, but together, they could take out the front line.

Four vampires stopped mid-stride and dropped limply to the ground, blood running from their eyes. Before she could help Gabby with the next wave, her hand was torn from her shoulder and she spun backwards into Zac's arms, Gabby falling limply to the ground. Liz was at her side in an instant, laying a hand protectively over her heart.

Aya felt the presence of power almost instantly. Turning with a growl, she saw the witch who'd subdued Gabby standing in front of the remaining vampires and Arturius, who was trying not to laugh.

A look of triumph was plastered on the witch's face —a look Aya wanted to rip off with her bare hands. She took a few steps forwards, her eyes opalescent as she sized up the woman.

The witch's expression faltered as she advanced, her attempts at subduing the vampire not working.

Aya laughed at her. "Do you really think your little mind tricks work on me?" Zac's blood had erased any footholds her magic could've taken.

Before the witch could reply, Aya was in front of her, fangs bared, ready to rip her throat out. Instead, she placed and hand on the woman's shoulder and smiled down at her condescendingly. As the witch pleaded silently with her, she plunged her hand into her chest cavity and tore her heart out. *No remorse for the betrayers.*

Dropping the useless organ to the ground, she looked up at Arturius, whose expression had turned cold. Peeling her lips back in a snarl, she dived onto the closest vampire, her fangs tearing into his throat, fingers opening the wound further until his head tore cleanly off. Aya didn't have to tell the others to take care of Arturius' minions, they were already on it.

She was vaguely aware of Liz standing over an unconscious Gabby, tearing into anyone who dared come close like a lioness protecting her cub. If Aya had been in control of her thoughts, maybe she would've retracted her previous opinion of the blonde vampire. Liz had finally stepped up.

She felt Zac tearing into someone behind her, but she disregarded him, knowing he would be okay. She advanced on the Roman who was content to watch the carnage unfold, her eyes blazing with anger.

Arms were around her neck before she could close the distance and she flipped her assailant over her head, her fist following them down and plunging straight into their chest cavity. The female vampire's heart was crushed instantaneously, her skin fading to grey.

Zac let out an angry roar of pain. Her head snapped towards the sound and she started towards him when she saw a stake protruding from his shoulder, blood soaking into his black shirt. Sam was in front of him a second later, tearing it from his brother's flesh.

"*Go*," he yelled at her.

Pivoting on her heel, she flipped one vampire over her shoulder, hardly noticing where he landed. She only had eyes for Arturius.

When another vampire appeared in her path, she lunged with her fangs bared. She sunk them into his throat and bit down with all her strength.

Her victim let out a strangled cry of pain as his blood poured into her mouth and down the front of her shirt, hot and sticky. Dropping him a moment later, she stepped over his inert body and lunged towards Arturius, her elbow colliding with his stomach, making the Roman double over in surprise.

As he lurched forwards, her fist came up and connected with his nose, the crack as it broke vibrating through her bones.

He was quick to correct himself as his head flung upwards with a snap, his bulky form behind her before she could twist to the side. Arturius grasped the back of her neck, throwing her across the yard with a roar as blood poured from his broken nose. As she slammed into the wall of the house, she felt her flesh bruise under the impact.

Landing face-first on the hard ground, she was hauled up before she could scramble to her feet. Arturius' fingers dug into the flesh of her shoulder, drawing blood. She cried out as the pressure crushed her bones, rendering her left arm nearly useless.

"You're nothing," he spat at her, pushing all his weight into her slight form, pinning her against the wall. "You've got nothing left." He leaned into her neck and licked her blood from her skin, his black eyes boring into hers as he drew back.

Aya couldn't speak, pain burning through her shoulder and back. She had to lead him on, let him think he was winning. If she fought back, it would only delay the inevitable.

"I know it took all of your strength to murder Caius. The centuries of drinking human blood to survive has eroded your power into *nothing*," he hissed, his hands crushing her ribs.

Twisting out of his grip, she tried to put distance between them, but he pushed her to the ground, a knee heavy in her back.

Looking up at the others, she saw Sam wrestle with a male vampire, his arms around his neck. She'd only seen him once in his vampire guise—the night they'd saved Alex in the gardens. Kindhearted Sam, all back eyes and scary fangs, blood smeared across his face.

And Liz. Aya never thought she could ever step up,

but there she was, plunging a stake into a male vampire twice her size and who knew how many years older than her.

Zac... He was covered in blood, the sound of it all over the yard. He was looking at her in horror as the Roman pulled her head back violently.

"No," she whispered to him, pleading him to stay away.

He couldn't help her now, none of them could. She wouldn't let this mismatched family suffer the same fate as her own. She couldn't let it happen again.

Arturius pressed his knee harder into her back and she cried out in agony as her spine snapped in several places, her legs useless. He flipped her over, his face plastered with triumph. Wrapping his hands around her throat, he squeezed, her pale skin bruising as her airway closed.

Aya smiled up at him, even as he tried to choke the life from her.

"Why are you smiling?" he cried.

"Because this is the last time I will ever have to see your face, dear Arturius," she whispered hoarsely, a tear trailing down her cheek.

Her power simmered just below the surface, burning her from the inside in its desire for revenge. All she had to do was let go and it would be too late for him. She looked into his black eyes one last time and surrendered.

Arturius stared in disbelief as his hands began to

glow with a pale blue light. It trailed up his arms, burning the life from him as it grew brighter. Trying to let her go, he found himself locked in position, unable to control himself.

"No!" he cried as he realised what was happening. "No! No, you can't!"

Aya felt the power coil tightly inside her, the power she had always called her rage. It was her Celestine power in a different guise.

Just as she was turned into a vampire, so too was her power turned into something just a little darker, but no less pure.

She now know it had a limit... and Zac was her lifeline. The universe worked in mysterious ways.

"Yes," she rasped, "*I can.*"

Arturius screamed in agony as her power enveloped him, his eyes sinking back into his skull. She hadn't the energy to lift her arm to pulverise his heart, but she wouldn't have put him out of his misery given a choice.

Triumph coursed through her as she watched the Roman desiccate. The vampire who was responsible for turning her into a monstrosity. The vampire who'd torn her brother to pieces. The vampire who'd almost destroyed Gabby and everyone she'd ever loved.

Her body jerked as she felt a burning sensation shock through her mind. Just as her power was entering his body, it folded back on itself and she felt it searing back into her. The pressure of it almost split her head in two and a trickle of blood ran from her nose, across her cheek, and into her hair.

This had never happened before. *Ever.*

Her eyes widened with surprise and she knew Arturius realised it wasn't meant to happen. But Aya knew she couldn't stop it. Once her power was set lose, it had to run its course.

There was no way of telling what would happen when it came down to this moment. After all, it was his vampire blood that ran with her Celestine. There was nothing for her to compare it to, no status quo. But there was no doubt in her mind that she had to do this, even if it meant destroying herself.

Arturius had to die, no matter the cost.

The fire continued to burn away at Arturius greedily, his skin becoming ashen, his veins protruding as he desiccated. He let out a strangled cry as he tried to draw in oxygen, but it was useless. When the life finally left him, his limp body fell on her, an empty husk.

Pushing him off with what little strength she had left, Aya let out a sob as her broken bones grated together.

"Zac?" she called out, but her voice had been reduced to a strained whisper.

"Aya." He was there, murmuring into her ear, his hand on her face, brushing her hair out of her eyes. His touch was comforting, her heart slowing its racing to a steady beat.

"I..." She tried to sit up, but she collapsed back onto the ground.

"Shh," he tried to comfort her. "It's over. Don't try to move. Not yet."

"Gabby?"

"She's fine."

Turning her head, she saw Liz on her knees beside her, just as she was before. A tear slid from her eye as the young witch stirred.

"Sam?"

"I'm here," he said, the sound of his voice coming from behind his brother.

"Alex?"

"He's waiting for us back at the manor." Sam was always on top of everything.

"Are you okay?" Zac looked at her with concern. His green eyes had a strange hue to them in the aftermath of her power. He wiped a thumb over the trail of blood that'd trickled from her nose and she closed her eyes.

"I will be."

What she didn't tell him was that she was afraid that something wasn't right. She'd killed her maker and who knew what that would do to her. What it had broken inside.

Zac leaned down and pressed his lips to hers and she felt the life creep back into her body. This time the roles were reversed. This time Zac looked down on her as she lay broken on the ground. This time he would save her.

"Let's get you home," he said, scooping her up into his arms.

"Home..." she murmured into the crook of his neck. "That sounds nice."

H e watched the city outside through the rivulets of water on the windowpane, the glow of the fire reflecting off the glass. The tail end of winter always saw the most rain, even though England was probably the dreariest country to be living in, no matter the time of year. How he longed to return to his native Ireland, but it was just as grey as here.

"Tristan," a male voice called behind him.

He turned away from the window and crossed the study, the shelves upon shelves of old leather-bound books watching his passage.

"Yes, sir?" he said in his thick Irish accent, approaching the armchair from where the voice came.

There was a heavy sigh before the man's voice broke through the patter of rain. "Arturius is dead."

He gave pause for a moment. *Caius, Katrin, and now Arturius?* "What would you have me do?"

The man turned to survey Tristan. His imposing

stature always gave him a healthy dose of fear, though his black eyes never gave anything away.

"You will find her," he said and Tristan understood who he meant. There was only one who could end the Romans, and it appeared she was still alive. "You will warn her of her imminent danger, and you will find those who have aided her."

"Yes, sir."

Tristan had served him for hundreds of years hoping to find her. Finally, he would come face to face with the woman who'd saved him almost a thousand years ago. He would do as he was commanded.

Death was on her doorstep.

Regulus was coming.

THE SHADOW'S SON
(The Witch Hunter Saga #3)

The hunter has become the hunted.

When a mysterious stranger from **Aya's** past shows up in Ashburton it's not all good news. **Tristan**, a man she saved almost a thousand years ago, brings a warning that will affect not just her, but her new family.

Regulus is coming.

To protect Zac from her greatest enemy, Aya has to destroy the best thing that has ever happened to her. She has to pretend that their love has been a lie. But is it the right thing to do?

Heartbroken again, **Zac** must surrender to the darkest places inside himself if he has a hope of coming back. Even if that means aligning himself with his greatest enemy and turning his back on everything he's worked for.

Lovers are torn apart, friends are pitted against each other and families are splintered. But what they find buried under the streets of London will change everything they've ever known about their world. Something that should have been left alone.

But what Regulus does is the most unexpected of all.

The Shadow's Son is the third book in The Witch Hunter Saga, an Urban Fantasy series entwined with vampires, witches, and the ultimate mystery of their true creation. In the darkness of ancient betrayals, can these unlikely allies find the light?

The Shadow's Son is OUT NOW!

ABOUT NICOLE

Nicole R. Taylor is an Australian Urban Fantasy author.

She lives in the western suburbs of Melbourne dreaming up nail biting stories featuring sassy witches, duplicitous vampires, hunky shapeshifters, and devious monsters.

She likes chocolate, cat memes, and video games.

When she's not writing, she likes to think of what she's writing next.

Follow Nicole Online:

Website: nicolertaylorwrites.com
Facebook: facebook.com/nrtaylorwrites
Newsletter: nicolertaylorwrites.com/newsletter